THE
STARS
FORGOT US

R.J. GARCIA

Midnight Tide
PUBLISHING

EARLY PRAISE FOR THE STARS FORGOT US

"With the help of her believable and relatable cast of characters, R.J. Garcia seamlessly blends the real and fantastical together with compelling results. This story is sure to resonate with Paranormal fans everywhere!"

— M. AINIHI, AUTHOR

"I was hooked from the start, totally invested in the MC's relationship, and blown away by the twists and fresh spin on the paranormal."

— H.R. TRUELOVE, AUTHOR

"The Stars Forgot Us is bone-chillingly beautiful! It delivered an emotional and unexpected punch. It is the characters that made me love it so much. Fans of Shatter Me and Twilight will love this one."

— GOODREADS REVIEW

"In the midst of this awkward teenage love story, darker things are brewing. It isn't long before the mysteries begin to pile, and the tension causes your mind to race with a myriad of possibility."

— GOODREADS REVIEW

The Stars Forgot Us
Copyright © 2022 R.J. Garcia

Midnight Tide
PUBLISHING

Published by Midnight Tide Publishing
www.midnighttidepublishing.com

Cover design by MoorBooks Design
www.moorbooksdesign.com

Interior Formatting by Book Savvy Services

Edited by Meg Dailey
thedaileyeditor.wordpress.com/editing-services

ASIN: B09RTPRJMG
ISBN: 978-1-953238-77-1

Dear Dad,
Thank you for always taking such good care of everyone. I
love you so much. This one's for you!

PROLOGUE

It began centuries ago. In screams. In bloodshed. When man first tasted human flesh in the bitter cold. It came from below. Consuming. Devouring. Growing stronger with the greed of men...

(1880)

Sunlight tunneled in through the twisted branches of ancient oak and elm. Though it was such a hot day, fear rattled in young Benjamin's bones as if he were cold. Flies buzzed above limp corpses. Dead rabbits alongside stags were laid out around the oak tree in a ceremonial fashion. The realization struck the boy hard.

He reached over, whirling his older sister, Emma, around by the arm. "Don't you see, Emma? The animals are a sacrifice for the thing we saw. That monster." A creeping sensation ran up and down his spine. "Who would do such a thing?"

"The others. Reverend. Even Pa. They wore beautiful red robes of satin brocade. We're not going to be poor anymore." A rustling in the trees made the boy jump. Emma said, "Unfortunately, it's still hungry. Better run, Benjamin." His sister's eyes grew dark like night.

A strange feeling overtook him. He ran through a dizzying labyrinth of trees. A fierce creature growled and tore through the foliage right behind him. A branch slashed the boy's face open when he tripped over a boulder. His cheek stung...bled. His hands skidded through leaves, twigs, and dirt before he stopped. He staggered to his feet. Something dripped from his chin. Sweat. The perspiration drenched and cooked him in his own heat. It had suddenly gotten eerily quiet. The boy took slow, tentative steps, feeling quite unsure. His heart beat like a drum. Monstrous trees paired with stiff vegetation were a uniform view from every direction. His head spun.

Then he heard it. Emma's airy laughter, which echoed from every direction. "Stop it, Emma, please stop it," he pleaded. Benjamin could not be too far from home, so he shakily pressed on, yet the laughter tormented and followed. Fog crept in from nowhere. The smell of animal and rot tinged the air. Each subsequent step felt heavy—wrong. A human-like figure sprang out from the cover of the trees. Benjamin tried to flee but could barely move. The boy froze in horror, his mouth agape as he beheld a pair of luminous eyes, a flash of sharp white fangs.

His slender shoulders shook as he bleated, "Mother!"

1

THE WRITING ON THE WALL

(Modern Day)

We had moved to New York so *Michael* could attend a day program. Now we were going back to Steely, Pennsylvania, so *Michael* could have family support. My older brother tended to be the common denominator in everything these days.

It was a long drive. Such a long drive, Mom planned her death on the way. "I want to be buried with Freckle's ashes." He was our deceased cocker spaniel and the best dog ever. Mom pointed her index finger. "And make sure you slip my cell in the casket in case I wake up."

I laughed a little. "You're not going to die."

"Everyone dies, and I'm being serious, Jacob," she insisted.

"*Okay*, Mom," I humored her.

I rode shotgun. Mom's tapered fingers tapped the steering wheel to the beat of a soft rock song. She was small with dark curly hair, so curly she inevitably passed it onto her offspring.

4 R.J. GARCIA

She concentrated on the road, but her eyes flicked to me on and off lovingly. My mom had dark circles under tired eyes yet never stopped being reassuring.

Michael was in the backseat. Medicated and snoring with his precious guitar in its case next to him, though he hadn't played since his junior year in high school. His 1960s Rockstar hair—left long and wavy—usually obscured one of his eyes. He could have been Jim Morrison from certain angles.

"You know, Jacob, it's not like we don't know anyone. You'll get to live by Lucas. Come on, he was always your best friend. You should be happy."

"That was two Summers ago. I haven't hung out with Lucas since forever."

"We saw them at Christmas. Now he'll be less than two miles away, and you'll go to school together again."

"Yeah, but who wants to start school in the middle of sophomore year?"

A sigh of weariness escaped her until she resumed the role of cheerleader. "It's going to be great. And guess what? We're almost there."

We turned off the highway, and Mom took her foot off the gas, slowing down as the road narrowed. Trees, mostly maple and oak, were colorful, with changing leaves crowded together to give the illusion of a forest. Instead, the trees and hills opened up to old houses with big yards, killing the chance for any actual woods to explore. Then the voice on the GPS announced we had arrived at our destination on the right. I eyed a rusted-out relic of a mailbox. The tires crunched along a gravel driveway, causing a plume of dust to ascend. I peered through the front windshield at a two-story brick house with dark shutters and creeping ivy. I remembered this house from my old bus route and always figured it was haunted.

"Oh wow, oh wow. This is amazing!" Mom gushed and cut the engine of our beat-up Subaru. "Your aunt did good finding us this house."

I humored her. "Yeah, sure." Was she even seeing the same house?

"Just look, you got your forest." Mom knew I liked the woods.

Behind the plot of land, trees shot out, leading to a full-fledged forest. I remembered these woods. "Not bad," I admitted.

"The mortgage will be the same as our rent."

"Is this a murder house? You get good deals on the murder houses."

"Don't start." Her voice fell to a whisper. "Michael will take you seriously."

"He's sleeping."

Mom shifted around to face my twenty-year-old brother. "We're here, sleepyhead." She always talked to him like he was a much younger kid.

The snores continued. His head hung, and curls cascaded back to reveal the rare sight of his forehead, which gleamed with perspiration. Michael always ran hot. I opened the car door and jumped out. My butt had molded to the car seat, so standing induced an involuntary sigh, and the October chill felt good on my face.

Compared to our apartment, the house was practically a mansion. There was a wraparound porch in the front held up by thick columns with chipped white paint. It was an abandoned-looking place, big and overwhelming. A sagging porch squeaked beneath my feet, and the cracked deck had lost all its shine.

My mom caught up to me, probably having given up on waking Michael, who slept like the dead. "We can fix it up!"

"You've watched way too much HGTV, Mom." We walked over to a trapdoor on the ground adjacent to the porch. I lifted it with both hands and got a whiff of a musty smell. "Creepy," I muttered, letting it slam.

"It's just a cellar," she countered.

We circled the house together. I opened the rusty gate to find a leaf shrouded lawn, and a garden filled with drooping plants and weeds.

Mom put her arm around me. "Look, we have a fence. Maybe we could get another dog."

"Yeah. We should get one of those huge ones that looks like a wolf."

"A husky. We'll see."

I flicked an eyebrow at her as the moving truck crunched up the drive, making things seem less desolate.

She led the way back to the front of the house and bent down to pick up a newspaper already on the porch. "Veronica got us a subscription," mom said.

"Of course." My aunt was a columnist for the local and dying chronicle.

Mom jammed the key in the door, and I held it open for her and the movers.

The first guy was big and bulky, loaded with an arm full of boxes. The other mover was tall and spindly and had intimidating tattoos of scorpions, skulls, and demons drawn down his arms. Only one tattoo was a bit more innocent reading, MOTHER, in all caps and block letters just above his T-shirt. He carried a living room chair, giving me a dirty look.

He might have thought I was staring. "Nice Tattoos," I said to let him know I was cool. Living in New York, I'd pretty much seen it all.

I walked in to see a human-sized coat rack the previous owner must have left behind.

Mom brightly said, "Check out the wood floor. Your Aunt Veronica had them refinished for a housewarming present."

The floor shined with a dark finish. "Nice."

"Yeah...And it's all ours." We crossed the room before she said, "I better get your brother."

"Okay."

She squeezed my arm affectionately and pivoted around.

I shot up the flight of stairs to explore. Truth be told, I had never wanted to leave Steely in the first place. Once I made it to the second-floor landing, my stomach muscles clenched, and I was unsure if it was dread or excitement.

By 6-ish, it had started to seem a little normal. Beds assembled, computer and TV hooked up. There was no cable, just Netflix, but really, who needed cable? Mom had picked up Wendy's, so we ate together at the two-leaf kitchen table. Right after I sunk my teeth into my burger, I complained, "God, Mom, there's ketchup!"

"In some faraway lands, people say *thank you*." My mom said this a lot.

"Whatever," I mumbled and spat out a mandatory, "Thanks."

I counted five or six hemp necklaces hanging around Michael's neck as he told us, "Fast food has too many chemicals—hormones."

"What are you even talking about?" I shouldn't have asked.

"The government is trying to control the population. One burger can make you sterile for weeks."

Sarcastically, I commented, "Not like I'm planning to start a family anytime soon."

"Jacob." Mom rolled her eyes at me and turned to my brother. "Please eat, Michael. You can't take your meds on an empty stomach."

Mike pushed his Southwest avocado salad away, saying, "I saw a shadow. Heard footsteps. I don't want to stay."

"Honey, you'll get used to the new house," Mom promised.

I bit into my hamburger to please my mom, and because I was starving. Well, it turned out ketchup wasn't half bad.

"No. I really heard this. There's someone else in this house," Michael insisted. His lips quaked, and nostrils flared. "This wasn't in my head."

When it came to my brother, Mom had the patience of a saint. She softly reassured him, "No, Michael, the movers left. It's just the three of us."

I was about to put a nicely over-salted french fry in my mouth as Mom leaned forward, tapping my knee. "Just stay with Michael tonight until he gets used to things, Jacob."

"No way! There are four bedrooms in this place, and you

promised I'd get my own room." I sounded a little whinier than I intended and jammed a fry in my mouth.

"I think it's for the best. I want to look after you," Michael said.

I crossed my arms and swallowed. "Really, Mike?"

A half-smile broke the deadpan look on his face. I gave him an *are you for real* eye squint. Then he became serious again and eyed our mom. "Tell him he has to."

"Only for a couple nights," Mom decided.

"Unbelievable!" I mumbled, "Too bad I'm not the crazy one." My eyes swung back to Michael, and his head dropped.

The guilt set in. Useless, annoying guilt got me every time. "Sorry, Michael. It's not a big deal. We can room tonight."

He got up, his chair screeching across the tile, and stormed up the stairs.

"Really nice, Jacob." My mom chased after my brother.

Even when I won, I lost. A surge of emotion stung my eyes, and I ate a few more fries without tasting them. Soon my eyes cleared, and I looked around the kitchen. It wasn't too bad, just outdated. The cabinets were dark and aged, and the old appliances a dingy white. The rumbling of the old refrigerator kicked off, and it seemed too quiet. Still, I wouldn't have bothered to go upstairs if I hadn't left my phone charging there.

I made it to the steps and heard Michael crying but went up anyway. Passing by, I peeked at him and my mom in his new room. He was strewn across the bed, convulsing in tears of furious sobbing. Our mom hovered, trying to comfort him.

Once down the hall, I slid into my room and sat on the

bed. The drama was Michael's now. He owned it. This was his world, and I was cast in a supportive part. Sometimes, I sucked in the role of a good brother.

As usual, I watched YouTube videos. It was getting dark outside, and Michael had gotten quiet. A blustery wind began to beat up a loose shutter outside my window. I overheard footsteps and then the clatter of my mom in her room unpacking. I played more videos. It was late when my mother walked into my bedroom and handed me a soft fleece blanket.

Immediately, I draped it out and over my legs. "Thanks."

Her eyes narrowed, mouth parted, thinking for a moment before she started talking. "I should've told you, the psychiatrist at the hospital thinks Michael has schizoaffective disorder and not schizophrenia."

I sat up straighter in bed. "Is that better or worse?"

"It's almost the same. There can still be paranoia and hallucinations, but there's a mood component. Highs and lows. We have to be there for him."

"I am." She had to see that.

"Good night, Jacob." Her tone had softened. She never stayed mad for long. "I put a few towels and soap in the bathroom so you can wash-up. And don't stay up too late. We're registering you for school in the morning."

"Oh, great," I groaned and then added, "Good night."

She gave me a sad smile and left.

I made my way to a Pepto Bismol pink bathroom. Mom had hooked up our old shower curtain with the silver dragonflies on it. After a quick scrub and rinse, the old pipes loudly screeched as they shuddered off. I dried and dressed before wiping away the steam on the mirror, analyzing my reflection. My hair was too curly, and my eyelashes too long. After being teased in the first grade, I'd cut them off, but they grew back with a vengeance. I continued to move my face to my most flattering angles and decided to stop being a weirdo and go to sleep.

I returned to my room to find the closet door was slightly ajar. It was closed before, yet maybe my mom had been here and put something away. I opened it and flicked on the overhead closet light. Nothing was there except for my clothes and two cardboard boxes I had put there earlier that read Jacob's crap. Only this time, there was writing on the wall in black marker. I would have noticed it.

I scratched my head and read the words out loud, "The sky was a dark tomb. The stars forgot us, but it didn't matter. We ran. We ran. We ran. And hid so no one would find us."

I swallowed thickly. What? Oh, hell, Michael. I shot down the hall and stuck my head in his room. "What did you write? Part of a story or something? Or are you just messing with me?" Only then did I remember offending him and added, "Sorry about earlier, just don't write on my walls. Okay?"

"I didn't write anything. Get lost."

Michael didn't lie about any of the dumb shit he did. On the other hand, I suppose there was a first time for everything. "Whatever," I mumbled and said, "Good night." Hesitating, I drummed my fingers on the doorframe. Mike still ignored me, so I darted off.

I was drawn to the closet again, examining each word. I couldn't be a hundred percent sure, but it didn't look like Michael's handwriting. It appeared loopier, almost resembling calligraphy.

Then I looked around the rest of my room. There wasn't much to see. I only had a full-size bed and a small dresser.

Still, my eyes inspected every square inch of the space. The weirdness hijacking my usual sarcastic edge. I closed the closet, sprawling out across the bed, and searched for *schizoaffective disorder* on my phone. It was pretty much what my mom described. I read the words *genetic component* and placed the phone on my chest, trying not to think about it. The wind continued to battle the shutter, and the rain poured. My eyes went to the window with the heavy, mustard yellow curtains we'd left up for now. Of course, the lights flickered, and a cold chill crept in. The house was full of bad omens.

2

THINGS THAT GO BUMP IN THE NIGHT

My eyes snapped open as three words surfaced in my sleepy brain. *You're not alone.* A cold settled into my flesh, making the fine hairs on my arm stand up. I sat up in bed, sucking in a deep breath, and stared into the darkness, unsure what had woken me. My lights were off. It was pitch black. Then the distinct pitter-patter of footsteps sounded down the hall.

"Mom?" When I got no answer, I jumped out of bed and scrambled for the light switch. The overhead fluorescent light blinked on, and I immediately noticed the closet door was partway opened again. I was sure I'd closed it this time, so I started off with slow, measured steps to investigate. I yanked the door open the rest of the way and hit the closet light. I scoured the walls to discover more writing. The single word, HELP, was written in the same marker on the wall. My pulse skyrocketed. It freaked me out.

I crept over to the bed and grabbed the blanket, swinging it around my shoulders like a cape, settling down on the drafty hardwood floor. With a shiver of anticipation, I kept my eyes pinned to the door, straining to hear the slightest noise. It was eerily quiet. Even the wind had died down.

Unexpectedly, I heard a girl's voice, so soft it was hardly audible, as it drifted up from the floor. It was only the word, "I'm."

I scooted over to the vent and whispered, "Um…hello?" There was no reply. It could have been a ringing or humming in my ear. Yeah, I'd only imagined it was a voice. Yet, I hadn't imagined the writing on the wall. I mean, what the hell? I got up and decided to have a look around. If someone was in the house, I had to know. I exited my room and began my search.

I stood face to face with a long and quiet hallway—doors on the left and right. My mind was a hot blank space as a thread of fear tugged me along. My mom's bedroom was kitty-corner to my room, so I stepped in just far enough to take in the visual of her tucked in bed. Her sleeping sounds were somewhere between wheezes and moans.

"Mom?" I whispered, but she didn't wake up, and I decided to just let her sleep.

I crossed over to the spare bedroom, smacking on the lights. There was only a desk and Mom's old computer in the corner. Determined, I was now on a serious hunt and rushed to the closet, flinging the door open. There wasn't anything. Not even writing on the wall.

Next on the list was Michael's room. I found him sitting up in bed with a vacant stare. The lights were off, but the blinds were open. Moonlight flitted in, creating shadowy outlines above the chest of drawers that appeared incompatible and menacing.

My gaze returned to my brother as I cleared my throat. "Were you just walking around?"

"No."

"Did you hear a girl's voice, Mike?"

He came to life. "Yeah. I heard her."

My mouth dropped. "Holy shit, I hoped I imagined it."

Michael stared at me with an unsettling intensity. "I heard her in the vents, the drainpipes, and in the walls. If you listen closely enough, you'll hear them all."

Oh great, I'm losing it too.

My brother nodded approvingly. Tension slid from his features, softening his mouth and jaw muscles. Misery loves company, I guess.

"Thanks a lot, Michael." More suspicious than ever, I flat-out accused him. "You wrote the word 'help' on my wall. Really cool. Well, you didn't scare me."

"Why would I want to scare you?" Michael asked.

"You tell me?" I smirked, yet my face heated. "There is no stupid ghost in the pipes, or in the walls...Got it?"

"She's not a ghost. She's a spirit."

"That's the same God damn thing, Michael." I rolled my eyes. "There's no spirit. Don't start with me." I threw my hands up in frustration and stalked off.

I gripped my head with my right hand and paced around my room. "Everything's fine," I said out loud. The words helped me gain some reassurance, but it was only momentary. Paranoia nagged me, and I had to double-check. I dropped down and planted both palms on the floor, speaking directly into the vent. "Hello—Um, hello. Is anyone there?"

I waited. Waited longer...Nothing. I puffed my cheeks and let my breath out with a pop, feeling a pang of relief. The hunt was over. I refused to dwell on it anymore. Finally, with a bit of effort, I decided Michael had written on my wall to get back at me, and I'd only imagined hearing that voice. I strode over to my bed and climbed in. My head sunk into the pillow, and fear, along with my thoughts, disintegrated into white noise. I fell asleep.

Friday morning, my mom stuck her head into my room, annoyingly cheerful. "Rise and shine, Jacob."

If life had been normal, I'd torture myself with snooze and wake up in a tiny yet warm apartment. Unfortunately, nothing was normal, and I woke up in this big, chilly house. On the plus side, I didn't have to go to school. On the minus side, I had to register for school, where I'd be the new, old student. It made for an awkward dynamic. People vaguely remembered you but were quite content to live their life without you.

After registration, we bought groceries and unpacked some of our stuff. Michael must have found more of his necklaces because now he had at least a dozen or so on. He also tied a bandana around his wrist like it was a bracelet.

The built-in bookcase in the living room was kind of classy. I had put so many of Mom's books away I'd lost count. It was an eclectic collection from nonfiction to suspense and fantasy. I set the hardback editions Harry Potter series toward the top. She and I read the first one together. Then from the corner of my eye, I watched as Michael methodically studied the cover of the novel in his hand before turning the pages. He was a lot of help. He'd probably only put three onto the shelf.

My mom held up an unmarked box filled with tangles of Christmas lights and ornaments. "Who packed this?" She gave me a questioning glance.

I shrugged. She directed me to put the Christmas tree and ornament boxes under the crawl space below the stairs.

I stooped down and slid open the door. There was kind of a funny smell like old flowers or something. I hadn't wanted to have to clean, so I decided to ignore it, jamming the boxes in. I stood there, slapping my hands together, jonesing for a break, when mom announced, "We're going to Aunt Veronica's for an early dinner."

3

RETURNING TO CAMELOT

A wisp of memories swirled around my chest, along with a slight unease that settled in my gut. We were seated around a large black dining room table with classy cloth napkins and shiny silverware. A big bowl of salad and breadbasket were being passed around. A pot roast with mounds of russet potatoes followed. My Aunt Veronica, or Aunt V, as I'd dubbed her, was a small-time journalist and the typical PTA mom, very well put together. She had the same dark hair as my mom but wore it in one of those straight, sleek bobs and got manicures. She had her snarky side and always had my mom's back.

My midget of a grandma, on the other hand, was my mom's biggest critic. "Sarah May, I'm not going to ask if you've been going to Mass. Maybe you're non-denominational now, like your sister."

Aunt V chuckled. "Christ. What's that supposed to mean?"

My mom quickly said, "We go sometimes."

"No, we don't," Michael blurted.

Grandma made a disappointed sound and fidgeted with her napkin. "Well, tell me the truth about something at least. Did you *really* quit this time?"

"Yes, I quit smoking," my mom replied firmly.

"The interrogation's over," my aunt said, her gaze landing on my uncle. "Where's Lucas?"

Before my uncle could answer, Lucas burst into the room. His eyes jumped straight to me, and his lips curled into a smile. "Hey, Jacob!" My cousin had grown into his teenage frame with hardening muscles while I just grew. He was the kind of guy girls swooned about.

"Hey," I said.

Lucas patted me a bit too hard on the shoulder, and my mom popped up to hug him. He kissed her on the cheek and said, "Hey, Aunt Sarah." Then he greeted Michael with a firm handshake. "How are you, Mike?"

Michael didn't answer and instead asked, "Does my hair look nesty? You know, like a bird's nest."

Why would he care? He never even combed his hair. Hell, he barely washed it.

"No man, you look great!" Lucas slid into the chair next to mine. He seemed a happy kind of hyper.

I looked at him funny, and my mom gave me a disapproving glance. "Jacob's so excited to see you, Lucas, aren't you, honey?"

I hated when my mom did this but nodded my head. "Yeah." She wanted everyone to be overly nice, like her.

"Let's hurry and eat." Lucas lightly jabbed an elbow into my arm. "So, we can go bike riding."

I was skeptical. Could it really be this easy? Could we just pick up where we left off? "I don't have my bike here," I said.

"You can ride my old one." Then we shared a look—the kind of conspiratorial look we'd shared back in the day.

"So, tell us, Jacob, did you leave a girlfriend behind in New York?" Grandma asked.

"No," I softly replied.

"Oh, Lucas always has some girlfriend," Grandma teased, looking over at him, and he blushed.

Michael broke in, "I liked a girl at the mental place."

"Nice, Michael," Grandma warmly indulged him.

I hunched in my chair. My sole goal was to clear the little bit of food I had on my plate, so I could go ride bikes.

Lucas shoveled his food in even faster than me, prompting Uncle Pete to tell us, "Whoa, boys, slow down. It's not a race." He had a deep voice, which boomed around him. "So, you run track, Jacob?"

"Uh, yeah."

"You should check out the trophies this one's got. He's breaking state records." Uncle Pete gestured to Lucas.

I nodded, and Lucas put his head down and said, "I don't have many trophies. Just ribbons."

My aunt grinned. "He's modest. And he didn't get that from me. I'll tell you I'm epic," she joked.

Clearly, my aunt and uncle were in the *Lucas fan club*. It wasn't necessarily a bad thing. I mean, he was a cool enough guy. My mom may have been right to bring us back here after all.

Lucas had cleared his plate and eyed me. I took a couple of quick bites and finished.

"Dinner was awesome as usual, Mom," Lucas said,

always knowing how to suck up to adults. "Is it okay if we go ride bikes now?"

"It's fine with me," she replied.

"Don't be too long," my mom added.

"Michael seems to be doing pretty good, but how is he really?" Lucas asked, concern etched around his brows.

The question made me uncomfortable. I just wanted everyone to remember my brother the way he used to be. "Different," I admitted.

It had never been easy for my brother. Early on, Michael was diagnosed with Asperger's. There was a sulky shyness about him, and he had trouble making friends. By the time he was in high school, he only wanted to play his guitar, and he mastered it. For the most part, he ignored me.

The realization hit me. "In a way, he's nicer now, but I miss the way he was, too. Now he seems like my younger brother."

The mood was sober until Lucas lightened things. "Remember what he used to call us?"

"Little Einsteins," I replied, and we both smiled.

Slightly unburdened and done sharing, I asked, "So, what's new with you?"

The garage door opened with a series of crackles as Lucas announced, "I'm thinking of becoming a communist."

I considered it. "Interesting," I responded as my gaze shot to the American flag on the side of the garage. "But your parents may not approve."

"They might not." Lucas disappeared into the garage and quickly returned, wheeling out his old ten-speed. "Here you go."

I climbed onto the bike, and a minute later, Lucas slid in next to me on his shiny new Schwinn bike with ape hanger handlebars.

A gust of wind cut across our faces as we pedaled furiously down the street, sort of racing. Then, slowing the pace, we splashed through a gutter clogged with soggy autumn leaves, surrounded by beautiful two-story houses, brick or stone. It was familiar scenery. I'd always known Lucas best from my peripheral. A buzz passed through me, and I vaguely remembered what real fun felt like. Riding our bikes transported me to a happier time. The cul-de-sac gave way to a maze of magic streets—we returned to Narnia. We were the cool kids patrolling the neighborhood. In second and third grade, we'd pretended our bikes were horses, and we were knights, or they were flying brooms, and we were wizards. It was stupid little kid stuff.

After an hour of riding, the barest hint of red showed on the horizon. The sun was setting, and we finally rested for a bit. Lucas took a drink from a bottle of water he had stashed in the pocket of his hoodie and handed it to me. I chugged it.

Then we circled the subdivision until his house came back into view. He pulled into his circular driveway, putting his kickstand up. I stopped next to him, leaning on the handlebars, slightly winded.

"I wanted to run an idea by you," he said. Then his cell chimed, and he held up a finger. "One minute. Park it around the side of the garage." I heard him say, "Hey," into the phone as he trotted off.

The kitchen window was partly opened, and I heard my aunt and uncle's voices over the clink and clank of dishes.

I strained to hear my uncle's low-pitched and even voice. "Michael seemed weird before, but now he's really lost it. And he looks bad."

"Don't be a dick, Sarah might hear you...Michael can't help it."

I turned away. Now I knew why I didn't feel comfortable here. My uncle used stuff like this to feel superior. This was just what I had been afraid of. Assholes judging my brother.

Lucas came from around the corner and said, "Hey, sorry, it was my sort of girlfriend."

"It's, um...cool."

He must have noticed I was distracted and asked, "Is something wrong?"

I forced myself to make eye contact. "No. Nothing."

Lucas tried to make small talk. I was too angry and mentally had checked out. Luckily, my mom and Michael appeared, and it was time to go.

On the ride home, a sense of dread brushed against me. I had another night in my strange new house to look forward to.

4

THE GRAVEYARD SHIFT

I inserted my earbuds and blared some rock music. After a few songs, there was a call from my dad. He hardly ever called anymore. Still, I didn't answer. I gained a sense of sick satisfaction from ignoring his calls.

My eyes shot to the closet, and I pushed myself into a seated position. I wasn't exactly scared. But I felt uncomfortable enough to get off my iPhone and head for the stairs. I hoped to spend a little time with my mom before she had to leave for work.

I passed through the half-lit house, finding Mom and some cookies in the kitchen.

Mom opened the cabinet and tipped a box upside down. "Did you eat all the granola bars, Jacob? I was going to take one for my snack."

I hurried to finish off an entire chocolate chip cookie I had just stuffed in my mouth. "No. Maybe Michael did."

"You know, he's not eating anything processed. It's his new kick."

This reminded me of the mysterious goings-on that had happened since we arrived. "There must be someone else here because I didn't eat them." I inserted a hint of firmness into my words, like she sometimes had. After swallowing the remaining crumbs, I added, "There was writing on the wall of my closet."

She appeared unfazed. "The writing must have been there before we moved in," she decided and tossed the empty box of granolas in the recycle bin.

"Yeah, but I thought I heard a girl's voice in the vent."

My mom seemed to freeze and stiffen. Then, curiously, our eyes met. She gave me an anxious, soul-searching look that freaked me out.

"I mean, it was, um, nothing. Michael was just playing videos." Quickly changing the subject, I asked, "Why do you have to work midnights?"

She exhaled and relaxed, casually slipping her hands into the pockets of her scrubs. "We talked about this, honey." I usually hated it when she called me sweet names but didn't mind it now for some reason. "Every new nurse gets stuck working midnights."

We strolled to the front door. She kissed my cheek and left to work the graveyard shift. I engaged the lock, turning my head toward the coat rack. In the dim light, it almost resembled a tall person. Staring at it made it morph into an unearthly, nightmarish form. What the hell? Blinking the vision away, I decided that coat rack had to go.

I sped off, stopping in the living room. Although our leather sectional and big screen were in place, it wasn't our living room at all. The dim, static glow of the TV only strengthened my discomfort. I grabbed the remote, accidentally raising the volume instead of turning to a channel. The hissing blared to a deafening shriek, making my ears ring. A strange human-like figure with horns flashed on the screen. I fumbled and shut it off, dropping the remote. It was probably from some cheesy horror flick. My heart still hammered as I jogged up the stairs—tonight was already getting the best of me.

Hoping to hang out with Michael, I stopped by his room. It wasn't even 11 o'clock, but he was already sound asleep. The repeated rattle of each of his snores formed a rhythm. Oh great, he'd probably be out for the night.

Michael could have made me feel better. I had reassured him plenty of times. Instead, he continued to snore. "Screw you, Mike."

Unexpectantly, footsteps crossed the hallway. My pulse quickened, and I paused for a few seconds before looking. By the time I did, no one was there. I rounded the corner and peered down the lonely stairs. It was useless. I had waited too long to check it out, and the person was gone, or my imagination was running amok. The latter made the most sense. Note to self, don't mention this to Mom.

Back in my room, I snapped on the lights and remembered my father saying, *'The same ugly that can get you in the dark, can get you when the light is on,'* which wasn't very reassuring. Hell, neither was he, and my lights were staying on.

I wasn't finished freaking myself out and went to look in the closet. Honestly, I hadn't expected to see more writing. Yet, there it was. "The world is small even if you crawl and no one knows you."

"Holy shit, is someone here?" I asked in response.

The same distant female voice said, "Yes."

I practically jumped out of my skin and dropped to the hardwood floor to be closer to the vent, breathing out a panicked, "Hello," and "Who are you? Where are you?" I waited. "Please? Say something."

"Hi," the voice weakly replied.

"Are you a fucking ghost?"

"Don't curse!" The girl's voice sounded stronger.

"Sorry," I said. "Who *are* you?" No answer. "Hello? Hello?" She had gone mute again.

Enough was enough. I bolted. The floorboards creaked with each hurried step as I made a mad dash to Michael's room. "Michael. Michael, there's a girl in the house!" I exclaimed, but he only snored in reply. I patted his shoulder blade. "Michael, wake-up. There's a girl in the house."

He groaned, "Lemme alone," and rolled over, placing the pillow on his face.

I picked up Michael's arms. They flopped back to his sides, and he groaned once more. It was like raising the dead, for sure. Then, somehow with ample whining, begging, and the threat, "I swear to God, I'll hate you forever if you don't get your ass out of bed." Michael got up and stood in his T-shirt and boxers, groggily slipping on a pair of rumpled jeans from the floor before accompanying me through a tour of the house. He shielded his half-closed eyes while I turned on bedroom lights, tore open closets, but didn't find anything or anyone.

Standing in the hall, the bathroom's leaking sink invited me in. My frightened face in the mirror startled me as I twisted the faucet shut. Shadows stretched out from corners of the wall, and a cursory glance behind me revealed Michael silently pointing to the closed shower curtain. Someone could be hiding there. Waiting. I jerked it, rings screeching against the rod. Nothing. Just an empty pink tub.

After checking out both the second and first floor, we convened at the foot of the stairs. My brother remained groggy throughout the entire search. "I'm going to bed," he slurred. His thumbs hooked idly in his jean pockets.

"We've checked out the whole place, right? Because I swear, there was a girl. She talked to me." I scratched my head.

With a tiny spark of interest, he told me, "We can't see her because she's an apparition. A phantom." He finished with a yawn.

I tried to stay calm. "Let's hang out in your room and see if we hear anything. Alright, Michael?"

He shrugged and seemed to come to life. "What did she say to scare you? Did she order you to kill me?"

"God, no." *What the hell were his voices telling him?* "She didn't want me to curse."

"You cursed at a spirit? What's wrong with you?"

I rolled my eyes at him. "Can you be sensible? The house was empty for a while. She's probably homeless, or a crack-head." Yet, I didn't even know what I was saying or what was going on.

Sarcastically, Michael countered, "Oh yeah, crackheads are invisible and outraged by swearing."

"Real funny." This was weird because sarcasm wasn't Michael's thing, but it probably wasn't intentional. He started up the stairs, and I followed.

Was the girl I heard a spirit? Or was I hearing and seeing things that weren't there? And which of the two scenarios terrified me more?

We were in Michael's room again when I suggested, "We should call Mom...or the cops."

My brother turned and blinked at me. "They're just going to tell you the same thing they tell me. It's all in your head."

An anxious feeling pitted in my stomach, and I swallowed hard.

Michael laid across his bed. "Do you hear her now?"

"No. I don't hear her now." I grimaced and lowered my head.

"Oh," Michael replied, almost disappointed. He knocked on his head. "I hear them."

"Sorry." God, that had to be terrible. What could be worse than having a haunted head? I didn't know what else to say and just stood there. A hush fell over the room.

Then my brother moved his tongue around in his mouth. His eyes half lidded. "My mouth's dry from this new medicine," he complained. It couldn't have bothered him too much because his sheets rustled, bedsprings squeaked as his snores recommenced. But, hell, for me, it was going to be one *long* night.

I sat at the end of my brother's bed, listening to him snore for about an hour. Finally, I tiptoed across the darkened hall to my room. The light was still on, and I closed the door with a sigh. It was chilly, so I snatched my hoodie from the closet. That was when an unexpected "Hello," jolted me, and I practically jumped out of my skin.

The voice still seemed to be emanating from the floor. Stooping down low, I spoke into the vent like it was an intercom. "Where are you? Who are you?" It was all I could think to ask this disembodied voice. My teeth carved into my bottom lip, waiting on a response.

"If it's okay, I want to meet...talk in person," the voice shyly said. "Uh, please don't wake your brother up? He kind of scares me."

"He scares you." I shook my bleary head. "Okay, I won't wake him. Come up. I want to...meet you too."

"Alright," she said.

I felt partly detached from the horror. What the hell? Was this really going down? I sprang up and paced. I was torn between making a run for it, yet anxious to get some terrible and inevitable fate over with. Then I perched at the edge of my bed with my cellphone in hand and the numbers 9 and 1 keyed in, just in case this meeting went south.

So, I waited, half expecting a pale ghost with hollow sockets where eyes should be. Or the girl from *The Ring*, hunched over, hair partly obscuring her ghastly dead and murderous face. Then the stairs creaked, and I concentrated on the footsteps coming closer and closer. My heart rate sped up, unease wrapped itself around my body, and I braced myself for *God knows what.*

5

ALONE

I anxiously listened to the brittle snapping sound of each footfall on floorboards rumbling closer and closer. Then, it got dead quiet before the sound of the footsteps resumed, increasing in tempo yet growing fainter. My frigging ghost was getting away. I dashed out of the room just in time to catch sight of a girl's fleeing silhouette.

"Wait!" I yelled.

I raced down the steps after her, but she was gone. Or had she ever really been there? Yet if you're losing touch with reality, doesn't some tiny part of you know it was all in your head? I went to each room, slapping on lights and calling for her to, "Please, come out!" Reasoning, explaining, "I just want to meet you."

I passed through the living room and stood at the foot of the stairs. I tried to stay calm, which was tough with my stomach churning. Whoever this girl was, she'd vanished into thin air. It left me chasing dusky shadows on the walls. Maybe there was never really anyone there, and it was just a hallucination. Then it hit me. There was one place my brother and I hadn't even checked out.

I had to go to the cellar even if it scared the crap out of me. It was your stereotypical dumbass teenager from every slasher movie's course of action. If there was really a girl in the house, where else could she be? I passed through the darkened kitchen. Neon green numbers on the microwave read 2:00. My mom wouldn't be home for hours, and I was sure Michael was still asleep.

I entered what my mom called a mudroom and hit the lights. The room was empty except for the washer and dryer and a flattened mouse that must have been crushed under a shoe. *Poor guy*, I thought, stepping around his tiny carcass to find myself directly in front of the cellar door. Honestly, part of me preferred to discover a band of homeless drug addicts living down there. Then I'd be able to make a run for it. It was better than being faced with the idea of losing my mind. Maybe my crazy decision to venture down there by myself was further proof that was what was happening. Yet, going down to the cellar seemed inevitable, like the unsealing of Pandora's box.

I felt an increase in panic as I twisted the doorknob, and it groaned in on its hinges. Since it was unlocked, someone could hide there and come and go with ease. I frantically felt for the light switch until I noticed a cord hanging and yanked it. A single light bulb eerily flickered back and forth, dimly illuminating the large, gloomy space. The dirty dishrag smell of the cellar intensified as I started down the stairs.

I gripped the railing and forced myself to keep going. One foot and then the next. As I made it to the final step, I paused, taking in a big shitty hole of a room. Shelves comprised of decaying wood lined the walls stocked with empty wine bottles. The other set of stairs was at the far end of the space, leading up to the trapdoor I had seen from the front yard. I remembered it hadn't even been locked.

Just then, my feet touched down on the concrete. It was cold and disgusting. I should have worn my sneakers, but at least I had my hoodie on. My hands stayed nestled in the pockets, and my elbows stuck out like broken wings. Curious items were strewn across the floor in the gloom. There was an old tricycle in the corner and a cardboard box. A blanket of dust covered the lid. I opened it, sending up a cloud of dust to discover some rusty tools, a screwdriver, saw, and wrench—possible murder weapons. A wooden toilet seat rested against the wall with a price tag of four dollars on it. I paid little attention to it.

Instead, I traced a straight path to a large doll. Her mock eyes and high arched brows were menacing. The thing had a mop of brown, chin-length hair and stood about three feet tall with a hand-written sign which read, $30, adding *She walks too.*

"Well, that's comforting," I mumbled and flicked its plastic doll head. Somehow, for a crazy minute, I wondered if a possessed doll could have been responsible for the voice and even the writing on the wall.

"Holy shit, Annabelle," I blurted in reply to my own whacked-out theory and slowly backed away from the doll.

They were probably simple garage sale rejects. I started searching the rest of the basement but sensed a presence. Someone or something looming...lurking. My feet pounded up the steps, thumping in concert with the beating of my heart. I swept the door shut behind me and shot off to the kitchen. The clock read 2:05. Damn, that had been a long five minutes. Again, I'd managed to freak myself out.

I trekked to the living room and surrendered, collapsing on the leather sectional, peeling off my damp and filthy socks, pleading, "Please, please just meet me."

I had to calm down and think reasonably. There was no such thing as a possessed doll, but what the hell? I pushed unexpectant tears away. I had to confront the possibility I was not well. I was hearing a voice, feeling paranoid, talking to myself, waking up my mentally ill brother in the middle of the night to go on a ghost hunt. "I'm losing it." My mom would have to take care of both of her sons.

Suddenly, the floor creaked, and I sensed a presence in the room and lifted my head to see a girl. A startled sound escaped me.

She was about my age. Her dark hair hung long, in loose, flowing waves, and she was wearing an old-timey dress, which clung to her thin yet hourglass figure. She had large clear eyes and full, pouty lips. I had seen that pretty face. After a beat, I stood and remembered.

"We went to school together. You stopped going to school in the middle of fourth grade. You had an unusual name. I can't think of it."

"You're Jacob Kelly and your cousin's Lucas McKay. You were good at the multiplication tables timed tests, but Lucas was the best. In Math, I always felt someone whispered the answers to me."

She was saying a lot, her voice trembling. What was she rambling about? My eyes followed her about the room as she wrung her hands and paced near the mantle.

"It seems like just yesterday I was that little girl," she said.

"You were smart, and uh, grew up nicely." My cheeks warmed, and I remembered now. She had been a weird kid and obviously still was. I had a little crush on her back then. She always wore a dress and was the cutest girl in the class. She tried hard to make friends but played by herself at recess. She had a unique name. "Ary. Your name's Ary Daniels."

"Nice of you to remember. It's actually Sanctuary. Only Ms. Collins suggested I'd be called Ary for short, and I liked it better. Sanctuary's such a mouthful."

"Oh yeah, Ms. Collins, our third-grade teacher." Her forgotten image flashed in my head.

"Did I upset you? You were crying?" she asked caringly, still keeping her distance, standing at the far end of the living room.

"Oh, no, hell no," I said, with a small uneasy voice.

She reprimanded me with a hand on her hip. "Don't curse."

"Oh, sorry." My mood shifted, and I felt confused and a little defensive. I took a couple of steps toward her. "Wait. Why are you in *my house*?"

"Just stay back. Alright?" She held out her shaky hand. Her posture straightened, and she seemed fearful and oddly pious at the same time.

"Okay." I halted.

A foot of space stood between us when she said, "I know about bad things." A flush of color crossed her cheeks, and her pink lips fell into a frown. "You're not one of those boys who likes to hurt girls, are you?"

"No, of course not." I held up my hands reassuringly before becoming more annoyed than ever and dropping my arms to my side. "I'm not the one who's suspect here. You had me thinking I was going crazy. Now answer the question. Why are you here?"

"I ran away. And Lucas...Lucas brought me here."

"Lucas?"

6

ARY FROM FOURTH GRADE

Really? Lucas brought her here. That must have been what he'd wanted to tell me. "Okay. So why did Lucas bring you here? Are you his girlfriend or something?"

She talked just above a whisper, with a voice as smooth as velvet. "I thought about Lucas all the time. I lived for Sundays. Mother let us dress up and go to church. It was a reprieve, a celebration, and there he was. Lucas McKay. He'd greet me with a glance, a nod, sometimes even a smile."

Her speech was oddly formal. Eloquent. No one talks like this, I thought. "You didn't answer either of my questions." I spoke gently. She was fragile.

"Sorry. What did you ask?" She rubbed her hands together.

"Why did you run away from home?" I asked. It seemed like the more important question, though I wondered about her and Lucas's relationship just as much.

"It's not a home. It's a haunted house." A few tears welled

until they broke free. She batted them away with a stroke of her hand.

"Haunted? Um, do you want to sit and talk?"

She nodded. I sat on the couch, and she settled a good foot away from me. "I ran away for all of us. If you could help me say things the right way, there's a chance we could get them out of there."

"When you say all of us, are you talking about your siblings?"

"No." She squinted in heavy concentration, but she still had difficulty getting her words out. "I don't know, uh—all their names. Ma-Mother fosters some…Kidnaps most of us. One girl said they took her from the tire swing in her back-yard. They come. They go. We aren't allowed to speak to one another. We're chained…and the silence is like a cold slab between us."

I felt weird inside. What the hell? Everything she said was hard to process. It was so wild I momentarily blanked on how to respond. She probably had mental health issues and was off her meds. If that was the case, why would Lucas bring her here? He was a smart, sensible guy.

"Mother and Gary hurt us. It's bad. Someone needs to stop them. But I'm not sure anyone can." She seemed smaller and shakier than ever.

"They should be in jail. Why didn't Lucas take you to the police station. You know, so you could report them?"

Her breathing became labored, and the palms of her hands ran up and down her arms. "I tried going the police once when I escaped, but Mother speaks so well, they believed her instead of me." We looked at one another, and I could tell she was genuinely scared. Yet delusions are real to the person experiencing them.

"Do you have a camera?" she asked.

"Well, yeah, everyone's phone has a camera."

"If anyone could help, you could. You were smart and popular. You always got picked right away in gym."

The way she put it was odd. "Sadly, I may have peaked in the fourth grade." I was almost brought back to the days of dodgeball, the shrieking links of the swing set, and the happy screams of recess.

"You were always funny."

"I was?"

Her lips twitched into a smile. "Yes. You're funny now, too." She neatly folded her hands in her lap. "I've been so lonely." Her right hand darted up to her throat. "My voice sounds strange, and I can't shut up. Am I talking a lot?"

Almost instantly, I felt oddly protective of her. "Yeah, but it's cool. Are you hungry?"

Her sad, aqua-colored eyes beamed at me, becoming round as quarters, and she nodded her head *yes*.

Sitting at the kitchen table, Ary nodded my way. My gaze settled on the elegant column of her neck as she tipped her head back, gulping down a glass of water. Her black hair had mocha highlights, and her skin was creamy under the fluorescent lights. She possessed a sweetness and innocence that gave her immediate charm—a kind of sparkle. Next, I watched her wolf down a cheese omelet. Utterly fascinated. Still, it was after 3:00 am, and despite being weirded out by the turn of events, my eyelids felt heavy, and I was starting to fade.

Her fork clinked down on the plate. "That was the best thing I ever had, next to chocolate milk." She broke into an even bigger smile, which revealed dimples. "I love chocolate milk." Then her expression changed, and she bent over as her lips fell. "I have a bubbly feeling in my stomach."

"Good bubbly or you're going to yak, bubbly?" I talked to her as if she was a child, and in a way, she was.

"I'm not sure." She nodded quite seriously, and a worry line formed between her eyebrows.

"That's not good." I told her where the bathroom was in case, she got sick now. Then it occurred to me she must have known since she'd been living here, and I had to ask, "How long have you been here?"

"I got here the night before you did, I think."

"Where have you been hiding? I couldn't find you."

"Under the stairs."

"Like Harry Potter." I was amused by this.

"Someone put boxes there, and now I can barely fit." She shook her head in exasperation.

"Sorry, I put the boxes there. If you want, I can take the boxes down to the cellar?"

Ary leaped to her feet, and her skirt twirled around as she did what resembled a pirouette. She stumbled as she came to a stop and let out a nervous laugh. "Really, that'd be great. I feel safe there. I can help."

"Okay. Let's do this."

I lugged the six-foot tree box, and she took the box filled with ornaments and lights. We arrived at the cellar door, and I propped the box against the wall in the mudroom. Ary noticed the dead mouse. She heaved in a couple deep breaths and shut her eyes.

I called her name a couple of times before getting her attention. "Mice freak you out. Sorry, I forgot to throw it away," I said.

"Throw it away. That's awfully cold. We should probably bury it and say a prayer. Every creature big and small has worth."

I was too exhausted to argue. "Let's put these boxes in the cellar and get some sleep, and I'll bury it in the morning." This was code for I'll throw it in the trash without her knowing.

"And say a prayer?" She added.

I hesitated and gave her a one-shoulder shrug. "Sure."

She said an exaggerated but sincere, "Thank you, Jacob Kelly."

"No biggie, and just call me Jacob." I opened the door and yanked the cord for the lights. Next, I placed the boxed tree on the stairs, letting it slide down.

Ary remarked, "Clever." She was a girl easy to impress. Before I could say anything, she did the same thing with her box. It tumbled halfway down, breaking some of the glass ornaments by the sound of it. My eyes shot around the shadowy room, and I decided to deal with the boxes later.

We didn't speak till we were back by the half-opened door under the stairs. "Do you have a blanket?" I asked.

"I found an old sheet in the cellar and hairbrush. That's all I have."

"I'll get you some stuff."

"If possible, could you get me a change of clothes?"

"Sure," I said and added, "And you can shower if you want."

She twisted her hands together excitedly and practically sang, "Thank you, thank you, thank you."

My eyebrows lifted. "No problem."

I made it to my room with what little energy I had left. First, I found my old sleeping bag and continued rummaging through several boxes until I located a hurricane lantern and a toothbrush still in its package. All things, I had reasoned, would be useful. Next, I stopped by my mom's room and grabbed a couple of flowy nightgowns. Gifts from Grandma that Mom never wore. They kind of looked like Ary.

I headed back down the steps, and almost expected that Ary would have disappeared. But she stood like a statue just where I had left her.

7

COMPLICATED

Sunlight sliced in through partly opened curtains. A glance at my phone revealed it was nine o'clock, definitely early for a Saturday morning. Usually, I'd bask in the warmth of the blankets and maybe revisit a dream. The excitement and anxiety of having a girl socked away under the stairs had me springing out of bed. After using the bathroom, gargling with a little mouthwash, and wetting my hair, so I didn't look like the Mad Hatter, I wandered down the hall, taking count of Mom and Michael in their beds.

Then I thumbed a quick text to Lucas. "I found the girl, or should I say, MET Ary. WTF? Call me"—and descended down the steps. *What's up with Lucas? What's with this girl?*

Once down the stairs, I wondered if Ary would be awake or even still be here. I kept expecting her to bail. Hesitantly, I lightly rapped on the half-door to the crawl space under the stairs. One moment of silence stretched into another. I knocked again as my cell buzzed. It was a call from Lucas.

I answered. "Hey."

"I got your text. Something about a girl?"

"Remember, Ary? Ah, the girl you brought to stay at my new house."

"What? I have no clue what you're talking about."

"Come on, you know, Ary Daniels, the runaway? I know she's here. The jig is up."

"*Jig*? Are you on drugs? I haven't seen Ary Daniels since the third, maybe fourth grade. Is she really at your house?"

The half-door swung open, and Ary stepped out and shyly stood before me, in my mother's nightgown, simply blinking.

"I'll call you back." I ended the call and slipped my cell into my jean pocket. The corner of my mouth edged up, and I squinted at her.

"Is the coast clear? If not, I can sleep longer." She clasped her hands together as if she was praying. "And if it's not too much trouble, do you think you could wash my dress and my sheet?"

"Sure—" Then I decided to confront her. "Just so you know, I talked to Lucas, and he didn't bring you here."

Ary crossed her arms and refused to make eye contact. Her expression was the slightly distant yet superior one. "Well, whether or not you believe me, Lucas was there with me every step. His face was what I saw with every heartbeat."

It was all getting too weird for me. "Whatever that means. Sorry, but I'm calling the cops. You can tell them what you told me." I lifted my cell, prepared to make the call.

Her delicate hand caught my wrist. Surprisingly strong.

"Please, please don't send me back. I'll do *anything*. I'll clean, do bad stuff with you." She blushed, shutting her eyes, and puckering her lips.

"Bad stuff. What are you even talking about?" She looked silly, and I halfway snorted. "Cut it out, Ary." She lowered her head, sniffling, and I tried to reassure her. "My mom and I can talk to the police with you and make sure things are investigated. Make sure you're safe."

"Please, please." She dropped to the floor, wrapping her arms around my calves. "You don't understand. I just can't."

"If you lied about Lucas, how do I know you're not lying about everything?"

She stared up at me and drew in the kind of breath you take before you're about to say something important. "It wasn't a lie. It was make-believe. I couldn't walk through those woods alone at night. I'd be too scared. I'm not a brave girl."

That made a weird kind of sense. I sighed. "Just stand up, Ary."

She reached for my hand, so I helped her to her feet. For a second, our fingers locked together.

"You're pretty brave," I told her.

She pulled her hand away, and her eyes flashed with an idea. "I have granola bars. Do you want one?"

"Geez, those are my mom's granolas. You stole them."

"I didn't know. Sorry." She shamefully bowed her head. "Just don't send me back. At least let me get dressed so I can run for it."

"The granola bars are no big deal. And run where?" I drifted away from the stairs and plopped down on the sofa. It was way too early for all this drama. Lucas was calling, but I decided to ignore the call.

Ary had followed and was hovering above me. "I'll go anywhere, anywhere but there."

I studied her. She was shaky, the kind of shaky even some theatrical chick couldn't fake. She was either mentally ill or telling the truth. If there was the slightest possibility it was true, it was terrifying. Tired and feeling bad for her, too, I just gave in. "I'll do your laundry, and we can hang out and think about things." This way, I'd get a better feel for her and the situation.

Straight away, Ary became all dimples and sparkles, and a few happy tears fell down her face. She wiped them away. Her eyes twinkled at me, and her long lashes stuck damply together. She decided with certainty, "This will be the best day ever."

"Yeah. Why not?" I went with it. "We can binge watch Netflix, eat hot chips."

"What's Netflix? What are hot chips?" She seemed like an eager student taking notes.

I wondered if she was for real. It didn't matter. I already liked her way too much.

I leaned back against the sofa, my legs stretched out and crossed at the ankles, feet on the coffee table. "Is your stomach better now?"

"I think so," Ary softly replied.

"Next time, I'll make pancakes. I excel at the art of breakfast."

"Pancakes." She nodded approvingly and brightened until I thought she might burst. "This is all so great." Then she studied me, mimicking my exact position. "Is this really what life can be like?"

"I guess," I replied. It was hard to tear my eyes away from her. She had on what looked like *A Little House on the Prairie* dress, with a high collar and puffy sleeves that tightened and stopped at her elbows. I examined her dress more closely. There were tiny purple flowers and greenery on the heavy fabric. Pretty stylish if you're Amish. Come to think of it, she wore these kinds of dresses in grade school. She was still pretty—like a cute girl from some history book.

She turned to face me. I hoped she didn't notice me gawking. "Thank you for washing my dress and for breakfast," she said, sounding grateful and surprised.

"It was nothing." Finally, in a quiet moment, reality sank in, and it was almost noon. "My mom will be up soon. Um, we could tell her that you're an old friend from school...and you stopped over to visit." It didn't seem believable, but I snapped my fingers, adding, "We reconnected on Facebook."

"Facebook?"

"Yeah, it's on the computer," I explained.

She thoughtfully rubbed her chin. "Anyway, I am your friend from school. So, it's not a lie." Her voice became a little wobbly, and she eased into her next words. "Uh...when your mom and brother wake up, I'd rather hide." I didn't reply right away, and she let out a sigh of relief, asking, "Now, are we going to watch Netflix?" She appeared cheerful, but there was a weariness just beneath the surface.

"Yeah." I grabbed the remote and turned the TV on. Of course, I scrolled to *Stranger Things*, the curiously odd similarities not lost to me. "You haven't seen it, right?"

Her balloon of enthusiasm popped, and she frowned. "You don't get it. I haven't seen anything, done anything."

"Right." I started the show, and Ary returned to life, throwing several excited looks in my direction during the previews but quickly becoming immersed in the TV. Her eyes were glued to the screen as she twisted the corner of a cobalt blue throw on the sofa.

During the third episode of *Stranger Things*, I popped up. "I'm going to get snacks."

She shushed me before apologizing. "I'm sorry, it's just so good."

"It's cool," I told her and then proceeded to the kitchen. When I came back, I handed her the bag, explaining, "I got you Cheetos cause hot chips are a little intense."

"Thanks," she said and began munching on them, stopping only to suck the orange off her fingers. I scrunched my nose up at her, and she noticed and blushed, extending the half-eaten bag my way. "Have some. They're delicious."

"No thanks." I fished out a napkin from my pocket and gave it to her.

She wiped her hands and said, "This day is—" she searched for the right word. "Perfect."

"Yeah, there's something innately relaxing about Saturday and binge watching someone else's life."

She scooted closer to me. I could hardly believe it. Her head fell on my shoulder. Enjoying the closeness, I grinned, and my cell buzzed. Ary's head jerked up as I read a text from Lucas: "I'm here." A knock on the door followed.

"Who is it?" Ary rubbed her eyes and swiveled to me. Her irises were shimmering pools of blues and greens.

"It's fine, it's just Lucas."

"Lucas! I'll hide." She scampered to her feet.

"Relax. You don't have to. I already told him about you." I paused the TV and stood next to her.

Ary latched on to my upper arm. "Jacob, you're the only one I can talk to. Please don't make me talk to other people," she pleaded with a nervous blush on her cheeks.

I kind of liked that she said this and briefly smiled. "You don't have to talk to him." The knocking resumed. "I better let him in, or he'll wake my mom." I caught a blur of Ary running away out of the corner of my eye as I walked over and opened the front door.

Lucas wore a wide-eyed, you're *freaking-me-out* expression as he walked into the house. "So, were you joking about Ary Daniels being here?" He asked and strolled over to the living room.

"No. She's here, but she must've gone back under the stairs. She feels safe there."

"Call her. I want to talk to her." Lucas faked a smile.

"She doesn't really want to talk right now." He ignored me, and I followed him as he walked to the stairs and bent down to tap the door.

"Ary, can you say hello?" Lucas asked, calling my bluff.

"Sorry, Ary, I told him you didn't feel like talking."

"Come on, say hello," Lucas pushed, but nothing.

It was an uncomfortable look. I knew he thought I was

nuts, and it got to me, so I tapped lightly on the door. "Please, Ary. Just say hi, then he'll buzz off."

Lucas bent down and opened the door, leaning over to step inside. Then, Ary's voice squealed, "Hello."

After Lucas responded with a strained, "Hi there," he reemerged, standing next to me again. His face reddened slightly. "She's here," he said in disbelief.

I folded my arms across my chest, satisfied.

His mouth briefly formed a circle. "That's Ary Daniels."

"Really, you don't say." I gave him my best shit-eating grin.

"What's she doing here?" he whispered.

Voices floated down from the second floor. Mom and Michael had woken up and were talking. I walked away from the stairs, and Lucas trailed me into the kitchen.

I tried to explain things. "She ran away. I mean, it sounds bad. She claims her foster mom and some guys are keeping her chained up...even beat her."

Lucas squinted, processing what I'd said. "Ary used to go to my church a few years ago, then just stopped. Her foster mother still does and seems...nice. She has this GoFundMe page because she takes in a lot of special needs kids. She has different kids with her sometimes, but always this older boy." He shook his head, gently adding, "Maybe Ary has psychological problems."

I thought about the odd way Ary acted. Still, I answered from my gut. "Yeah, she has issues, but maybe because of how she's been mistreated. Why did her mom stop sending her to school, taking her to church?" I decided, "I want to at least meet this lady for myself—and go to the house and check it out."

Lucas rubbed his hands over his face, and his lips twisted into a grimace. "You're not qualified. A social worker should be the one to check things out."

"Yeah, but if her mom is such a pillar of society, and Ary's a runaway, she'd probably get sent back there."

My mom suddenly walked into the kitchen. She was wearing her light blue terrycloth bathrobe with the coffee stain and immediately lit up at the sight of Lucas. "Hey, you," she reached up and stroked his cheek. "What a nice surprise."

Lucas said a warm, "Hi, Aunt Sarah," and asked, "How do you like the new house?"

Mom said, "I like it. But if you could excuse us, I just need to have a word with Jacob. Alone."

This wasn't good. Had she seen Ary and me together? Overheard us talking?

"Sure thing," Lucas gazed briefly at me and exited the room.

Mom microwaved a cup of water, and the silence ate at me. So, I asked, "How was work?"

She said, "Busy…Labor and delivery usually is. I got to wrap up not one but two beautiful babies in their birthing blankets." Mom dreamily smiled as the microwaved dinged.

"That's awesome, Mom."

She sat down at the table, dropping a tea bag into the hot water. Instead of joining her, I hoisted myself onto the counter and let my feet dangle.

Then she started with a "Jacob, what were you thinking?"

My stomach squeezed in on itself as I waited for a little more information.

"Why did you wake Michael up in the middle of the night? You've got him all freaked out. You know, Dr. Feldman said we're supposed to be positive. Reassure him."

Oh, that. "I just thought I heard something. My bad. Of course, I'll tell him there's no one in the house."

Mom put her elbows on the table and rested her chin in her hands, carefully studying me from across the way. "What's up with you, Jacob?"

"Nothing." I tried to sound extra normal. "Everything's fine." I slid down from the counter and stood on the worn linoleum.

She took a sip of tea. "Alright, Jacob. Go have fun with your cousin." Then, she smiled at me in her loving way, and I felt a little bad not letting her know about Ary. We were a close family and hardly ever kept secrets. Yet, I left the room and didn't look back.

8

HARBORING A PHANTOM

Lucas sat on the couch. His head whipped around to me. "Now what?" he asked. "Come on, we can't just leave her under the stairs all day."

"She likes it there." I shrugged and admitted, "It's crazy, I know." Next, I peered out the living room window at the gray expanse of sky and a *police cruiser* pulling up in the drive. But I hadn't called them. "Hell no. The police."

Lucas jumped up and came over by me.

I whispered urgently, "Help me convince them Ary's not here."

"No, I don't think so. I'm not lying to the police." Lucas shook his head and exhaled loudly. "It's aiding and abetting or something like that."

"Dude, she's not a criminal," I scoffed.

An officer was walking up the drive and saw us framed in the window. Crap, I had wanted to draw the curtains, but it was too late.

"Dah. Running away is against the law," Lucas hissed, and

then there was a hard knock, and we immediately stopped arguing. Lucas stayed rooted in place while I hurried to the door.

The cop was a tall, intimidating character. His head was clean-shaven, exposing a wrinkled skull. He didn't speak at first, but frowned at me, lumbering his way into the house. I hadn't expected him to come inside.

I told myself to chill out and tried to sound friendly. "Um, hello officer. Can I help you?"

"Good afternoon." The officer continued, "A sixteen-year-old girl has run away from home."

My mom walked up, cinching her robe, attempting to find out what was going on. "Excuse me officer, I work midnights and just woke up. Is there a problem?"

"Hello, ma'am. I'm Officer Damler. I just informed your son that an emotionally disturbed young girl has run away from home. She lives not too far from your house. She's sixteen years old and believed to be dangerous."

So, was this how they were going to spin things? No way.

"Have you seen or heard anything unusual?" the officer asked.

Mom started to answer, "Well, my sons thought they heard—"

"No. It was a mouse. I found a mouse," I said, interrupting her.

Mom wrinkled her nose, completely repulsed. "We have mice. Why didn't you tell me, Jacob?"

"I was going to."

The officer handed my mom his card. "Well, if you see her, please call."

"Of course," Mom said.

Lucas stepped in. "Excuse me, how exactly is this girl dangerous?"

The officer paused. "I'm not really at liberty to say. Have you seen her?"

Lucas hesitated. "No, Sir, just curious."

The officer's eyes suspiciously darted between Lucas and me before his attention settled on my mom. "Well, I have taken up enough of your day."

"Anytime, officer," my mom replied.

He politely nodded and left. I was happy to close the door behind him.

My mom tapped the officer's card to her chin before she slipped it into the pocket of her bathrobe.

It was a strange scenario. I had gone from trying to find the unknown phantom in the house to hiding her. Liking her. Sure, a tiny doubt snuck in. I loved my mom and Michael and wouldn't risk their safety for anything. But Ary wasn't dangerous.

Mom still wore her thinking face, now lit with suspicion. She wagged a finger at me. "Let me see that writing on the wall."

"You know, I think you were right. It was already here when we moved in."

"I'd still like to see it," she insisted.

Lucas and I exchanged a passing look before I followed my mom up the stairs. I was still on her heels as she entered my room.

"The writing was in your closet, right?"

"Yeah." I felt unsure how to act and scratched at a loose cuticle on my thumb.

Mom's slippers shuffled across the floor until she bumped the partly opened closet with a terrycloth hip.

"There's a lot of writing here." She squinted, reading to herself. Then she said, "Jeez. These are creepy. God, that disturbed girl was really in our house."

Disturbed. What a terrible and generic label. My mom should have known better. I tried to compose myself and only managed to make a "Hmm" sound.

My mom turned to me, hugging herself, seeming spooked. "This writing was all here when we first moved in, right?"

"Yeah. Definitely." It's almost to be expected once you lie, you will have to lie again. Really, I was too panicky to keep up with it for too long. How well did I know Ary? Yet I trusted her, but it was more than that. I was already falling for her. So, I said, "Me and Michael searched the whole place. There's no one here now."

"Even so, we probably should've told the officer and had him look around—And we have mice, too?" She sighed. "Well, I'm going to go take a shower. Go hang out with Lucas."

"Okay." I let her walk out of the room first.

I booked it down the stairs to see Lucas coming out of the crawl space. "Um, what are you doing, genius? I could have been my mom." I was alarmed but kept my voice down.

"I just wanted to talk. Relax." Lucas flashed me an empty smile. "No one saw. By the way, you're lucky I'm keeping your secret. It seems wrong, though."

A twinge of jealousy crept in. "Uh, what did you and Ary talk about?" Lucas would probably think she was odd.

"She's sweet," he said. "She didn't say much and mainly gave yes and no answers." I felt good about that part until he added, "It wasn't light enough to tell for sure, but I think she was blushing."

I didn't appreciate his tone or the vibe I picked up on. He was like, 'I'm Lucas, and I make girls blush.' Who cares?

He added, "We had this little thing in the fourth grade. I used to draw her pictures and sit with her on the bus."

"It probably means you'll get married," I sarcastically commented. Could he still be thinking about her after all these years?

"What's eating you, Cuz?" He raised his eyebrows, seeming annoyingly chipper. "Come on? Out with it?" Lucas sat down on a step.

"Nothing," I said and rested my arms on the stair rail. "Hey, aren't you supposed to have a girlfriend?"

"That's what I was going to talk to you about. It's Jamie's birthday tonight and of course, he wants you to come."

"It'll be great to see him."

"Yeah, but the girl I'm seeing—well, she's older—popular." He nervously finger-combed his hair. "I found out she's going to make a move on me tonight, and I should feel excited about it, but I just don't."

"Damn, it's tough to be you." For some reason, I just couldn't stop being an asshole.

"Can't you be like you used to be?" He asked, and his eyes narrowed, and his gaze somehow darkened. I hated to darken him.

"Sorry." I stood straight. We used to tell each other everything, and I missed it.

"I can't admit this to Jamie. He'd probably die laughing." He hesitated and sputtered out. "I'm not ready yet." He looked up at me, waiting for judgment.

"Really. What's the rush?" I offered. I wanted to start with second base and work my way up to a home run. Also, if I were going to be with someone for the first time, I'd want it to be special.

"Well, I thought you could be my depressed cousin who I'm stuck hanging out with."

"I can do a pretty good depressed." I grinned. "So...you don't hook up tonight, won't she still want to another time?"

"Just come tonight. I'm going to break up with her soon."

I didn't like parties but wanted to see Jamie and help Lucas out. "What about Ary? She's alone." I couldn't leave her.

"Yeah, you're right." Then his eyes flashed with an idea. "You could bring her."

"No way." I lowered my voice to an annoyed whisper. "She's too nervous—fragile."

"Your probably right." Lucas shot up.

"You're going?" Somehow, I didn't want to be alone in this.

Lucas patted my shoulder. "Yeah. I'm taking off. Let your mom and Michael know I said bye. Call me if anything changes."

"Wait. Don't you need a ride?"

"Nope. Got my bike."

After Lucas left, I lingered near Ary's hiding spot, and even though it was risky, I couldn't resist.

"It's just me," I whispered as I slipped under the stairs, careful not to alert my mom.

Ary had kept the small light on. Her long hair cast

shadows on her face, making her appear mysterious, almost haunted.

"Hi." She sat up on the sleeping bag, her shapely legs stretched out. She must have been eavesdropping since she asked, "Are you going to the party?"

"I'd rather hang out with you." I stood slightly hunched because that was all the space allowed in the ceiling arc.

"Sit," she said.

I took the spot next to her.

"You have to go. I overheard Lucas telling you some girl likes him. Maybe you should tell Lucas I love him. He may not feel the same anymore, but he has to know," she said.

This wasn't how it was supposed to be. How could she not see this was the beginning of our story? My heart dropped and thudded in my stomach. I argued, "Ary, you barely know him."

"What are you talking about? Well, I've practically known Lucas forever." A smile shaped her lips, and her tone became happy. Dreamy. Sickening. Her dimples carved below high cheekbones. "In the fourth grade, Lucas drew a picture of a bird with intricate wings."

"What a creative guy. I mean, drawing a bird with wings. How outside the box."

"What box? Are you being mean?"

"No."

She decided, "Yes. You're being mean."

I knew it was stupid, reckless to be here. Anyway, I felt like crap. "I'll see you later."

"Thank you, Jacob. You're my best friend." Clearly, she formed bonds quickly. Why was I the best friend? She turned to me and leaned forward, and we fell into a hug. Then, for reasons of self-preservation, I slid away.

She breathed into my ear before whispering, "Hold me a little longer."

I wrapped my arms around her, and it felt good. Too good. Scattered noises soon caught my attention. First voices, followed by descending footsteps on the stairs. I broke out of the embrace and rose to my knees, putting my index finger to my lips. Ary nodded, silently telling me she knew to be quiet. Of course, she'd known. She had gone unnoticed for this long. My mom called my name. Suddenly, there was a nervous feeling in my chest. My legs began to stiffen from kneeling too long. Drops of sweat formed on the back of my neck. There was little ventilation. How could Ary stand it here? My mom called again. Since Lucas had left too, she might think we took a walk or something. I had to wait it out and dropped back down to a sitting position.

It was as if the floodgates of touching had opened. Ary bravely took my hand and placed it to her face. Her skin was cool to the touch and baby soft. I guess she thought this kind of thing took place in platonic friendships. Her fingertips glided over my cheeks, nose, and lips. Then she tousled my hair, wrapping the curls around her fingers, innocently smiling like a preschooler with a new toy. What was with her? When she started rubbing my chest through my shirt, I told her, "Uh, Ary, cut it out." My voice was low and breathy.

She moved in, and her mouth drew enticingly close to my lips. Feeling tentative, I needed personal space. Truthfully, I was attracted to her and fighting a growing urge to kiss her.

"Sorry, please don't be angry at me," she mumbled and drew her knees up to her body, hugging them.

"Believe me, I'm the opposite of mad."

She tilted her head. Confused.

I was prepared for disappointment but needed to double-check. "You're still into Lucas, right?"

"Of course," she said. "I'd be too shy to touch him."

"I see. You only touch the boys you don't like." I had the impression my sarcasm was lost on her. It was frustrating. Regrouping, I listened. I couldn't hear my mom anymore. She must have gone into the other room, so I whispered in Ary's ear, "I gotta go. But I'll see you later." The corner of my mouth awkwardly inched up, and I gave her a little wave, so she'd know everything was okay. When her mouth spread beautifully into a smile, I made a break for it.

9
TOUCHED

Ary

I was unsure what had happened. Maybe I simply gave into a magnetic and overwhelming urge. A zip of electricity passed through me. I trembled. It had been the irresistible touch of the mother and father I never knew. The feel of another I had longed for all those years. And yes, it was the touch of a boy that sent a giddy and unknown rush through my body. A desire lingered, and I wanted more.

We parted, and Jacob smiled his sweet, crooked smile. I was memorizing his grin. The way one corner of his lip hitched up first as if he was shy about a joke he just told. I had to smile in response, struggling to control my strong emotions. And then he was gone. The door shut. But how I'd wished, he stayed. I could grow accustomed to being in his company forever.

My voice rasped out, "Please—don't go."

Jacob radiated warmth and kindness. After being in the

dark for so long, there was a blinking, fuzzy sense of reality that was hard to put into words. Jacob was touchable, palpable, present. With him here, life almost seemed possible. Maybe I could return to the world which had gone on without me.

I hugged my knees and rocked back and forth in the small, warm space. I sat there for hours and hours, humming with a slow-burning zeal. Holding onto memories that anchored the mind to life. Thoughts of Mrs. Collins, Lucas, and recess played in my head. Lucas handing me the picture of the bird he had drawn for me when we were on the bus.

A memory of fourth grade unexpectedly flittered in. It had been a movie day where the other students had brought snacks. All the kids except for me, I think. Yet Jacob, not Lucas, turned around and handed me a bag of Cool Ranch Doritos.

I muttered, "Thank you." He just blinked at me and turned back around. They were delicious. The memory was so vivid, I still tasted them on my tongue. Why had he done this? I had to know. Was it because his cousin liked me? I shook my head, puzzled.

Counting to one hundred always helped time pass. It was what I did. Now I pushed thoughts of Mother and that place away. Instead, I'd remember happy things. Again, the reel of Jacob turning around at his desk played like a scene from a movie. I stretched out on the floor. Unsaintly fragments of memories arranged themselves into horrific scenes. Lurid nightmares, though I was still awake.

I was four years old. I poured the cereal into the bowl, but the milk sloshed and spilled. A puddle quivered on the counter. I left the mess along with my half-eaten bowl of Corn

Flakes and stood in the center of the room. I noticed it. The line of salt around the parameters of the kitchen had blown away near the back door. Gramma always prayed and sprinkled it there. The still and quiet cottage held its breath. I swallowed hard, and my bare feet scampered across the cool parquet floor. I had to let her know.

The stairs leading to the second floor were narrow, confining, and creaky. I felt the curve of the doorknob twist in my small hand. My eyes glided over lovely eggshell-blue walls in the small square room. The air was usually warm and cozy, only now it was tainted with a foul smell as if Gramma had an upset stomach. I caught sight of the sewing machine with floral material left in mid stitch and made my way to her. Her body stretched out across the length of the bed. My hands held two fistfuls of the comforter. Wet with water, not blood. Then I reached up and shook her shoulders, making the row of wrinkles on her neck jiggle. Yet her sweet but sagging eyelids stayed closed.

"Gramma," I said, scared.

A tall lady appeared. Her reddish-blonde hair was twisted in a curious knot.

I started to shake my grandmother harder. But nothing. Panic flooded my chest. Tears fell as I gazed over at the lady. "Help her. Help my Gramma."

The lady calmly said, "Humans die and soil themselves. You are in part like them, Sanctuary. But you are also from a noble, superior bloodline. As far as I know, one of a kind. And I'm taking you home."

More images skidded in. I was getting into a dark car. Digging the little tips of my pink fingernails into a stiff leather, watching the scenery pass. First, I glimpsed the woods and soon a pretty house, after pretty house, until we finally pulled into a twisty drive. A beautiful house out of a fairy tale materialized. I beheld the place in wonder.

Once I got out of the car, the air was scented with a fragrant aroma emanating from enormous lilac bushes, which nearly blocked the front windows. A garden gnome peeked at me from an overgrown azalea bush as Mother led me by the hand. We entered, and ceilings soared twenty feet high, appearing so much bigger from the inside. It must have been an illusion. I walked down a long rectangle of pale gray carpet onto a hard and polished wood. Mother threw the heavy front door shut, making the floor tremble under my feet. My gaze flitted to a pair of oversized leather chairs fit for giants facing one another while gaudy art cluttered the walls. One painting, in particular, caught my attention. A bloody battlefield in the sky. Angels and demons in mortal combat.

"Do you like it?" Mother asked, but I didn't answer.

I felt like I was a small animal in an open field, ready to be pounced on and devoured at any moment.

"Well, come along," she instructed.

At the top of the ascending stairs, there was a long corridor lined with closed doors. The jittery feeling accompanied me as Mother led me down that hall. Finally, she opened a door to reveal a pink canopy bed and red roses on the wallpapered room. There was a built-in shelf full of beautiful dolls and teddy bears, a jack-in-the-box, and wind-up toys. Somehow, this lovely room felt like a cage.

She feigned a smile. "It's all for you."

"I just want Gramma."

Mother dropped to her knees and forced me close to her

chest, encasing me in a firm embrace. She let go and said, "You are mine."

I was cold and shaky. I bowed my head but didn't dare argue.

However, I refused the copious requests to drink a strange, thick nectar. One day in the kitchen, I tried to resist, but Mother seized my hand, twisting it until I surrendered. She forced the glass to my lips and down my throat. It burned. I choked. My stomach twisted, and I vomited it back up. The red mixed with bile spattered my dress.

"I've never given a child this many chances. Through no fault of your own, you came out wrong...weak, worrisome. You need to drink this for your own good or be punished." The words were later accompanied by Mother's slaps which progressed to fists. She grabbed my hair and yanked out a handful, and I cried out.

Not all the cries were mine. I also heard agonizing cries from the basement kids who haunted the house.

Another picture sprung to life. Mother and Gary skillfully shepherding a row of kids up the staircase. Even when I'd see them for myself, they'd remain phantoms, ashen and frail. Most of them were older than me but so listless a strong wind could topple them. Ghostly children, not allowed to speak or unable to, were propped up on the high-backed chairs at the formal dining room table—a sprawling table seating twelve.

Gray smoke came, filling eyes and lungs. Mouths opened like scarlet flowers, and Mother savored limp bodies in her arms.

Days were threaded together by cries. By blood.

But the memories were never solid, only distant and surreal, like I might have dreamed them all.

10

THINGS YOU REMEMBER

JACOB

I ran it past my mom. She thought going to the party with Lucas was a great idea. A way to get reacquainted with old friends. Then I retreated to my room, feeling the subtle dip of the mattress as I sprawled across my blue quilt. My mind was a mix of thoughts about Ary and tonight's get-together. Ary, Lucas, and Jamie were all part of some lost time. I had been almost as close to Jamie as I was with Lucas but hadn't really talked to him since I moved. Not a spoken word, at least.

There were a few text messages from Jamie that read "Hey," and "What's New York like?" and "Dad's drunk. Same old. Miss u."

And "Are u watching *The Flash*? U should watch *The Flash*, and we can talk about it." But I kept forgetting. Then nothing. It's weird how friends you had once seen every day can become only a few memories you lock away.

Lucas was the quiet, little smart boy everyone liked. I was

Lucas's best friend, which made me a semi-popular guy and a little cocky. Both variables were related to my association with him. Lucas preferred to fade into the background, but the spotlight always found him. Everything Lucas touched turned to gold. If my cousin took a test, he aced it. If he ran a race, he came in first. It kept me at the top of my game. I studied hard to get almost as high of a score as Lucas and ran my ass off only to come in second.

In fourth grade, Jamie was the new kid in school. He had dirty blond hair and was taller than Lucas and me, which already made him cool.

I liked him because he was the polar opposite of Lucas. He sucked when it came to grades and sports. Behaviorally, it was Lucas the good and Jamie the bad. He was so bad, in fact, he succeeded in getting Lucas into trouble a couple of times. Adding to the dynamic of our grade school trio was Jamie's desire to be a superhero. Mainly he did villainous acts like smashing pumpkins on Halloween and stealing candy bars from gas stations as he blabbered on about wanting to have superpowers.

Deanna Mulling was a pixie-haired, apple-faced girl. Despite being smart and bookish, Deanna always had the lowdown on everyone. During a morning bathroom break, she stopped Lucas and me in the hall to inform us about Jamie.

"You'll never believe what I heard." Her sour smirk turned to a knowing nod. *"The new boy got expelled from his old school. He stabbed his teacher in the eye with a pencil."*

"Wow, I wonder what the teacher did to make him so mad," I responded. *"Or if he's just a psycho."*

"It was probably an accident," Lucas reasoned, always giving people the benefit of the doubt.

As timing would have it, Jamie came up to us, holding up a blunt number two pencil, and we both flinched. He asked, "Where's the pencil sharpener?"

With wide eyes, Lucas pointed to the other side of the classroom. After Jamie walked off, I gave Lucas a "Good job. Now you'll be an accomplice."

He shrugged. "You know, I'm just polite."

It turned out the teacher was abusing several of the students, and Jamie accidentally stabbed the teacher in the arm, attempting to get away.

Jamie was a nice guy. Just being in his company was fun. He and I were prone to fits of laughter at the most inopportune times, like in the middle of class. Faces red from trying to contain the uncontainable. Lucas would turn away, pretending not to know us.

I don't think Jamie had it great. He didn't seem to have a lot of anything. His worn-out second-hand clothing was too small and made him seem taller than he was. Handprints in purples, blues, and yellows were often displayed on his arm. A shadow of a bird's wing on his cheek was recurring.

And I would never forget the first time I visited him at his house. *The trailer had a broken screen door that never got fixed. His dad inherited it from a great uncle. My eyes shot to a stack of dirty dishes posed next to a leaky sink. A row of empty beer bottles cluttered the counter next to a white refrigerator, which bore no magnets. Some adults must have been around to install the imperfect plumbing and even drink all the beer, but there was sure no sign of them now. "Where's your mom and dad?" I asked.*

"My dad sleeps a lot since he got fired, and my mom died when I was three," he said casually enough.

"Sorry." I tried not to tear up.

He asked, "You and Lucas are my best friends, right?"

Lucas and I had been tight since nursery school. But I liked the idea of having two best friends. I also felt bad about him losing his mom. What could be worse? I upped the scales. "Best friends forever."

"Damn straight, it's forever." We fist-bumped there in that disaster of a kitchen to make it official.

The little voice that stopped people from doing crazy things didn't talk to Jamie much then. We were in the sixth grade. The images of what happened in the park were seared in my head. We had snuck out, which already added a mysterious layer to the night. *A cold wind rattled dark branches— the kind of wind that brings leaves to their doom. We searched the sky, but the stars were a no-show, and a bluish-gray fog blew in, lending an unwholesome impression.*

"Autumn is the best assassin because she makes mass murder look beautiful," Jamie said, kicking a pile of fallen leaves with his sneaker.

I called him out. "You probably read that on Instagram."

Lucas nodded again.

Jamie replied, "Yeah. So?"

The swings and monkey bars appeared in our line of vision. We stopped walking and stood around, forming a huddle. The playground was deserted, with only a solitary streetlamp for light.

"Let's go back to my house and get my bat," Jamie suggested.

"No more smashing pumpkins. It's rude," I said, "and it upsets Lucas."

Lucas grimly nodded his head. It had bothered him a lot, and he'd appointed me to be the spokesman. It always seemed easier to defend one another than to speak up for ourselves in those days.

Out of nowhere, a high-pitched scream pierced the air. It was then we saw a teenage girl with long red hair running toward us with a tall man behind her in hot pursuit. Quickly, He pounced on the girl, propelling her down to the wood chips below, only feet from the swings. Lucas took cover behind a large oak tree, and I quickly followed his lead. He held his phone up in his shaky hand.

"Call 9 1 1!" I frantically said.

"Yeah." He nodded, pausing before he asked, "Wait. Where's Jamie?"

We exchanged a look.

The sounds of the attack shifted. Now adding to the clamor, I heard Jamie's voice, yelling for the guy to "Get off her, you bastard!" I peered from around the tree at the unforgettable sight of five-foot Jamie on the six-foot-tall guy's back.

The man's voice raged, "You're dead, kid!"

"Holy shit, now what?" I asked Lucas, whose expression went blank in response.

The girl got halfway up but was dragged back down to the ground. Now she and Jamie were pinned under the big guy's knees. The guy took turns. First, he punched the girl, and then he'd clobbered Jamie.

Lucas stood there vibrating. "What should we do?"

"Call 9 1 1 now!" I reminded him and ran over to help my friend.

The big guy raised his arm, ready to strike the girl again. Having no actual fighting moves or plan, I yelled, "Get off em! My friend called the cops!" and somehow managed to wrap my eleven-year-old self around the maniac's thundering frame until he stood up and peeled me off, throwing me to the ground.

From there, he towered like a mountain above me. I gazed up at his shadowed and bearded face right before he began stomping up and down on my stomach... my rib cage. He was easily 200 pounds and wore a pair of big workman boots. It felt like I was trampled by a herd of elephants. I quietly moaned with what little air I could muster, and he ran off into the night.

I sat up in bed, making the mattress squeak. Even recalling the pain made me shudder. I blinked hard. But the weight of the memory dragged me under again.

A bloody-faced Jamie kneeled over me, holding his sleeve to his nose, asking, "Are you alright, Jacob?"

It required a heart-straining effort to speak. "I'm dying. Call my mom."

Next, Lucas loomed over me. "Wait, do I call Aunt Sarah, or do I call the police?"

The police never caught the guy who assaulted us. The girl was in serious but stable condition. I suffered from over a dozen broken ribs and came dangerously close to rupturing my aorta and really dying. Jamie had a busted nose, along with two black eyes. Yet Lucas received more than equal attention as he was quite "Shaken."

Surfacing back to the here and now, I mumbled, "Freaking

THE STARS FORGOT US

Jamie." He was either fearless or crazy. Who else would have jumped on the guy? Then an image of Ary flashed in my brain. I knew. Going to the party tonight was the right thing to do. After all, Jamie was the best guy to go with me to Ary's house and check things out.

11

THE PARTY

JACOB

The same old rusted Camaro without wheels remained propped up on blocks in Jamie's front yard, and the screen door remained partly unhinged. There was a jack-o'-lantern with the top of its head smashed in. Its lopsided smile welcomed us. I wondered if Jamie had whacked his pumpkin a couple of times with his trusty bat or if karma finally caught up with him. At any rate, the place was a dump. I couldn't quite believe we had been allowed to hang out here. There was hardly ever adult supervision, but Lucas's parents and my mom totally trusted him. And, we did have a tight curfew of eleven o'clock. How much debauchery could really happen before midnight?

I'd only gone to one boy-girl party before. My main objective had been to kiss a stranger in the dark. Goal accomplished. Tonight, I had other objectives. I was here to reconnect with Jamie and persuade him to accompany me to Ary's house. I was also here to play the role of Lucas's depressed cousin.

We made it to the door when Lucas suggested, "Your New York girlfriend dumped you."

"Okay," I agreed, "Under one condition—she has to be super-hot."

Lucas played along. "Oh yeah, I saw her, and she was smoking. And wait, wasn't she a model?"

"Hell yeah." This imaginary girl wasn't half-bad. Yet, even if she had been a real, living, breathing person, I'd still be thinking of Ary.

Jamie's sixteen-year-old face appeared through the screen. Two female silhouettes were right behind him. Instead of dressing in clothes too small, he wore a baggy T-shirt and jeans worn out and torn at the knee. Music played loud but not at an ear-shattering decibel.

Lucas went in right before me. Jamie gave him a quick arm pat before asking, "Jacob, where the hell have you been?" His hair was darker or maybe just a little oily. I was as tall as him now, both of us about five foot eight. We looked up to Lucas, who hit six feet.

"Dude, it's great to see you!" I barely resisted the urge to tackle-hug him.

"Love ya, Jake from State Farm," he gave me a one-armed hug, careful not to spill his beer. He proudly held it up. "You guys want one?"

Lucas took it upon himself to answer for us, saying, "No thanks, we're good. If my mom smells it on our breath, we'll be grounded for life."

But I'd never had a beer and thought I'd give it a try. "Sure."

Jamie's cheeks lit, and he shot off toward the kitchen.

"Come on, my mom can't even find out there was alcohol here. Be cool, Jacob." Lucas pleaded.

"It's not like your mom kisses me. I'll just have one or two. It's a depressant. It will help my acting." I smirked.

Lucas rolled his eyes at me as Jamie reappeared, handing me a can of Bud Light. I didn't want to get drunk and puke in front of Ary, anyway.

It almost felt like I won when Lucas let it go, introducing me to a couple of semi-cute girls named Madison and Kylie. I remembered them anyway. Madison was short with smooth caramel skin, dreads, and glasses. While Kylie grew tall and rail-thin, flaunting black eyeliner and the cat-eyed look. She had the same blonde frizzy hair hanging to her shoulder blades, only now she added a blue streak near her face.

The two girls talked over one another, responding, "Oh, right, you're Lucas's cousin."

I nodded and took a drink. Unfortunately, it was bitter and way worse than I expected. Turned out I'm more of a Sprite guy.

Jamie knocked his shoulder into mine. "So, did you watch *The Flash*?"

"That shows still on?" This was his first question after years apart. I had to smile. "I think you're gay over *The Flash*." His eyes had the same old spark.

Jamie grinned. "Totally," he joked.

"Um…where's your dad?"

"He's working midnights at the gas station."

"Are these his beers?" I had only talked to his dad on a few occasions, but knew he was a little scary. Drinking his beer didn't seem like a wise move.

"He got me a six-pack for my birthday."

Lucas stopped talking to the girls to sarcastically remark, "Oh, yeah, and the legal drinking age is sixteen." He was all cool about Jamie drinking but had a different set of standards for me. He leaned in closer to me, whispering, "Just one, okay?"

"Whatever you say, Mom," I replied, and Lucas slugged me in the arm, and I returned the favor. Sure, the beer tasted like piss, but I didn't want Lucas thinking he could boss me around.

Jamie started in. "What good is it to turn sixteen without a car? I'll never get that piece of shit to run."

"You could get a job. Save for a real car," Lucas said.

"Who'd hire him," I joked.

Jamie turned to me. "Maybe you can get me a job at State Farm." He always ran that one into the ground. Then he turned to Lucas. "Anyway, too bad you're not turning sixteen till June. You know, your rich old man's getting you a car. And you ain't gonna have to work for shit."

A buzz filled the air as years of being apart evaporated. It was just like old times. Jamie the Bad, Lucas the Good, and me in the middle, taking a little from columns A and B.

Jamie leaned in closer to me, placing his hands squarely on my shoulders. "It's so good to have you back, dude," he said. "It's been boring as hell without you."

"Thanks a lot," Lucas said.

Jamie's eyes panned to Lucas. "You're welcome, bro." He had a few zits scattered around his chin and dropped a lot more f-bombs, but he was still the same old Jamie. He'd be my willing accomplice.

Lucas handed him an Amazon gift card. "Here's your birthday present, dork."

"It's from me, too. Happy birthday." I hadn't known about the card but lied for fun, smirking over at Lucas. He shook his head but didn't say otherwise.

"Wow. Thanks, guys."

A VW rabbit's headlights flashed in the front window, followed by the clink and clank of a car door opening and closing.

"This girl is obsessed with Lucas. He's been trying to break up with her for weeks," Jamie said.

"How did she even hear about the party?" I asked.

Jamie's lip edged up into a mischievous grin.

Lucas's eyes darted between us. "I really need new friends."

Then the girl walked in, came straight up to Lucas, and kissed him on the lips. Once they parted, she gave me a quick once over. "Oh, this is your cousin."

"Yep, this is Jacob. Jacob, this is Alissa."

"Hi," I said.

She was kind of pretty but wore too much makeup and sported the drawn-on eyebrow thing. Her nose was a little big but not as large as her lips or chest. She didn't seem like Lucas's type, but hell, he was so frigging polite, he might wind up marrying her.

"Hey. Sorry to hear about you and your girlfriend," she replied.

"Yeah. I've been thinking of ending it all."

Lucas wore a startled expression before cocking an eyebrow as if to say *relax*.

"Over some stupid chick? Come on," Jamie said, clearly

emotional. I guess we should have filled him in on the plan.

Alissa said, "I'd probably be the same way if Lucas quit me. I know he's my forever."

Lucas's face strained. No wonder he hadn't broken up with her.

The two other girls greeted Alissa as Jamie said, "Well, I'm here for you, bro," as he dragged me into the kitchen. "You're a cool guy and you got a lot to live for." He opened a creaky cabinet. "You need to meet my friend Jim Beam."

"Um, I'm not drinking that. I made up the suicide thing, so Lucas would have to hang out with me and not stalker girl."

My eyes shot around the messy kitchen. Empty beer cans and old mail cluttered the counters. Dirty plates piled up in the sink, and a stub of a cigarette floated in a coffee cup of murky water.

"Jeez, clean your house," I mumbled.

Jamie stood there silent and squinty eyed under the fluorescent glare of the lights. "Wait, sooo—" he was just figuring things out. "You didn't get dumped?"

"You're buzzed. And no. I never even got picked up." Then I wondered, "Who else is coming to this party?"

"No one. It's low key, ya know. But there are three girls and three guys." He made a clicking sound with his mouth and pointed at me, finishing with, "You're welcome."

It wasn't a real party, which was alright with me. But I wasn't into the idea of some hookup or triple date either.

"Do you remember..." My heartbeat thudded. "Ary Daniels?"

He thought for a second. "Yeah, the weird girl from grade school. Did she die or something?"

"God, no, she didn't *die*." Even the idea was a little upsetting. "Why'd you think that?"

"Uh, just not seeing why she's relevant." He leaned forward, and his entire torso was plastered against the counter, bored and deflated. "Come on, we should be getting wasted."

"Can you just listen?"

He straightened up, clenching his beer in his fist.

We were alone. This was my opportunity. "Ary ran away from home. It's bad there. She's ran away in the past, but the police just send her back."

"I didn't know you kept in touch with her." He put his free hand on the base of his neck and took a sip of beer, looking confused.

I decided to skip the long story of her staying at my new house. "These people keep foster kids chained in the basement. Some of the kids have been kidnapped."

"There are rumors of devil worship in Steely. And the cops just found a calf sacrificed in the woods. But no kids in town have gone missing that I heard about."

"They can abduct kids from other towns," I reasoned. "Animal sacrifices." A fuzzy memory poked its way up. "Like how we found the dead goat tied to a tree."

"We were ten," Jamie remembered with a hard frown. "Yeah, fuckin' unnerving."

"Not to mention the girl who was attacked in the park."

His voice became a little thick. "I'll never forget that night."

"Steely has always been a little off. I just need you to go with me to Ary's house to see what's really up."

Jamie guzzled down a long drink of beer while he let it all sink in. "Just so I get this straight, we're talking about breaking and entering?"

I hadn't thought it out. With a jolt of surprise, I realized how serious this could all be. "Possibly," I admitted. "Because we need pictures and maybe a video for proof."

Without hesitation, he said, "I'm in."

12

AFTER HOURS

JACOB

We watched, *A Nightmare on Elm Street*. Alissa hung on Lucas all night long. His neck was a swarm of hickies, but she didn't have her way with him. Girls can be perverts, too. Kylie stared at her phone until she and Jamie coupled up and made out a little. Madison sat by me. She fidgeted with her clunky glasses and confessed she liked Lucas, which was fine with me. Since Jamie had agreed to go with me to Ary's and check things out, I considered the night a success. And in a way, it was almost as if I had never left.

My aunt picked Lucas and me up at eleven o'clock sharp. It started to drizzle as we got in the warm car. The windshield wipers clanked to a fixed beat. We drove in silence because we never liked talking in front of our parents.

When we got close to my house, Lucas said, "Call me later tonight or tomorrow."

"Will do." And I told my aunt, "Thanks for the ride, Aunt V."

"No problem, kiddo."

The BMW rolled to a slow stop. They dropped me at the end of the driveway just after eleven. The guttural accelera-tion made the engine rev in a higher note. I watched the red taillights as the car sped off.

The rain had stopped as quickly as it came and painted the night sky an ominous purple black. I lingered there, observing a tall figure in the shadowy fringe of the woods. It's not like we owned the woods, but it still seemed weird for someone to be there by themselves late at night. I rushed up the driveway to the door and fumbled to get the key in. Still feeling uneasy, I creaked my neck to get a strangled look at the figure but could no longer see anyone.

I stepped into the house and flicked on the lights. A drowsy stillness had invaded the space. My plan was to go upstairs to see my brother, but I paused once I walked past the foyer. I figured I could just say a quick hello to Ary and check on my brother after.

I tapped on the half-door to her hiding place as a hand brushed my shoulder. Startled, I spun around to see Ary right behind me.

"I scared you," she said.

A relieved smile spread across my lips. "Nah. It's all good."

She let out a whoosh of breath. "You are a sight for sore eyes. I was just missing you."

My eyebrows flicked up. "Really?"

She held up a bottle of water. "May I please drink this?"

"Of course. My casa, your casa." I started taking Spanish this year and had the vocabulary of a toddler.

"You mean, mi casa, tu casa."

"You know Spanish?" I asked.

"I know all the words."

"No one knows all the words," I mumbled, confused.

Ary struck a rigid pose and abruptly asked, "Did you talk to Lucas for me?"

I let out a disappointed breath. "We didn't really get a chance to talk. I will. Promise."

She nodded and seemed okay with it. "I've been nervous for nothing," she admitted.

Only then was I able to tear myself away from the conversation. Away from her. "Wait for me in the living room. You can stay here. Michael only leaves his room to use the bathroom and my mom is at work," I explained, so she wouldn't have to be cramped in that small space.

"Where are you going?" She gripped the water bottle with both hands, holding it up to her chin.

"To check on my brother."

I zipped up the stairs to get this visit with Michael out of the way. He was standing in the corner of his room, looking tall and gaunt. He had scraped his unkept rock musician hair into a stubby ponytail. It made him almost unrecognizable. "Michael, what's the matter?" He was trembling. His dark eyes were deep set, sculpted into the sockets, appearing paranoid beneath arching eyebrows without his bangs to soften them. His face was marred by fatigue. He had barely been eating. Seeing my brother like this was disturbing enough, but he spat out several nasty curse words, angrily talking to himself.

"Michael," I said firmly.

He asked, "Why'd you leave me alone?"

"I went to Jamie's. It's his birthday." I hadn't even told Michael I was leaving. In retrospect, it was pretty shitty of me. I held his gaze respectfully. "Sorry, I should have said goodbye." I took him by the arm and led him toward his bed. After a few steps, he stopped and rubbed his forehead with his long, nervous fingers. Then he turned and pointed. "Someone wrote in my closet too."

"What?" I crossed over to have a look. Beyond a sea of T-shirts and jeans, the word *evil* was carved in deep scratches on the wall several times. Why would Ary do this? Michael was terrified, so I decided to lie. "I wrote it on the wall to get back at you for always being a prick," I said to make him feel better. It was messed up logic, but he was just frigging scared.

"I'm a prick?" His expression shifted from scared to mildly annoyed and a little sad.

Good intentions aside, it felt all wrong. "No. You're not." I should have come clean and told him about Ary. But I couldn't because he would tell mom for sure. He could never keep a secret. "I screwed up." I shook my head and helped him get into his bed.

He let me tuck him in and adjust the blankets the way he liked them before complaining, "You're the worst brother ever. I hate you, Jacob."

I ignored him and instead noticed his old baseball bat propped against the wall by his bed. "Come on, even if there was a ghost, you can't beat her to death," I said, alarmed, and snatched the bat, putting it in his closet just to be cautious.

"Why'd you do that? I need it for protection." He pouted.

"It's not a ghost, it's some kind of monster. I saw it for just a second, and it's small and hideous."

"No. There's no monster." Ary was kind of small, maybe five foot four, but super cute. He must have been flat-out hallucinating. Now I had to talk to her more than ever. I mean, what the hell? Why would she carve the word 'evil' on my brother's wall? "Go to sleep, Michael. Okay?"

He didn't answer, and his eyelids looked heavy. I decided to let him rest and flipped the switch. The room went dark except for a thin ribbon of light that came from beneath the shade.

"Why the rush? Stay a minute."

I should have known it wouldn't be that easy. If I wanted my brother to stay up, he fell fast asleep, and if I wanted him to go to sleep, he stayed up. I moved closer to him. "Sure."

"A voice in my head is saying it's not safe to sleep, but I'm bored and tired," he admitted.

"It's safe, I promise." I heard the creak of the floorboards. Had Ary come upstairs? She may have become impatient. I craned my neck and caught a flash of someone passing down the hall.

"You heard it too," Michael said.

"Yeah, but it's just old house sounds. They settle." It was a vaguer version of what our mom told us. Even with my hoodie on, a chill feathered up my spine. Yet I knew if I made Michael talk, he'd relax and fall to sleep. "Tell me a story, Michael."

"I know the one about Achilles."

"Sure. I like that one." It was a story he'd spun often enough I'd memorized it. The same story he told the same way.

"Achilles was prophesied to die at a young age. So, when he was only an infant, his mother brought him to the River Styx." Then, curiously, Michael changed the narrative. "The sky was pink and blue, bruised and strangled above the valleys, she hid in. Now she waited in a box. But after the door opens, the world will be hers."

"What? Who, Michael?"

"I'm not sure," he mumbled.

I attempted to lighten the mood. "Well, skip to the good part. Helen of Troy. She must have been pretty hot, huh?"

"You like girls now?" he asked.

"Yeah, I've always liked girls." I grinned.

"Has one liked you back?"

"Not so much. I never liked any girl enough or had the nerve to pursue them." Until now. Until Ary. She was special. Even the thought of her triggered warm feelings in me. Why not tell him? "Now there's a girl from school. I've sort of reconnected with. But you've got to tell me about this girl at the hospital." The corners of my mouth hitched up teasingly

"Well, I liked her a lot, but she was a social worker and couldn't date a patient. She told me, uh, I was handsome...You know what? You're a good brother," he said through a yawn. Peaceful. Relaxed.

"You are too, Michael. Good night."

I felt a cold draft in the hall and kicked the heat up. For an intense moment, I thought it over. Was there a chance Ary was dangerous? Maybe I couldn't see it because of a stupid schoolboy crush. I barreled down the steps, anxious and wanting to talk to this girl and see what was up.

13

A VISITOR

JACOB

I found Ary cocooned in a flannel blanket on the sofa, chewing the pad of her thumb, all shaky. Weeping. I scratched my head. "Um…are you okay?" Clearly, she wasn't, but I was awkward about these kinds of things. She didn't answer at first. So, I sat down next to her, about half a foot away, to be respectful.

"I just have this bad feeling going back is inevitable." She looked up at me with wide and shiny eyes—chest heaving.

"I talked to my friend tonight. We're going to get the proof."

She dried her tears away, sniffling. Her expression slowly brightened. "Your friend? You mean Lucas?"

"No, another friend. His name's Jamie, but Lucas might tag along."

"Jacob, I'm not sure. I thought it over. It's too da-danger-ous," she stammered.

"It's all good. We've got this." I assured her. Pretending to be much more confident than I was inside.

She pulled in another breath, which calmed her just a little. "But... they're evil."

Then I remembered what I needed to ask her. "Is that why you carved the word evil?" She looked lost. "In my brother's closet?"

"What? No. I didn't." She jumped up. Her eyes animated with fear. "It's Elijah. He always writes that word. He's here." She clapped her hand over her mouth, muffling a gasp.

"Oh, crap." She was scaring me. "Elijah? Who's Elijah?"

"He's one of the kids. He used to be good. But now he's as bad as them. He does *whatever* they say. His face is scarred, and he likes to wear scary masks. He's small for eight, but don't let his size fool you. Elijah's a force to be reckoned with."

A shot of nerves twisted in my stomach, and now I hoped she was delusional. "And what kind of things do they tell him to do?"

She shook her head. "Bad things. We need to leave *now*," she said urgently. "Please, Jacob."

Could this kid really have gotten into the house? I stood, too, and began to think out loud. "My brother saw someone, and I think I heard them upstairs. I better check on him."

At that very moment, a faint sound swelled into a scream. The intelligent thing to do would be to run in the opposite direction of the scream. Unless the scream was coming from your brother's room. I charged straight for the stairs, and Ary trailed right behind me. I burst into the bedroom, and she stayed just outside the door. I hit the lights.

Michael moved to the edge of his bed and with a shaky voice, said, "The monster was just here. It ran down the hall." He stumbled to his feet and took a tentative step. Ary came in. We all met in the middle of the room, facing the open door. My brother said, "I saw it. It's a creepy, little thing."

"It'll be okay. It's just a kid," I offered, unsure what else to say.

Ary's uneasiness colored her skin, but she nervously introduced herself. "Uh, I'm Jacob's friend from school." She came closer and snatched my hand, her loose grip quickly tightening.

Michael gave me an approving nod. All three of us peered out the door. "Stay here, and I'll go find the little shit," I told Ary, and my adrenaline accelerated.

"Be careful." She whispered to me, "He always carries a razor, or a knife."

Her words crawled like insects on my skin, and I changed my plan. I quickly lurched forward and shut the door, leaning my entire weight against it. I eyed my brother. "Help me move the dresser. And we'll call the cops."

Ary grimaced at the suggestion of calling the police. I moved with Michael to get the dresser then, in perfect timing, footsteps sounded down the hall. My jaw clenched, and I rushed to open the door and caught a glimpse of a small shape running down the stairs. I wasn't sure why, but I chased after him. Maybe because he was only eight. The minute I reached the last step, I spotted a small boy of wiry proportions opening the front door. I continued my pursuit, taking two steps at a time down the stairs, and arrived at the first floor and didn't stop. Soon, I was outside and had eyes on him once more and kept going in a reckless dash. But the boy crossed into the woods, and only then I remembered seeing another person there earlier and slammed the brakes. I strained to see. The darkness had quickly swallowed the kid, and I lost sight of him completely.

The breeze drifted, humming through the branches, and I bent over to catch my breath. I noticed his rubber mask had fallen on a sketchy spot of grass. I was tempted but didn't pick it up. No longer feeling bold, a panic unexpectedly rose in my chest. Now I sprinted back toward my house as if I were the one being chased.

Once inside, I closed the front door and locked it. A swell of nerves continued to jolt through me. I dug my fingernails into my scalp, hyper and fidgety. After a few deep breaths, I hardened my reserve and was on a mission to keep my family and Ary safe. In the kitchen, I grabbed a chair and entered the mudroom, wedging it against the doorknob. Now no one could gain access into our house through that dismal cellar. Next, I pinged around the first floor, a pinball of energy—my gaze bouncing around every room and every inch of space downstairs. So, I returned to my brother's room. Michael was seated at the edge of his bed, and Ary was still standing.

"He's gone. I chased him into the woods."

Ary exclaimed, "Jacob, you're so brave!"

But I wasn't really. Hell, I almost peed myself. "Thanks, but I'm not too sure about that."

"I'm so glad you're alright," she added.

"Me, too," I admitted. Yeah, the kid was small, but he may have had a knife or a razor blade, both equally troubling. If I couldn't get it from the little weirdo right away, he'd do some real damage.

"Who was he?" Michael asked.

Ary stayed quiet, and I was blank on how to answer. "Um, I don't know."

We all hung out in Michael's room with little conversation. I nibbled at a hangnail. Ary kept giving me anxious looks. A crease indented her forehead.

Finally, Michael said, "If you two don't mind, I'd like to be alone."

"Okay. I'll be right down the stairs," I reminded him.

As soon as we made it to the first floor, Ary said, "I was wrong about your brother. He's got a pure heart. But—" And then she said what I was thinking. "They know. They know I'm here."

14

HOW MANY SECRETS CAN YOU KEEP?

ARY

We sat next to one another on the sofa with a growing space between us, and I had a lost and sinking feeling.

Jacob said, "Alright, Ary. I'm in this thing pretty deep. You have to tell me everything."

I turned my head away. Jacob was just that decent and good. It was hard to look at him and think of bad things. "I told you, Mother and Gary keep kids chained in the basement. What I need to explain to you is there are upstairs kids, too, like Elijah and this older kid, Ren. I stayed upstairs at first, when I went to school." My stomach turned sick with heat at the details I dared not utter aloud. Anyway, he'd never believe me. I couldn't stand it if he thought I was crazy like the others had. I paused.

"I'm here. I'm listening," he gently coaxed.

"Mother thought I could grow to be like them. But I couldn't. She would get angry."

A memory flamed. Mother's statuesque outline flickered before me like a dancing shadow on the wall. Her dark silhouette knelt, and her face loomed closer and closer until I saw her like she was here. I turned away, but she snatched my jaw and lifted my head, forcing me to behold her shiny white skin and long elegant nose with eyelashes so clumped together with blood, they resembled caterpillars. Then a ghastly decaying face began to show. Nose flattened and skin all but decomposed with patches of fur and bone. Horns sprouting, parting the cloud of human hair—her true monster self. I recoiled at the sight of it.

"You like to tell your teacher tall tales. Tales they will never believe." Mother held onto my chin with her cold clawed hands as she spoke. "You can shower and dress and come willingly." Impatience crept into each word. "Or you can stay down here and rot. It's up to you, Sanctuary." Then she lifted my head up by my hair, almost ripping it from my scalp. "Answer me, you weak, worthless waste of space." She gritted her teeth, and her eyes lit. "What will it be, you little nothing?" Her disarming charm and temperate coaxing had long gone.

"I'll rot." I'd never give myself willingly to such perversion. I had learned long ago what upstairs entailed.

I was enthralled with the numbness that had overtaken me from hours upon hours in the dark. Days of seclusion, hunger, and loneliness brought a numbness, which helped me endure the pain as Mother dragged me up the steps by my arms. Moonlight peeked in from the narrow window with a long burgundy drape, and I looked at hard angles and modern furniture. Carved moldings decorated an arched ceiling. The subdued flames crackled and flickered in a quiet dance in the

stone fireplace as visitors arrived in an orderly fashion. Sure,
they looked human, but I knew better. Mother made sure the
children had been bathed and were presentable and waiting
for them. Music softly thrumming. Guests talking, smoking.

"Ary?" Jacob said, and I returned to the here and now. "I
kept calling your name. It's like you were somewhere else."

"I was." I hugged myself—grateful he had brought me
back. Until he insisted.

"I need to know exactly what to expect if I'm going
there."

"It's worse than you can imagine." I sensed his frustration
and confusion. The longer I was with him, the more the fog
lifted. Remembering terrified me. "I don't want to be there,
not even in my mind. It feels like a giant hand is squeezing
my lungs and I can barely breathe."

"It sounds like you're having a panic attack," he calmly
said.

"Can we forget about it tonight? Just for tonight." I
clenched and unclenched my trembling fist.

Our eyes only met for seconds, but the way Jacob looked
at me was soft and reassuring. "We'll talk when you're ready.
We can watch TV for a little while. It relaxes you, right?"

I nodded.

Surprisingly, Jacob said, "My mom stopped at the gas
station, and I got you a little something." He got up and
walked off to the kitchen. Full of anticipation, I slid to the
edge of the leather seat. Jacob returned, holding a bottle.

Fidgeting with my hands, I didn't take it but nervously
inquired, "Will I get drunk? I don't want to get drunk."

He smiled, explaining, "No. It's Yoo-hoo. Like chocolate
milk from school."

"Chocolate milk." It sparked fantastic memories. "I love chocolate milk."

"I remembered." He twisted off the yellow lid, handing the bottle to me.

I allowed myself to experience a small hum of excitement and took a wimpy sip. It tasted beyond delicious. What a random act of kindness. "Wow," I exclaimed, and took a bigger drink. "You always were full of surprises. You had those sneakers with blinking lights on the sides of them."

Jacob smiled his contagious smile. "Jeez, my mom always got me light up shoes. Only they stopped being cool after kindergarten."

I chugged half of the bottle and leaned forward to set it down on the coffee table. Then and there, I had to know. "Why did you give me your Cool Ranch Doritos?"

Confused, he asked, "I did?"

"In fourth grade, during movie time. Right before we watched, *Despicable Me*."

He shrugged. "I'm sorry. I don't remember."

"Oh." Probably because I was Lucas's girlfriend, I decided. Then I wondered out loud, "Did he miss me terribly?" My heart pounded to know.

"Did who miss you?" He asked.

"Lucas, of course."

Jacob shrugged. "You'd have to ask him." He cleared his throat. "I probably gave you my chips because I liked you. Yeah, I had a crush on you."

He liked me. "Jacob!" I exclaimed in sheer disbelief and looked down at the floor. My face heated, and my limbs felt weird and loose. I moved around on the sofa. "Well, you better not let Lucas know. He'd be so jealous."

Jacob frowned and shrank away. But what could I do? I couldn't come between cousins and was certain Lucas and I were back together or soon would be. Always, I had thought only of Lucas. Once comforted by the longing for him, I had now felt in some way suffocated by it.

Jacob turned the TV on, and I was relieved. "This is Antenna TV. They play a lot of old stuff," he explained.

I drank more Yoo-hoo and stared at the screen. The picture was in black and white. A man and woman kissing flashed across the screen.

My gaze flicked to Jacob. I squinted, focusing in on the curve of his lips. "Girls must want to kiss you a lot," I blurted.

"Oddly enough, some have managed to resist," Jacob softly snickered.

He was funny… and kind. He made believe we had all the time in the world, even though deep down, I knew we didn't. What had I brought here with me? I quivered, and Jacob handed me the blanket.

The credits on the screen rolled.

I wanted to take in as much of Jacob as possible. "First, tell me more about you. I know you have a mom and a brother. What about your father?" I asked.

"Well, my dad and mom split up when I was twelve." His voice went flat, and his shoulder slumped. "I hardly ever see him." He tried to sound casual, but I could see the sadness in his eyes.

"I feel bad for him. He's missing out on time with you."

He choked back a little laugh. "Yeah. I'm awesome. So awesome, you're all into Lucas."

"And you love him too," I reminded him. They were best friends. Family.

Jacob shrugged one shoulder but didn't argue. He knew it was true. "All pettiness aside, I want you to be happy," he said.

I was starting to wake up even more. My mind swam in curious thoughts. Was Lucas just an idea I'd held onto in the dark? No, it was more than that, wasn't it?

Jacob deftly returned the question. "Where are your parents?"

"Me?" I shook my head. "I never had any."

"Well, who took care of you when you were little?"

"My earliest memory is of an old woman. I thought she was my grandmother. But there's…things I can't remember." I felt detached from it.

"Do you remember how you ended up living with Mother?"

"Mother showed up the day Gramma died. She only wanted me to go to parties and help her open the door."

Somberly, he said, "I think I know what kind of parties you mean." There was a subtle change in his expression when he lifted his head toward me. "If they want to open a door, why can't they just break it down?"

"It can't be opened like that." My heart raced wildly. "Mother cut my throat." I brought my hand to my neck, reliving the strike of the blade. "I was hurt. Bad." My head jerked in nervous beats. "There was so much blood. But the door still wouldn't open."

"That's terrible." Jacob seemed to examine my neck, but I knew there was no scar.

"I got better. I always get better. On the outside."

"I still don't understand." His voice softened, tender enough to warm me. "I'm sorry they hurt you." Jacob's face clouded with another thought. "Michael mentioned a door."

I flinched. "Your brother talked about the door? Mother can sometimes send messages through people. The vulnerable, I think."

"Just forget I mentioned it, okay?" Jacob rubbed his temples.

"Okay." I knew all about not wanting to talk. Even with my stomach in knots, I asked, "Will you teach me how to make pancakes?"

"It is morning." He stood, and so did I. "We might as well." He bit his lip, a prelude to an awkward smile.

In the kitchen, Jacob said, "Welcome to Pancakes 101." He slapped a box of pancake mix, a glass bowl, and a measuring cup on the counter.

When we finished, we sat across from one another at the table. Despite telling me what to do every step of the way, he awarded me all the credit. "These are the best pancakes I've ever had. You're a natural."

"They are pretty good." I beamed, fighting to keep my feet on the ground.

Soon, we settled on the sofa, closer this time and exhausted. His head touched down on my shoulder, and I heard his breathing change. He had fallen asleep. It seemed like we were safe as long as we were together. But the more I ignored the darkness, the more it crept in.

15

THE MORNING AFTER

JACOB

An unwelcomed light shined in through the safety of my eyelids. I heard my mom's voice say, "Good morning, Jacob." It occurred to me my eyes were closed, and I should probably open them.

My lids sprang open, and I lifted my head off Ary's shoulder to discover my mom standing over us. She was still in her dark blue scrubs, her hair windblown, curls falling in ringlets from her ponytail, car keys clenched in her fist. My mouth unfastened, but I couldn't say anything but, "Mom."

Ary woke up, and her face fluttered in shock.

I rubbed my hand over my chin. "Um, this is my friend, Ary." My mom squinted. "We reconnected on Facebook."

Next, my mom contemplated a silent and terrified-looking Ary. "Good morning," she said, softening her voice.

Ary meekly replied, "Morning."

Then my mom homed in on me. Her eyebrows pinched together, seemingly in confusion and mounting outrage. "I'd like to have a *word* with you in the kitchen, Jacob."

Oh crap. How had we been careless enough to fall asleep together in the living room? Our mess from making pancakes was spread all over the kitchen. Powder on the table and floor. Mixing bowl and two dirty plates in the sink. I assembled a story in my groggy brain. "Ary came over for breakfast."

"It's only seven," Mom said.

"Yeah, she came over at six." I gestured to the mess. "We made pancakes. Sorry. I should have asked first."

"Jacob, did she spend the night?" Her hand dramatically flitted to her head.

"No, Mom," I replied, sounding overly innocent. My mouth felt sticky with syrup, yet dry from sleeping.

"So, you got up at six o'clock?" she asked in an accusatory tone, raising a sharp black brow.

Stay with it. Stick with it. Breathe. "Yeah. It was too early. Probably why we fell asleep."

Our eyes met in a sort of staring contest until I faltered and looked down.

"I know I'm a pushover. But always ask first. Got it?" Mom tapped her foot.

"I will."

"Clean this mess up. I'm gonna jump in the shower and go to bed." She turned around to leave but stopped. "What's with her dress? Is she religious or something?"

"Yeah, she's very religious. Um, that's why it had to be early. She goes to church." The story was starting to flow.

Mom thought for a second, then gave in to her exhaustion.

"Alright." She made her way back to the living room. I followed.

Ary was gone. "Where did your friend go?" she asked.

"She's probably in the downstairs bathroom."

"Okay. See you later, Jacob." Mom wore a slight smile but looked beat. She dragged herself up the stairs.

A fresh spike of worry hit me when I realized she'd have to talk with Michael at some point. He'd tell her the truth. Ary was here last night, along with the strange visitor I chased away. I laced my fingers together, nervously cracking my knuckles, and paced. What should I do? And how the hell did my life get so weird?

I knew where Ary had gone. Still, I waited until I heard my mom in the shower. Sucking in a lungful of air, I entered Ary's hideaway, closing the door behind me. It was more cramped than I thought in here. Her shoulders hunched, and her hair hung down on both sides of her face like a dramatic wig. She gestured for me to come closer, patting the spot next to her. I inched over. There was just enough room for me to sit beside her. Our hips touched and legs stretched out. She shakily handed me a sheet of notebook paper. The lantern I had given her eked out enough light to read, "I won't tell." The words were scribbled in childlike writing.

"Do you think he's telling the truth?" I handed her the paper back.

"We were in the dark together for a time. He was a good boy. I don't know." She clenched the paper to her heart. "He's not exactly the same kid anymore."

I felt a shiver of something and was as confused as ever. The question I had been holding in simply spilled out. "Do they kill people?"

Her head hung low, and she brought her legs in and tightly hugged them, making herself small and inaccessible. The spot below her left eye twitched. "Do you want to make more pancakes?"

"Stop it, Ary. We can't just keep ignoring things."

"I'd be happy to live under your stairs forever. I don't eat much."

Clearly, neither of us knew what the hell to do and were in way over our heads. "You're changing your mind again. For real?" My phone buzzed. A text from Lucas read, "Are you still going to church?"

I thumbed in a quick, "Yes," needing to check this lady, Ary's foster mother, out now more than ever.

Lucas replied, "Leaving in a few. Will pick you up."

I slipped my phone into my pocket. I had to consider the possibility that the answers weren't with Ary. But why would her foster parents send a little boy in a Halloween mask to our house? Or had he come on his own? The more I thought about things, the more questions I had. Ary only gave half-answers and pretty strange ones. "I've got to get ready for church. We'll talk more after," I told her.

"Do you regret letting me stay?" She stared down, frowning, obviously scared and anxious.

I answered, "No." And I meant it.

She twisted her head to look at me. "Thank you, but it's hard when you leave." She was silent for a moment before she said, "Promise me one day we will walk outside together. I'm afraid to go by myself. I might disintegrate if I ever see the light of day."

I had an idea. "We will go outside together as soon as I get home."

Her wide eyes radiated fear and excitement. The fear took charge. "*Da-don't* even look at Mother," she stuttered. "If you're on their radar b-bad things will happen...To answer your question from earlier, she's capable of anything."

Whoever this lady was, she'd sure done a number on Ary. "I'll be cool. No worries."

I wrote my mom a note telling her I was going to church with Lucas. Luckily, Uncle Pete didn't come. I was still annoyed at his lame-ass comments. When I slid into the backseat, Lucas handed me the newspaper. I quickly scanned the page, locating an article about a missing girl, Sanctuary Daniels, and a close-up photo. It looked more like a mug shot than a school or family picture. She was beautifully sad, her lips set in full pout. It also listed an award of 10,000 dollars for information leading to her safe return.

I uttered, "What the hell?"

Lucas mouthed, "I know," in reply, and loudly huffed.

I was still freaking out inside when my aunt asked, "What are you two conspiring about? You always were as thick as thieves."

"Nothing, Mom," Lucas firmly said.

We got out of the car. It was a really nice day. Even though it had been a chilly October, today oddly seemed like Summer, almost hitting 70 degrees. The ornately glazed doors of the church were propped open. A small older man, maybe sixty, welcomed us on our way in and handed my aunt a program. I walked alongside Lucas. He was dressed in a crisp

white button shirt and khakis. I was the slacker who had just
thrown on a pair of black jeans and a T-shirt. The building
opened to a huge lobby. People sat at tables with sign-ups for
outings, and there was a café off to the side, resembling a
Starbucks. Clusters of voices buzzed on all sides of me. Two
girls with lattes in their hands excitedly shouted, "Lucas!" He
waved. The place almost seemed more like a community
center than a church.

My aunt led Lucas and me to the worship center. There
were no statues of Jesus, Mary, or even a cross. The three of
us settled into a pew. Immediately, I searched for a lady who
might be Ary's wicked mother. The crowd consisted of fami-
lies, young couples, and empty nesters. Most of the seats were
already occupied. Over a hundred had gathered.

"Is she here?" I impatiently asked Lucas.

He shook his head. "No, I don't think so."

I wasn't even sure what seeing Ary's foster mother would
really tell me. Finally, a tall, willowy lady with rosy blonde
hair in a French braid entered, catching my attention. There
was something stiff, almost mechanical in her movements.
Sure enough, a small, thin boy walked at her side. His face
appeared damaged by a fire or serious accident. He could
have been the small figure in the mask, Elijah. A tall, lanky
kid, a little older than me, came in right after her. He had corn
silk blond hair and powder blue eyes. They all sat in the pew
across from ours.

An empty feeling unfolded in my chest.

Lucas elbowed me. "There she is," he whispered, but I
already knew. I just knew.

I peered across the way, and holy shit, the lady looked
right at me. I may have psyched myself out because my

nerves tingled. I tried not to stare, not wanting to end up on her radar.

The service began. After a blessing from the graying yet zestful minister, the parishioners were asked to shake hands with their neighbors. Welcome them. Lucas reached for my hand, and my aunt did the same. It was kind of nice. Then my gaze shot to the lady and boys across the aisle. To my relief, they didn't cross over to greet me. I was conflicted because, in a way, I'd wanted to get a closer look, a better impression. Of course, you could probably shake hands with a serial killer or cult leader and be none the wiser.

A couple turned around and shook my hand, saying, "Welcome."

I mumbled the word back, hardly registering their features. Next, an old woman, slack-faced and empty-eyed, leered at me. She rasped out a phrase in a creepy-sounding Latin, tightly grasping my hand.

"Huh?" My voice cracked, but she had turned away. I swallowed hard and told myself to stop being paranoid. People spoke other languages.

Then a chubby lady at a keyboard started pounding out an upbeat hymn. A hippie-looking guy playing the tambourine joined in. People sang along, clapping, raising their hands in excitement. I again sought out the lady. The one called Mother. I watched as her lips remained slanted in a half smile though they never opened to sing along. It didn't matter. Somehow, she completely glowed and completely belonged.

Of course, the preacher's sermon would be about honesty. What were the odds? He talked about a little league game where a seven-year-old admitted he didn't tag another player.

I'd have told the truth about it too. Probably. Then the minister recited several scriptures, making me question if I'd burn in hell.

Then, after a few songs about Jesus, I wasn't any surer about what to do and was sweating a little under my pits.

Curiosity got the best of me. My gaze briefly flicked to Mother again just as she turned her head, and our eyes met. *Oh crap.* My stomach did a heavy flop, and I stared down at my Converse sneakers.

The minister ended the church service with an even more direct message. "If anyone has information about Sanctuary Daniels, please notify the police immediately. Now let us pray for her safe return."

A flurry of anxiety circled my head like a fog, and sweat bubbled across my forehead. What if my mom saw the paper? Of course, she would recognize Ary. What if Ary's foster mom and this Gary guy were human traffickers capable of hurting my family? Lucas and I exited the church through a side door, letting Aunt V stay behind as she chatted with a lady about her age.

"The shit's hitting the fan," Lucas said. His face was streaked with unease, and he hissed to me, "We need to tell someone."

"No. We can't." We hurried across the paved parking lot. "I need to check things out first."

"You just have the hots for her," he said as we made it to the beamer.

"No," I replied, explaining, "They're really weird. The little boy was in my house the other night wearing a creepy mask."

Lucas made a slight "hmm" sound, attempting to process

it all. When he couldn't process it in his genius of a brain, he asked, "What was the kid doing there?"

"What are you boys talking about?" Aunt Veronica asked, pointing out, "You two are acting even stranger than usual. What's going on?"

"Nothing," we replied in unison.

16

WHEN YOU LEAST EXPECT IT

JACOB

I arrived home at eleven o'clock. After some coaxing and encouragement, Ary stood with me in the kitchen by the French doors, which led to a small cement patio. Probably the nicest part of the house.

Her expression was deadly serious. "It's too soon," she decided, teetering on a pair of wobbly legs. "I can't!" She whirled around, her back now toward the patio door. Her small shoulders were hunched, and her hair concealed most of her face like a protective shield.

I gently brushed her long tresses away to see an undercurrent of worry on her trembling lips. "I'll be with you every step of the way," I promised.

"Alright," she said, pasting her mouth into a rigid smile.

I reached and took her hand, and we were palm to palm. "Better?"

"Yes. Better. And I don't even have to pretend you're here."

"No. You don't," I said.

I stayed with her, though she moved with glacial slowness. Our feet shuffled past a slab of cracked concrete as a gentle wash of fresh air greeted us. It was a bright and sunny day with a pale blue sky. At first, Ary only looked at the ground. Until finally, she shut her eyes and lifted her head. She clearly enjoyed the warmth on her skin but kept a tight hold of my hand. We strolled along the yard.

"It's been over a year since I've seen the sun. It stings a little, but it's wonderful."

"And guess what? You're not disintegrating," I cheerfully remarked.

"I'm not." She let go of my hand and spun around, laughing. Yet, in less than a minute, she'd reclaimed my hand as though it were oxygen, and she couldn't breathe without it. "Stay close, Jacob. Please."

"Sure."

She bent down to pick up one of the many burnt orange leaves which had fallen from a large oak in the yard. "May I keep this?"

"Of course."

She slipped it into her pocket as her eyes flittered all around. "The world's beautiful."

The blades of grass shimmered in emerald green. It was like I was viewing it through her lens. Everything held an extra appeal. "Yeah, you're right."

Then she surprised me, venturing ahead until I joined her in the garden.

Just days ago, I hadn't even glimpsed signs of buds. Now,

flowers that had been missing in action had unfurled and blossomed, overtaking the bed of weeds. Stunning pink petals, fiery at their edges, gleamed in the sunlight.

I scratched my head, having an irrational notion that her very presence had magically brought them back to life. "These weren't here before."

"Some flowers bloom in the fall," she replied.

Admittedly, I didn't know anything about flowers. I squinted at them. They were stunning. I inhaled their fragrant scent, and a sense of peace stole over me.

"They're nice." She drew a deep breath before abruptly reclaiming my hand. The easy-breezy feeling evaporated. "How was it?" She gulped. "How was church?"

"It was weird seeing your foster mom."

"*Don't* call her that." Her nostrils flared.

"Uh, sorry," I mumbled. Then I remembered how the newspaper had Ary's photograph. People were looking for her, and now anyone might recognize her. "Do you want to go inside?" I asked, thinking it was a good idea.

She said, "Yeah. We should."

On the way back inside, we paused and faced one another by the French doors before I opened the door. Her hand slipped free of my grasp. She entered the house but craned her neck to ensure I was still behind her.

"Do you want to see something cool?" she asked.

"Always."

She practically ran through the house to the mudroom. I picked up my pace to keep up. She dropped to the floor just near the cellar door. "Look at them."

I joined her to see a line of ants marching through the cracks in the tile's caulking.

"Aren't they orderly?" She sounded utterly impressed.

"Orderly? This house has mice, ants. It's pretty gross." She was cute. I smiled at her. "What's wrong with you?"

"I don't get out much." We laughed and sat there on the worn-out checkered linoleum, grinning at one another.

"No kidding." I started thinking out loud. "We could go to movies, the park, the museum, a Broadway play. Me and mom see one every year. It's like a live movie."

"That'd be great." She moved her face closer to mine, our lips so close they almost touched. My lips involuntarily puckered until she jerked her head away.

"Sorry." I wasn't actually sorry. I wanted to kiss her more than I thought possible. Even as weird as the situation felt, she was pretty, sweet, and innocent.

"It wasn't your fault." She paused for a second, her brow creased. "I always dreamed of Lucas. Only Lucas for all those years, but I—" Her voice trailed off.

"What? Tell me." Was she starting to feel it too? This thing between us?

My cell buzzed. It was Lucas, of course. What *perfect* timing from the *perfect* Lucas.

I was planning to blow him off, but his text read. "The cops are coming. Meet me in your backyard with Ary. NOW."

I jammed my phone into my jeans pocket. "You've got to go with Lucas for a little while."

"Why? Did I upset you?"

"No." I was lightheaded and had trouble thinking clearly. "The police. They're coming." I jumped up first and helped her to her feet. "Lucas is here," I explained and sailed toward the kitchen. Ary followed. Through the patio door, I saw

Lucas. And in a matter of seconds, I heard distant sirens coming closer. I threw open the door, instructing Ary to "Go with him."

She looked at me briefly and was out the door. Lucas took her hand, and I spun back around. Bracing myself, I proceeded toward the screaming sirens and shrieking brakes.

As I approached the front of the house, the sirens had halted. The door was jolted and rattled by the pounding. I threw it open before it was knocked off its hinges. The same bald police officer loomed there. "We have a warrant to search the premises." The officer scowled, thrusting his way inside. I briefly raised my hands in response, inching away from him.

He looked me up and down. His eyes crawling all over my skin. Dark eyes, shining with a desire for violence. "You know why I'm here."

"Um." I cleared my throat. "Are you looking for the, uh, runaway?" I tried to sound nonchalant but felt shaky inside.

He proudly informed me, "I'm close personal friends with Mother."

Mother, he called her *Mother*. "Is she *your* mom?" I mumbled the question.

The front window framed three police cruisers in the driveway with lights flashing as I watched a fourth patrol car pull up. Oh, crap. It now looked like a scene out of a crime show. What the hell? More officers entered my house.

Hearing my name called, I turned around to find my mom squinting at me in her robe, with Michael standing next to her in his sweats and a T-shirt. Mom asked, "My God, what's going on?"

The police officer said, "I have a warrant to search the house." Then he abruptly walked off.

"A search warrant. For what?" Mom looked at me.

I avoided eye contact. "Dunno," I managed to say. A strange and itchy feeling came over me as the police invaded our house. Two police officers, one a short guy with a monobrow and a chubby white lady cop, disappeared up the stairs. A third cop, a young red-haired guy, was looking around the first floor. Loud voices and the blare of walkie-talkies were all around. I glanced back at my mom and Michael, a step behind me. My body bristled, and my hands were trembling. The atmosphere thickened with tension.

The bald officer, Damler, advised my mom, "You better tell your son not to interfere. He's already in enough trouble."

"In trouble?" I squeaked.

"What's going on, officer?" Mom demanded. "How is my son in trouble?"

"We have reason to believe your son has been harboring the runaway."

"He wouldn't. Jacob?" Her voice rose in volume.

I turned around. Mom's gaze sharpened on me. "No. I haven't." I blinked with concentrated effort.

Michael started telling the officer, "There was a monster and a ghost here."

My mom explained, "He has schizophrenia."

"Jeez, Mom, why'd you say it like that? Anyway, they changed my diagnosis. And Jacob saw them too," Michael protested.

I drew my bottom lip into my mouth, refusing to help my brother out.

Michael let it go and asked, "Can I go to my room now?"

"No, honey," Mom said. "Just relax."

We all stood there for a couple of crazy minutes, dazed.

After a frantic search, a second female officer with short brown hair briskly emerged from the kitchen. I hadn't even realized she was there. She reported to Damler, "Nothing, Sir. No sign of the girl."

"You searched the cellar?" he asked, slightly agitated.

"Yes, Nico did."

We had stood right by the stairs the entire time, and somehow no one had searched Ary's hiding place. She didn't have to go with Lucas in the first place. I guess I should have been relieved. I mean, they'd have found the sleeping bag and the note. All things that would have been pretty hard to explain.

The officer sniffed and rubbed his forehead. "Sorry, Ma'am," he tipped his chin at my mom. "We have to follow every lead. This is about a missing teen who is believed to be dangerous."

"I understand," my mom replied.

The police left.

Mom closed the door behind them. I watched the stress roll off her shoulders as she turned to me. "That was weird. Can you believe it? Like you'd bring a strange girl into our house. Crazy, huh?"

My stomach tensed a little. "Yeah. Crazy."

17

IN THE SUNLIGHT

ARY

We ran, my vision blurred in the wake of a thousand tiny suns. Cool gusts of wind ruffled my skirt and whispered my name. *Ary. Ary.* Over and over again. Once at the tree line, Lucas put his hand on the small of my back as he piloted me through the shadowy woods.

The last time I was here, a blanket of darkness covered the world, and the wind's nighttime chants sang as my legs swayed with fear, and my whole body shivered beneath the starless sky. All the while pretending Lucas was by my side. Now he was here, and we walked in the daytime. Yet it was equally terrifying. Light streamed in misty and unreal shafts. Twisted branches on giant trees reached for me with gnarled limbs. Trepidation crawled up my legs and arms like demonic vines.

Lucas himself had been in my mind for so long, the flesh and blood boy seemed strange. Taller, older, and unfamiliar.

His features were sharp but attractive, and his charisma was disarming.

"A little farther," he coaxed, commanding the pace with his confident stride. My heart pounded from the excitement as I strained to keep up. The delicate bones in my ankles felt ready to snap, and the muscles in my shaky legs ached and burned. I'd never have made it if I hadn't snuck a small snack earlier. Still, I pushed myself, walking faster and faster uphill to keep up with him. Soon my senses tingled as the warning bells rang out. We were dangerously close to the house, *Mother's house.*

I stopped in my tracks, digging my feet into the ground, entrenched in the spot. "I ca-can't...I won't."

"Alright. I suppose we're far enough." He pulled his arm away and attempted to make eye contact, but I picked at my fingernails and looked down at my hands. "We'll chill out for a bit before I take you back to Jacob's." His voice sounded low and sweet, but not like I'd imagined it.

Unable to find my voice, I thought *yes* and rubbed my throat.

"Are you okay?" he asked, running one hand through his dark, wavy hair. He was handsome enough that he could have been a jerk, and the world still would have accepted him, but he was nice. Kind.

I felt shaky, and tears clouded my vision.

"You're trembling," he said, fumbling to take his jacket off. Then he placed it over my shoulders.

It made me wonder if he had loved me too all these years. But I must have seemed pitiful. I was crying a little, and my nose was dripping from the chill in the air.

"It'll be okay," he said, his voice steady and reassuring.

Yet, I cried even harder. My vision blurred, throwing my surroundings out of focus. Lucas presented me with a napkin from his pants pocket. There was confidence in his stance and character that painted a portrait of a person always prepared. It should have calmed me, but it didn't.

I dabbed my tears away and cleaned my nose. Unable to stop the panic, my heart thudded, and the trees seemed to spin round and round. I would have fallen if it weren't for Lucas holding me up. Grateful, I let my head lean on his chest. We stayed in the embrace. It was the fantasy that had kept me going.

Then he asked, "What can I do for you?"

And my head cleared. I pulled away. Realizing I wanted— needed—to be with my friend. I only managed to say one word, sounding primitive, "Jacob."

"I'm taking you there, but I want to make sure it's safe first." He gestured to the pocket of his jacket as if to ask permission.

I nodded.

He retrieved his cell phone, explaining, "I'm going to wait until Jacob calls. The police might still be there."

I nodded again.

"Wow, this reminds me of our conversations, from what was it, fourth grade? I'd say something, and you'd nod."

My lip twitched up involuntarily, briefly warmed.

"Oh, you can smile," he playfully said, slipping his hands into his pants' pockets. "It's been a *long* time. You sure grew up."

"I did?" The smile died on my lips as I experienced a sudden jab of pain over a life stolen. "How old are we?"

"We're sophomores. I'm fifteen, but a lot of kids in our class are sixteen already."

"That is so old," I blurted. How could I be that old?

Unexpectedly, there was the sound of breaking twigs, footsteps. Lucas's eyes darted from side to side, making me also scour the strange surroundings.

He decided, "It was nothing. Probably a deer."

Then it was quiet, and I had that haunted feeling of being watched. A bundle of nerves gathered in my chest.

Lucas held his phone. And there we stayed, so still and quiet. Finally, he asked, "Was it bad for you there? At your foster home?"

My mind flinched and jerked against the chaos of memories from my time in dark places. I couldn't answer or even nod. After a few seconds elapsed, I told him, "I... I can't."

"No, I'm the one who should apologize. It was a stupid question. I didn't mean to upset you," he said, tugging at the collar of his shirt.

Lucas was every bit as nice as Jacob and as handsome. More importantly, Lucas was the one I'd always loved. Yet, he'd seemed like a dream I tried to remember. It felt unnatural. Forced. Prompting me to act like a zombie around him. I was, after all, the undead—a ghost in a way. Somehow, Jacob had fooled me into thinking I was alive.

In that cellar, good memories faded away. A dull pain thudded. My driftwood bones fragile inside an immobile body. I curled up and strained to make myself smaller and smaller, wishing I'd become so insignificant, I'd disappear altogether. My heart had even stopped beating for hours at a time. Only I wasn't good at dying.

Lucas's phone chimed. "Hey," I heard him say before he

paced away. After a few minutes, he shuffled over to me and announced, "It was Jacob. The coast is clear. We can go back now," and by the slight turn of his lip, I could sense his relief.

I was relieved too. The heart had a mind of its own. And I knew I didn't love Lucas, and I cared about Jacob. A lot.

The return trek was better for many reasons. First, the sun was no longer in my eyes. Second, my legs easing down the slope of the hills fared much better than that strenuous uphill climb. Third, sweating but no longer exhausted, I experienced the swooshing of my blood through my veins, like a sweet song of determination. Lastly, the mere idea of seeing Jacob and retreating to my refuge under the stairs inspired me to happily march on.

We were almost there. I took Lucas's jacket from my shoulder and handed it to him. "Thank you," I said.

Lucas put his hands on my waist and helped me climb over the chain-link fence. I saw Jacob standing there in the backyard—waiting. We smiled at one another, and the closeness made me feel like I was home for the first time. It hit me all at once. My relationship with Jacob had changed me in some utterly significant and intangible way. There was almost hope in that moment. I knew what I needed to do. I had to tell Jacob *everything,* and I had to make him believe it.

18

WHEN SHE RETURNED

JACOB

Ary and I just looked at one another for a few long seconds. I had no idea what she was thinking, or if she and Lucas had felt a spark.

"I'm glad you're back," I admitted, and having enough close calls for one day, cautioned, "Um, my mom is asleep. So, we better be super quiet."

Once inside, Ary looked beat. "Come and see me, Jacob, when Lucas is gone," she said.

"Oh, okay."

She immediately slunk away.

Lucas stayed a few feet behind me, closer to the door. They didn't seem to have coupled up. I was happy, but still hoped he hadn't broken her heart.

When the half-door closed under the staircase, Lucas gestured for me. "Let's talk."

We had made it to the living room when he said, "I don't

know what we're doing here." Lucas lowered his voice to say, "Sorry to be blunt about it, but she's weird." He slumped down onto the end of the sectional.

I flopped down next to him. "Hell yeah. You'd be weird too if you hadn't seen the light of day since the fourth grade. Think about it. It makes sense why she's fixated on that time." Lucas and I had switched roles. Now I was the sensitive guy, and he was the cynical a-hole.

"Maybe, or she may just be delusional, Jacob."

"That's why I want to go there and see what it's like for myself."

"Are you two...You know?" he asked.

"No." I shook my head.

"You like her." His voice and eyebrows climbed with the accusation.

"Yeah... I like her." I shrugged, trying to sound casual.

"And of course, she'd cling to the first person who helped her."

"It isn't like that," I argued, my voice rising in volume, but it probably was. It was Lucas she liked, anyway. But I was still her friend no matter what.

Lucas sighed.

"I still can't believe the cops didn't even look under the stairs." Then I wondered, "How'd you know they were coming?"

He rubbed his hands together, his face registering the distress.

"How?" I pressed.

I sensed a hitch in the air, hesitation brewing in Lucas's eyes before he said, "It was, uh...Jamie...He called for the reward."

"No frigging way!" I stood up, putting my hands to my head in a mix of disbelief and outrage. "How did he even know she was here?" I scowled at Lucas.

He just sunk into the leather. "He thought maybe she was, and I guess I confirmed it." Then he sighed and slowly stood. "Sorry, Jacob. I didn't think he'd, well, you know."

"I'm going to kick his ass!"

Lucas smirked. "Have you ever kicked anyone's ass?"

I shot him an irritated look. Then I remembered. "Wow, and that idiot pretended he was going to help me. What a joke."

"It was wrong, but you gotta think about it. Ten thousand dollars. It's a lot of money and Jamie's *poor*," Lucas said, defending him.

"Yeah, well, you don't sell out your friends." I felt choked up and tried to rein it in.

"You don't even really know Ary."

"You're wrong. There're people you can meet and just know, connect with them in a few days, hours even. It's Jamie I don't know. Not anymore. He's dead to me." My words even struck me as harsh right after I said them. I backpedaled. "I mean, I didn't think he'd do something like this."

"I'm gonna take off. Call me later." He stood. Whenever possible, Lucas assumed the neutral position. He never liked controversy. I couldn't even say this was a bad quality, and the guy was always there when I needed him.

"Okay." I only gave him a half-hearted, "Thanks," and watched him walk away, deciding to go and check on Ary.

After saying a shy hello, Ary politely asked, "May I take another shower?"

"Sure. My house, your house, remember?"

"Thanks."

"But make it a quick one. My mom left to go on errands."

So, I sat in the hall outside the downstairs bathroom listening to the trickling water as she washed up, and I played the part of lookout. Then the landline rang. I hurried to get the call so I could return to my post.

"This is Ted, from Bob's Exterminators. I'm calling to confirm tomorrow's appointment."

"We have to cancel," I quickly said, thinking of Ary. She couldn't very well be there when he was fumigating the house, and it would be risky to sneak her out again this soon.

"Do you want to reschedule?"

"No," I replied and hung up. That was a close one. When I looked up, Ary was there. A fluffy blue towel enveloped her frame, and her hair was wrapped up in another towel, genie style. Her hand rested on her collarbone, which glistened with drops of water. The scent of the strawberry body wash wafted off her skin. Her legs and arms were shiny and exposed.

"Uh...hi," I muttered.

"Are you alright?"

I took a breath, fighting a rush of attraction. "Um, me, yeah, g-good," I stuttered.

"We need to talk later tonight once I'm proper." She tilted her chin up, and her small, slightly upturned nose was almost aristocratic. Her full pink lips set in a pout.

We stared at one another like we were under a spell until Ary's eyes blinked back to life. "I'm...I'm going to tell you *everything*." There was a slight quiver in her voice. She turned away, dashing off to resume her place below the stairs. The small door closed just in time as my mom's voice jolted me.

"Hey, Jacob," she said.

I spun around. "Mom? Hey, *you*."

"I picked up a pizza and got Michael a salad. Come and eat. I need your help with something." She sounded a little frazzled.

"Sure."

We sat next to one another at the table. Mom hardly ever cooked, yet we always ate together. "Okay. A Facebook friend of mine's grandmother is dying, and I accidentally sent the ghost emoji instead of a heart." She handed me her phone. "Fix it."

I cringed, sharing my mom's discomfort. She was such a screw-up sometimes. Just another reason I loved her. "I don't know! I'm not on Facebook very much. It's for old people."

"Quick, just delete it," she demanded.

"You can't delete comments, only posts. This is *bad*." I groaned.

"It's okay, Mom," Michael said. "Sending the ghost just shows you believe in the afterlife."

"No. It's messed up." I shook my head. "Oh wait, I did delete it." I handed her the phone back. "Now comment something and add the hearts. Lots of them."

My chair made a scraping noise as I scrambled for a slice. Mom typed on her phone and said, "God, it's been such a weird day."

"Yeah," I exhaled.

Mom sucked in her right cheek, a telltale sign she was thinking. "The girl that was here—what was her name? Was it Airy?"

Had she read about the runaway? Be cool. Be cool. "No. It was Arie. For Ariana."

Mom made a 'hmmm' sound, seemingly unconvinced.

Michael's eyes inspected me, but Mom seemed to relax. We lapsed into silence. Michael picked at his salad, and despite the fizzy feeling of treachery, I began pigging out.

After dinner, I started towards the stairs. I knew things couldn't keep going on like this. I needed answers, yet my pulse raced at the prospect of learning everything.

19

EVERYTHING

ARY

Jacob's mom had left for work. We stood side by side, our elbows touching. It was chilly outside, so Jacob lent me one of his mother's jackets and a pair of her leggings. The stars gleamed like diamonds, and I could have easily gushed about how beautiful it was but dialed it down and began with simple pleasantries. "It's a lovely night."

He grinned. "I never notice that stuff, but yeah, it is." And then, he surprised me by asking, "Do you want me to talk to Lucas? You still like him, right?"

I gathered my thoughts. "My fourth-grade self will always love Lucas, but I like someone else now." My gaze fell to the ground. "Well, you probably know who I mean." I brought my head up to see Jacob looking confused.

He pointed at himself, asking, "Is it me?" with little confidence.

"Yes. You." We smiled in sync.

"I like you, too," he said, his voice soft and clear, but I already knew.

"I want you to kiss me." My own words made me happy, excited, and scared. A swirl of emotions soared as he moved closer, ready and willing to kiss me on the spot. It was all happening too fast, and I panicked. My knee jerked up, connecting with his private area.

He bent over in pain. "What did you do that for?"

"Sorry! It was a reflex. Don't be mad."

He grimaced but stood up straight again. "I'm not mad."

"Try again!" I said, louder and more demanding than I intended.

"I don't think so...Ary, there's no hurry. I'm not going anywhere."

"Please," I pushed.

He hesitated. "Okay." He slowly bent down and brought his lips briefly to mine. Tentative. Shy. His chin brushed against my hair as he backed away. Probably worried I'd assault him again.

There was always a softness to Jacob's sweeping dark locks, boyish way, and openness. It invited me in. I moved closer, reaching up on my tippy toes, and our lips met. This one lasted a little longer. Lips tasting lips until I ended the kiss.

With the sudden hammering of my heart, I decided to say the words that had me sent to the psych ward and back with Mother. I needed to warn him so he'd know just how dangerous they were. "Jacob, they're *not human*."

"What are you talking about?" His eyes pleaded for me not to go there, not to be crazy.

I couldn't tell him what I wanted to. "Kids come and go." My jaw tightened. "They want us to do bad things."

"Ary," he sighed, though it was scarcely audible. "I wish I could change things. But you need to know, you're the sweetest, purest person I've ever met."

Jacob had gotten a little teary as his cheeks flushed. It was plainly written on his face. He felt sorry for me. But did he understand? I had to say more. His phone beeped, and he snatched it from his pocket. "It's just Lucas."

"You can take his call."

Jacob shrugged. "I'll just talk for a minute." He strode away from the patio.

I twisted my hands together. Memories screamed at me, tearing through my brain. I flashed back to my first party.

A blond boy named Ren sunk into the sofa next to me. He was a foul-mouthed kid who had been seventeen years old for as long as I had known him. My empty stomach became a pressure cooker of anxiety.

Vampires strolled in through the front doors, ghosts and demons crept up from the stairs. Black candles were laid out all around. Music softly thrummed, and the guests talked and smoked.

A ghost of a girl whispered, "I just came to say goodbye. I have to go to the light."

The apparition was just a little older than me at the time, maybe ten, when she was alive. A frail thing, almost transparent. I knew this girl had been chained in the basement. I'd even helped spoon feed her on occasion before her demise.

I told her, "I thought about you. You just weren't here one day. How did you die?"

"It may have been starvation or blood loss," she mournfully replied.

"Lucky you," Ren said.

"I'm sorry," I told her. She and I exchanged a look of sick understanding.

Ren snapped, *"Stop feeling bad for her. We've got our own problems."*

Mother's squared back turned to us as she wheeled and dealed with two adults—a well-dressed man and woman with beautifully alarming faces and shiny skin as white as bone.

"This is why they keep us weak, so we can barely run." Ren's forehead creased. *"It's cold in here, and I'm sweating bullets."*

"What are they going to do?" I asked him.

"They're going to make us do bad things."

The ghost-girl nodded in somber agreement.

"I won't." I shook my head.

Mother spun around, and in a flash, the little girl vanished. She ordered Ren and me to *"Stop talking,"* Then she spoke to the couple. *"You can take the boy and drink all you want. Just leave him immortal."*

Mother lowered herself to the couch and grabbed Ren's arm, pulling him to his feet. *"He's of noble bloodline."*

He chuckled. *"My mom? My mom's a prostitute. And my dad was one of her johns, and I'm pretty sure he ain't noble."*

"What about the girl?" The couple looked curiously at me and inched in closer. *"I've never breathed in such sweet blood."*

I gripped the velvet arm of the couch.

"Now that...that would cost you... for the tiniest taste," Mother said, gesturing for Ren to sit. He obeyed.

The pretty stranger assembled on the other side of him. She gently smoothed the clammy hair clinging to his forehead. Her head popped up, and she addressed Mother. "He has a sixth sense. He may be quite powerful if I change him." The lady's eyes were bright blue and dead of any emotion.

"I'm aware," Mother said.

"Ary, Ary," Jacob repeated, pulling me out of dark places once more. "Are you alright?"

I blurted, "Little kids who die eventually find the light."

"What? You mean, they kill them?" Jacob blinked at me. "They kill kids?"

Words kept pouring out of my mouth. "Some of the kids change and start drinking the blood, too. It's rare. They must come from a certain lineage to become the upstairs kids, like Ren and Elijah. And they're allowed to go places, visit the school, stores and go to church. They let me stay upstairs for a while. But I kept telling people about the bad things they did." He probably assumed I was crazy. He didn't reject me outright but caressed my hand in a sympathetic gesture.

We didn't speak for a couple of minutes, but I could practically hear Jacob's mind ticking like a clock. Then he said, "There was this evil cult of cannibals I heard about. They killed and ate people, and thought it made them immortal. They were just crazed drug addicts. It could be something like that. And I think the one police officer is in on it. He called her Mother, and it's not like she's a nun."

My heart sprinted. Amazed. He believed me. "They all call her Mother." I leaned in, explaining, "Even the adults who visit the house."

"Freaking creepy. Yeah. And there have been animal sacrifices in this town. It all sounds cultish."

In a way, he was right. "I shouldn't have brought you into this." A throb of emotion permeated my voice. The wind sighed. Again, I had a creeping, sneaking feeling, like we were being watched. "Let's go inside."

A startled Jacob turned and bashed his shoulder on the patio door before opening it for me.

I had barely told him anything. Barely warned him at all. I couldn't stand it if he'd rejected me.

He secured the lock, and we walked into the living room without saying a word. I sat on the sofa. My palms were spread flat on the cool leather when he joined me, sitting a foot away.

"It's going to be okay," he said, his voice steady.

We kept swiveling our heads around, exchanging glances.

Jacob moved closer. "I like you so much," he said.

I struggled not to say, 'I love you.' It seemed too soon. And after all, I'd thought I'd loved Lucas for years. Who knew what my heart would do next? I settled for a sincere, "Me, too."

Feeling a magnetic pull, we turned purposefully and leaned in. Our lips met. His arms wrapped around my back, and I put my arms over his shoulders. Our lips met, and his tongue touched my tongue, which shocked me at first. Still, I kissed him. Fiercely. Wishing the kiss could fill the emptiness. Hoping it could banish the ugliness I'd seen. Thirty or so minutes came and went, and an addictive heat grew between us.

All of a sudden, he broke away. We panted like we were both coming up for air after being underwater for too long.

He mumbled, "Ary," sounding breathless.

"Can we kiss more now?"

His face flushed, and he grinned. "I think I need a *wee* longer break. I want to take things slow, but it's hard to stop kissing you."

We sat silently for a while, only hearing our breath. He sat with a pillow on his lap. I dared bask in the glow of him and in the idea of being a regular girl. A girlfriend even.

Jacob had a dreamy air about him. He moved in, kissing the silky soft spot beneath my ear. "I think I'm ready," he whispered.

A smile crossed my lips at the passing goosebumps he gave me. "No. Not now." I put two fingers on his lips, and then I ruined things. It was what I did best. "How do you kill vampires? Demons?"

"Ary…There are no such things as vampires. And if there are really demons, well, they're in hell."

"Yes, but Mother summons them. They want to open the door, but they can't…ever."

His lips pinched, and his eyes narrowed, thinking. "Please tell me something I can understand. Explain what you mean? Who comes over, and what *door* do you keep talking about?"

"I'm not sure what to tell you. Or how to explain things that don't make sense. Please don't think I'm crazy." I snatched the sofa pillow from him and hugged it.

"I don't," he said.

I dropped my head against his shoulder.

"Do you want me to make you eggs or pancakes?" he asked.

My stomach growled. In truth, I only kept half of what I consumed down. I was half monster. A wretched creature— bound to bring darkness wherever I'd go. Jacob had no clue. Dropping the pillow, I followed him, exploring a homey kitchen. One wall had white tiles with a couple of copper pots held up by hooks. Next to a deep stainless-steel sink on the counter, several kitchen knives were stored in a wooden block. I took note of them while Jacob busied himself gathering all the ingredients.

We were two ordinary teens, playing house and sharing smiles that made us blush—buzzed on the simple high of liking someone who liked you back. Yet all the while, I knew something wicked was coming. A beautiful beginning, ready to burst at the seams. I gazed out the window at the night sky framed by cheerful yellow curtains. The horror creeping up on me again as Mother's words played in my head: "I will always find you."

But she already had. I could feel it.

20

MAGIC

ARY

Jacob had gone to sleep two hours ago, but I felt antsy and hadn't withdrawn into my small space. Not tonight. After all, I was no longer sequestered. And my brain wouldn't shut off. I started thinking about all the things I had wanted to forget. I curved my hand around my stomach, which rumbled with curious longings. Cravings I'd dare not utter aloud. A brown shape streaked across the living room floor by my feet. I snatched it, and crept into the kitchen, flicking on the buzzing fluorescent lights before discarding a now lifeless mouse in the trash. My eyes stayed downcast, feeling loathsome and repentant. My mind spat out, *I'm sorry*. It was comforting to think I was like Eleven from *Stranger Things*. Then again, she never squeezed the life out of a defenseless mouse.

I padded across the linoleum and snatched the smallest knife from the collection. Holding the blade just above my skin before I sliced it into my hand. Blood felt warm beneath the cool metal.

It stung, and I even bled red blood—human blood. Closing my eyes, I concentrated. Warmth broke out across my hairline. When I opened my eyes again, there was only a smear of crimson on my flesh. I placed my hand under the faucet and rinsed the blood away. There was no longer any sign of a cut as pinkish water slid down the drain. Squeezing out a drop of dish detergent, I scrubbed my hands. Something as simple as soap was a luxury. I grabbed a maroon checkered dishtowel from the counter, drying my hands. Healing myself was not enough. I needed to know. What otherworldly things could my monster self do?

I opened the creaky oak cabinet and grabbed a pink coffee cup with a candy skull drawn on it. Placing it firmly on the kitchen table, I extended my arms like Frankenstein and— wiggled my fingers. Static electricity tingled and crackled at the tips. My body temperature elevated, and I fell headfirst into a feverish trance. I squeezed my eyes shut and thought *up, up.* I blinked at a kitchen table hovering in the air and then gasped as it crashed down with a bang. The silence magnifying the sound. The cup was on its side near the table's edge. I held my breath. "Shhh," I reminded myself. Luckily, it seemed like the house still slept.

A rich flash of recall arrived. It was not so much a memory at first as it was a scent—the wonderful fragrance of white sage and rose petals simmering on the stove. *Gramma's face briefly manifested as her voice floated in my ears. "Remember you have magic." Her words had astonished me then and now.*

Maybe I wasn't so wretched after all. I have *magic.* Now I needed to learn how to control it. Since I had lifted the table, I surely could raise that cup. Bare feet planted squarely on the kitchen's grayish linoleum. The sensation of heat rising inside. Hands up in the air, I focused only on the coffee mug. Again, an inner drive swelled until the cup skated across the table and exploded. Bits and shards scattered about the kitchen.

The words, "Oh, oh, crap," spilled out, and I placed my hand over my mouth. I had been hanging around Jacob too much. Just then, I heard something—a sound at the top of the stairs. Shaken, I nervously turned and just waited. A few heartbeats later, a sleepy-looking Jacob appeared.

"Sorry. I made too much noise, huh?" I said apologetically, stepping toward him and right onto one of the bigger shards of glass on the floor.

Jacob made a guttural noise in his throat and winced. "Oh, Ary, you're bleeding." He carefully tiptoed around the minefield of broken glass and grabbed the towel. The little blood which waded around my foot seemed to alarm him. The next thing I knew, he ushered me to the kitchen chair. For a moment, his eyelashes distracted me. They were a soft black, and so long they were a little tangled. He stooped to the floor and wrapped my foot up in the rag.

"I'm fine, Jacob." I focused, and my foot tingled. "Uh, I was just practicing magic. Using my abilities. Like the girl on TV, Eleven." I hoped referencing the show made it sound more normal. Acceptable.

"I guess it didn't go too well, huh?" His mouth curled into a grin.

It was hard to answer. "Well, the mug wasn't supposed to break." I yearned for him to know me but had trouble telling him about my strange and ugly parts. "Look—look at my foot. It's healed." I started to bend to unwrap it, but he stopped me, placing his hand on mine.

"Give it a little time. Feet bleed pretty bad," he insisted, sitting down next to me. He lowered his voice. "Um, Ary, you do know *Stranger Things* is just a TV show?"

"Yes. I mean, no." I lifted my foot and unwrapped it. "See, there's blood, but no cut. I'll go wash it off…show you. Prove it."

"No. Stay put." Jacob stood up, reaching for a broom, and swept some of the fallout away. "There's antibiotic cream in the bathroom. I can get it."

"No. I'm fine." I jerked my shoulder like it was no big deal. He didn't understand, or he didn't believe me.

There was a creaking. Movement from upstairs.

"Michael's up, and my mom will be home any minute from work. You better go to bed. Um, I'll finish cleaning this mess up," Jacob said, sounding slightly panicked. "Anyway, I start school today."

"Oh, that's right."

"You should stay off your feet. Is it alright if I carry you?" He propped the broom against the table.

I bit my lip at the idea of being in his arms. "Yes. I'll show you my magic later."

Jacob possessed an innate sense of chivalry without realizing it. He swooped me up in his arms like a groom carrying his bride. We didn't speak, and he set me down by my hideaway. He bent down and lowered his head as I reached up. An awkward peck ensued. I wanted more of a kiss. More of a conversation. More of Jacob.

Instead, he whirled away, and I climbed into my small, dusky refuge.

The front door opened, and Jacob's mom came in. I plunked my ear to the door and strained to listen to the real world. Footsteps. Voices. Cabinets opening and closing, the hum and ding of a microwave. And it brought a tinge of dismay because I'd never really been a part of it. Not really.

I heard other sounds too. Sounds from my world. A crash, skidding of claws, a fierce growl. Then unrestrained, hollow laughter. Helplessly and absurdly, I cowered under those stairs praying Mother wouldn't find me.

21

CANDLES AND CULTS

JACOB

After I cleaned up the mess, I took a quick shower and dressed. It was October 29th, Monday, and my first day of school. The whole morning, I kept replaying last night in my head. The amazing kiss and Ary's strange confession. A confession that honestly made little sense. It felt like I tried to swallow something small but jagged enough to catch in my throat.

I missed the bus. My mom didn't complain and gave me a ride. We parked in front of the two-story red brick school.

"I'm going home to sleep. Have a good one." She gave me a half smile, and I flicked her a grumpy look in return.

"Ugh. Do I really have to go?"

"Yeah, you really have to." She ruffled my hair. "Love you, Jacob," she said.

Automatically, I said it back and got out of the old Forester. Though it wasn't even winter, the wind made a cold sound, like hums or moans, and a chill had crept in.

I wished I'd stayed home with Ary and talked more, kissed more, figured something out.

Inside the school, I checked in with the lady at the front and was buzzed in. I hitched my backpack higher on my shoulder. The halls were mostly deserted as I charged up the steps to room 233, registration paper in my sweaty hand. Oh crap. The classroom door was already closed. The only thing worse than being the new-old kid was being late on top of it. I double-checked the schedule and opened the door. I blinked in a room full of students at their desks. Sure, I recognized some of their faces. All eyes went to me, making me a tad light-headed. The teacher's long red nails scratched her neck until she snatched my paper, looking it over before handing it back to me. "Okay, Jacob, there's a seat in the first row. I'm Ms. Trex and class starts at eight o'clock. Got it?"

"Yeah." Being stuck in the front row brought a small ripple of paranoia. I slid my backpack off and sat down, anyway.

The teacher rattled on about Hamlet as a girl whispered, "That's Lucas's cousin."

My ears perked up to hear, "He's cute."

My head swelled a little, but then the other girl countered. "Yeah, he's alright, but he's not as cute as Lucas."

Story of my life. Until now. I scribbled down Ary's name in not-so-large letters on the corner of my folder. Her beautiful face flashed in my head. Yet, thinking about what she told me made me sweat. I wondered what an intelligent guy like Lucas would make out of this crazy story. Could there really be a cult in Steely, Pennsylvania?

I surveyed the clock when I wasn't daydreaming about Ary. Even the memory of our kiss excited me. Sure, I wished we'd met in a more normal way, at the mall or a party, even online.

In each class, I'd scribble down Ary's name on my folder again. People who remembered me at all said, "Hey, it's Lucas's cousin." Sixth grade was a long time ago. I was surprised they remembered me at all. After fourth hour, I saw the blond boy from church in the hall. Our gaze intersected as we passed, and he said, "Hello, Jacob. I'm Ren," in an overly friendly and sarcastic voice.

My pace slowed as I turned to him. An ominous smile crawled across his face. Ary had mentioned him, but how did he know my name?

He disappeared down the crowded hall. I swallowed the unease and bumped into a girl who barked, "Watch where you're going, dumbass."

It was the prissy little girl, now all grown-up: Deanna Mulling. She still had those round cheekbones, but her hair was shoulder length now, and her brown eyes were more prominent with a touch of makeup. She didn't seem to remember me right away.

"Sorry," I offered.

It was then her eyes widened and lit with recognition. "Jacob Kelly." Her hands splayed out on the hips of her short plaid skirt, paired with long wool socks, so no skin showed. "Your mom bought the old house on Wesley Road."

"Yeah." Seriously, how did she always know everybody's crap? "Deanna Mulling," I said as Jamie walked up.

"Oh, the boys are back in town," she dryly remarked, tossing a thin smile Jamie's way.

"You know it." Jamie's chest puffed but deflated when his gaze met mine. He asked, "Hey, what lunch hour do you have, dude?"

My chin tilted, and lips tightened in defiance. I declined to confront him with Miss gossip girl there but spotted my next class and abruptly ducked inside. I sat next to Lucas, who was settling into a desk near the back of the classroom. He took off a canvas bag he was shouldering and let it drop to the floor. Only Lucas could have a man purse and still be cool.

"Hey, Cuz!"

"I have to tell you something." My shoulders sank in relief at having someone I could talk to about things.

"I bet I know about who," he said a little warily.

"Well, yeah." I dropped a folder and notebook on the desk. I had to tell someone. So, I just came out with it. "I like her a lot."

"I know." He clicked his ballpoint pen twice. "Hey, what lunch do you have?"

I picked up my schedule. "A."

"Me, too." He toyed around more with his pen, thinking. "I have to tell you, Jamie feels bad. He's really sorry."

"I'm not talking to Jamie."

Lucas told me, "Just give it time," and snatched my schedule, giving it a quick once over. "We've got the rest of our classes together."

"Really?"

He nodded, and I smiled. This made everything more promising.

At lunch, Lucas and I grabbed trays and sat next to one another. Soon, a boy named Hunter sat down. Lucas introduced us before they started talking. He was a halfway good-looking guy, the athletic type and possibly my replacement. Then none other than big mouth, Deanna Mulling sat on the other side of me, and within seconds, the girls from the other night joined us, too.

Madison said, a friendly, "Hey, Jacob."

"Hey," I smiled her way.

She picked up the bun to see a plain patty. "Everything about this school is underwhelming. Wait, is that a word?"

"I think so," Kylie responded.

"Are you Dumb and Dumber?" Deanna asked, tossing a couple of ketchup and mustard packs onto Madison's tray.

Jamie approached the table wearing a baggy and wrinkled T-shirt like he just didn't care. He thumped a tray with a slab of mystery meat and tater tots down, announcing, "The party can start now. I'm here." He settled in across from me. We stared at one another, my eyes narrowing and his widening in apprehension.

"What's going on between you two?" Deanna pointed a stalk of celery at me and then Jamie.

"Come on, Jacob," Jamie pushed.

I crossed my arms and sighed.

"You used to be cool," Deanna said and asked, "So are you on downers now? Or just an asshole?"

"Just an asshole," I replied.

Madison piped up, "Shut up, Deanna. He just broke up with his girlfriend. She was a model." She shot me a sympathetic look.

"Yeah, right." Deanna wasn't buying it and told me, "No one even cared that you were gone."

"I cared," Jamie dramatically exclaimed, making me seem like more of a dick.

"Me, too," Lucas piped in before glancing over to Deanna and adding, "Come on D, this is between them."

More conversations shot off all around me.

Hunter asked Jamie, "Did you see how Mrs. Quinn looked at you?"

Jamie laughed and seemed proud. "I know, dude. It was so funny." Whatever this was about led to other obscure references about last Halloween.

Kylie chuckled.

Madison lifted her hands up. "You are all bad."

"Not me. I had no part of it," Lucas added.

In the past, we had been a small trio of friends who had rarely sought the company of others. Now the group had readily expanded and gone coed. I didn't fit in or belong. The lunch break was filled with inside jokes. I was the outsider, not having the energy to try to break into the clique.

Then unexpectedly, Deanna said, "What's with all the parents being so into *Mother* from church? Hell, she's not my mother."

Shocked, I dropped a spoon full of mashed potatoes on my pants and quickly wiped it, listening intently.

Deanna crinkled her nose at me as Madison agreed with her. "Yeah, it's weird. My mom set candles in a circle for some kind of prosperity spell because Mother told her to."

Kylie smirked over her iced tea, squeezing her lemon wedge. "My mom did, too and claimed my dad got the promotion."

"All the parents are into it." Hunter leaned back and steepled his fingers beneath his chest.

"Not my old man," Jamie countered.

"Uh, and that's why you've got no prosperity," Deanna joked.

"Freaking cultish," I whispered to Lucas, who gave me a wry smile. I quietly asked him, "Do your parents light the candles too?"

"They're just candles." His lips fell into a pensive frown.

22

NO GOING BACK

JACOB

After lunch, I was more suspicious than ever but managed to survive the rest of the school day. Restless and exhausted, I just wanted to be home. So, I grabbed a seat by myself on the bus and had just started to doze off when I heard, "Hey, Cuz."

I opened one eye first and gave Lucas a look. "Seriously? Can't you see I'm resting?"

Lucas ignored me and sat down as the bus groaned onward.

"I barely got any sleep last night," I admitted through a yawn.

Lucas just kept talking. "I came up with the best analogy during Government class. You know how we have Burger King and McDonalds? They feed the masses. We're used to eating there and they get the job done, but are they really good for us?"

I asked him a hard, "What?"

"They're kind of like the Democratic and Republican party," he added.

"You really are a commie?"

Lucas laughed a little. "No. Just an independent thinker."

I flicked my eyebrows at him. "Whatever. I just wish I could be homeschooled. Be a mental shut in with," I lowered my voice to a whisper, "Ary."

"You are obsessed."

"Maybe…Yeah," I admitted, and I always hated that love-struck sap of a guy. "Have you ever been that way over a girl?"

The question made Lucas finally shut up. He mumbled, "Not exactly."

We just sat there in silence.

The bus brakes shrieked to a stop, and I popped up. Luckily, my house was one of the first stops.

"Call me later," I told Lucas and practically ran off the bus.

My new house was too big to take in all at once, but I saw someone at the second-floor window—Michael's room. I figured it was my brother. I stepped inside and slapped my keys on the hook. The house was still. My gaze longingly flickered to Ary's secret spot before I climbed up the stairs to check in.

First, I poked my head into my mom's room. The scents of smoke and wax drew me in. I tiptoed in to have a closer look. Mom was out cold. Her crazy curls spilled all over her pillow. Her mouth was partly open, with a string of drool hanging off the corner of her lip. When I turned around, I noticed a row of candles in formation on Mom's dresser. Black candles burned down into puddles of wax.

"Mom? Mom?" I repeated.

She moaned, "Let me sleep."

"Mom, did you burn these candles?"

"No. Check with Michael." She barely opened her eyes, and a sigh fluttered through her lips. "And make sure he doesn't have a lighter." She rolled over to resume her nap.

Of course, I recalled our lunchtime conversation about Mother and the *candles*.

I was tempted to wake my mom and tell her something weird was going on, but I couldn't find the words. Anyway, she'd never believe me. So, I rushed to my brother's room.

"Hey, Michael, did you light candles?" I asked. "Mom says you can't have a lighter." I paced around his room, but even the space itself was cold, unfriendly, dim. I hated it being this way. "Sorry, I've been distracted. I'm here if you want to hang out. Come on, Michael. Say something. If you're pissed, just say you're pissed." Frustration made my face twitch. "Tell me where you got those God damn candles?"

He didn't respond but continued to stare into space, sitting on his unmade bed. He looked a thousand miles away.

"Nice chatting with you," I sarcastically commented and began rummaging for a lighter or matches in his dresser drawers. I didn't find any and had already started to leave when I heard Michael say, "Mother's not happy with you."

Wait. We never called our mom *mother*. I turned around to face him. "You mean Mom? Our mom?" My voice squeaked. I had a bad feeling.

"No. Not Mom. I said, Mother, you worthless little parasite," he sternly replied.

"What the hell?" I flopped down at the end of his bed.

"Why are you talking about Mother? And why'd you call me a parasite?"

"I didn't," Michael protested, not even seeming to recall what he had just said.

I inhaled and exhaled, leaning in closer to my brother. "Were they here? Did they get to you, Mike?"

"Just shut up, Jacob," he whined, sounding like my brother again. He laid back down and shrunk into his covers.

Now that he'd freaked me out, nothing seemed right. In the hallway, I uttered, "What's up with you, Michael?" Anxiety continued to occupy the atmosphere, and I could feel something...or someone looming.

I started down the steps, needing to see Ary. Every step I took felt off. I may have been overreacting. I mean, Michael said weird stuff all the time, but what about those candles? Ary might know what to do and what this all meant.

The kiss played in my mind along with a fever of attraction all day, but an unease had taken over. I rapped on the door, then not waiting for her reply, I slipped inside. But Ary wasn't there. Her sleeping bag and her light were in their usual spot. I noticed every little thing. For one, her toothbrush was there, yet the letter from Elijah was gone.

I wandered to the living room. The room was also empty and undisturbed except for the one black-and-white picture, which hung slightly askew. I kept moving and found the door to the downstairs bathroom open and the room empty. From there, I slunk into the kitchen. A note on the fridge read:

Jacob,
Wake me at 4. And get Michael a snack.

Hope you had a good day at school.
Love,
Mom

I passed into the mudroom. Nothing. Only a heap of lifeless mice in the corner that appeared flattened, almost deflated, yet I had canceled with the exterminator, so what killed them? The broom was leaning against the wall. So, I swept the mice into the dustpan and tossed them in the garbage. On the way, I caught a draft, and it chilled me. I looked over at the open door leading to the cellar. It invited me to investigate. My breath clenched as I preceded down the steps. "Ary!" I called. A panicky feeling set in, and I searched the cellar for her, but she was nowhere to be found.

I bolted up the stairs to the first floor again. Through the kitchen window, the backyard was slightly visible. Ary probably wouldn't be brave enough to venture out alone unless she absolutely had to. I kept moving and burst out the patio door to ensure Ary wasn't there. My gaze shifted all around. Only dead leaves rattled around the yard, and oddly, the garden area was again overrun by weeds.

"Are you kidding me?" I said to myself. There was no trace of the flowers. My pulse continued to skyrocket.

I came inside and went into the living room to text Lucas. "Please come over. Ary's gone." God, were they in my mom's room to light the candles? And what the hell was up with Michael?

I sat on the steps and glimpsed at a tiny streak of pink, a pastel smear, barely visible on the shiny surface of the banister. Was it a streak of blood that had been all but wiped away? For a few intense seconds, my mind blurred in confusion.

Bzzt. Bzzt. Lucas had texted, "Only if Jamie can come along too."

Jamie must have been over Lucas's. *Greedy little bastard. Ugh.* "Okay." I reluctantly replied. Lucas's brain was a sponge. His power of observation was so keen he only had to see something once to capture a permanent picture of it. He'd be able to help me. But how? This wasn't a frigging story problem. We needed to act, and he was chicken shit.

Then it hit me, and my hands curled into protective fists, and my heart pounded faster. The boy named Ren's smiling face and the note Elijah left flashed in my head. They knew where Ary was all along. Now they'd came and got her. They did this. The police thing might have been a ruse, so they could say she was never even at my house. It was odd how they hadn't checked under the stairs. Sure, I missed it when I looked for her, but they were professionals, taught to search every square inch.

I needed to go to Ary's house tonight. If I didn't, who knows what they'll do? Maybe it was good Jamie was coming over. He'd go with me. Hell, even Lucas might come along if it was the three of us again like old times.

We sat around the kitchen table. I had finished rambling, and the guys just stared at me. "So…will you go?"

Jamie was the first to talk, sounding nonchalant. "I'll go."

"Thanks." I nodded at him. Honestly, I didn't have the luxury of time to hold a grudge. Next, I focused on Lucas. "I need you to knock on the front door of Ary's house. You're a concerned friend from church who wants to know if you can do anything to help find her. This way, we can see if they even admit she's there. If they lie about it, it means they might have hurt her." I winced.

"You've got it all figured out. Huh, Sherlock?" Lucas rolled his eyes.

"Not at all," I said. "I need your help."

Lucas played the role of devil's advocate. "How well do you really know her? You have to admit she's not stable. She may have run off."

"She wouldn't run off," I argued. A feverish weight pressed down on my chest like I was in love or something. "She just wouldn't. And she doesn't have anywhere to go. Ary told me she'd rather die than go back there."

He thought about it for a minute. "It must have been really bad for her," he said, and it surprised me.

"It was."

Jamie zeroed in on Lucas, too, rapping his fingers on the table. "Come on, McKay."

Lucas groaned, "Ugh, man. I don't know what we're doing here. We should have just told the truth in the first place. I'm not knocking on the door. It's too weird. Why wouldn't I have offered to help after church, or even called? But I'll go with you."

"Yes!" Then I had another idea. "This lady, Mother, has never seen Jamie. He could be selling candy bars for his football team or something."

"Hell yeah. I'm a great actor." Jamie stretched out his arms like he was Moses parting the Red Sea. "Let's do it." It was a game to him, like everything.

Lucas cast a wary eye between us. "We're not going to do anything crazy. I'll wait off to the side and Jacob, maybe you can get a look in the window. Agreed?"

"Agreed." I nodded gratefully. "Okay, let's tell our moms we're going to Jamie's." It was a flimsy plan. But I held on to it, thinking it would make everything alright and bring Ary back to me. I didn't even show the guys what I thought was old blood. Lucas would want to call the cops. The weird association Damler had with Mother and the bogus search made it seem like that wasn't the right thing to do. I had no idea what door I was truly opening, or who I was dealing with.

Lucas had given Jamie the address, and he plugged it into his phone's GPS. Clearly, the place Ary had escaped from had been within walking distance since she had made it to my new house on foot. Lucas and I moved somberly and slowly, shoulder to shoulder. Jamie had gotten a couple feet ahead of us, but we could still hear him rapping and doing the beatbox thing with his hands and mouth, hyped up at the idea of adventure.

The land rose as we entered the woods. Trees, mainly oak and elm, were all twisted or bent, seeming to be survivors of a great storm. They had distorted limbs all tangled together. A lot of brush, broken branches, and garbage was strewn on the ground. The wind howled through the branches and stirred the leaves, moving the lighter trash around. The trees thinned out and then got thicker again. My entire body felt charged, and my heart beat harder than normal, in almost painful thuds. I just had to know Ary was alright.

It was almost six o'clock. The sun hadn't even set, but gray clouds obscured it and made everything look shadowy and dull. Jamie slowed down, walking with us, and asked, "Did you ever date a model?"

"No. I told you we made it up." What the hell? I decided to tell them. "Ary said she liked me just last night. And I like her—a lot."

"I didn't know she was your girl," Jamie said. "Uh crud, I'm such a screwup."

I shrugged, carefully maneuvering through the brush, avoiding the low-hanging branches, and just stayed focused.

Jamie added, "I would have split the money with you."

I was pissed off all over again. "I wouldn't want the money." I turned my head. There was still a bitter taste in my mouth. "You could have sent her to a really bad place." I shot him a dirty look, feeling lost. "I guess she ended up there anyway." Intuition told me Mother and Elijah were more than a strange family-- something evil. "Let's just drop it."

He didn't. "Did they beat her? For real like my dad does? With fists? Or worse?"

It was a disturbing inquisition. "I don't know. I think so."

"It's probably worse to beat a girl. You said they kept her chained in a basement? That's like torture."

"It's not *like* torture. It *is* torture, idiot." I stuffed both fists in my jacket pockets.

Lucas said, "You're just making Jacob feel worse." A concerned expression flitted across his face, and he stared at Jamie. "Your dad hasn't hit you again, has he?"

"Nah. I'm getting too big for his crap. It's cool."

But who knew what to believe? Jamie always fluffed it off. Thinking about it, I wondered why I hadn't told someone who could have helped him. Back then, it felt like I was doing the right thing by keeping his secrets. I had fallen into the same useless train of thought. I should have just gotten Ary help. Now there was no proof she was ever at my house.

"So, is Ary hot now?" Jamie asked.

"She's pretty," I answered. It didn't feel right to use the word hot. She was too special.

"She's very pretty," Lucas agreed.

After about ten more minutes of walking, Jamie groaned theatrically and complained, "Let's take a break already."

A mix of determination and fear stopped me from feeling tired at all.

"We haven't even walked a mile," Lucas pointed out.

"Well, I'm cold." Jamie hugged himself. He was only wearing his hoodie.

"If you stop walking, you'll be even colder. And why didn't you wear a real coat?" Lucas asked and tugged his own black leather jacket's collar.

"This is my coat," he replied.

Jamie and Lucas kept talking, but I wasn't listening. The growing ache in my temples and the empty feeling in my chest consumed me. A creaking noise from a canopy of branches above snapped me to attention, and I watched as a large bird flew away. It resembled a hawk. Next, I noticed the letter "W" carved in the tree. No, it was a sideways "M," maybe for Mother. Before I could point it out to the guys, a foul scent wafted in.

"Something stinks," Jamie said.

I inhaled another whiff of a kind of organic decay which slowly sickened into the smell of rot. I wrinkled my nose. Then, not watching where I was going for a few seconds, I almost tripped on the carcass of a fawn.

"*Damn*. What killed Bambi?" I asked, and my heart dropped, and my stomach twisted.

"Uh see! It's like what we were talking about, bruh," Jamie said, almost excited.

"Looks like it's been gutted." Lucas breathed into his shirt and kicked it with the toe of his shoe. The poor creature's legs folded. Its limbs a rubbery misshapen mess. The chest cavity was compressed like an inflatable Christmas Santa with no power. "Even its bones are gone," Lucas added.

We followed his lead, hoisting our shirts over our noses, and stepped around it. Our eyes flicked to the side to find several more deer in a decaying pile. As if someone gutted all their innards and skeletons, leaving their meat to rot.

I grimaced. "Something sucked all the life out of them." They reminded me of the dead mice. "This is frigging weird. What happened to them? Even if it's another bizarre animal sacrifice, how can anyone remove the bones and leave the meat and fur?" I turned to Lucas and Jamie.

Jamie looked utterly dumbstruck, his mouth gaping ever so slightly, while Lucas turned a curious shade of white, admitting, "I have no idea."

Jamie said, "I need to get out of this town," as we passed the small massacre.

We kept walking. These people were in some cult. Cults do animal sacrifices, I reasoned, feeling chilled by my own thoughts.

"I should have brought my dad's gun," Jamie decided.

With a level voice, Lucas said, "Let's not go too
crazy."

Jamie led the way as we stumbled onto the tree-lined sidewalk of a small subdivision, he said, "Oh, this is Heaven's
Gate."

"Ironically named because they built it over hell," I kind
of joked.

Lucas played along. "It'd be a good way to throw off the
masses."

Homes lined up on equally tidy plots of land, like doll-
houses, watching us. Each house, all with wavy trim, were
exact replicas except for having different bright colors of
siding. As we arrived at the corner of the cul-de-sac, there was
a noticeable drop in temperature by at least a few degrees, and
the wind picked up.

Jamie shivered a little and held up his phone, the GPS
telling us, "You have arrived at our destination, 7220 Morning
Glory Road."

"Morning Glory, seriously?" I mumbled. The street
names, like each house, were saccharine enough. I had
expected a house in a lonely part of town, with a big iron gate
where one must be buzzed in. Only now had I remembered
seeing these houses when I rode the bus home with Lucas.
Even then, they appeared to be out of a fairy tale, just too
sweet for real life. Now the artificial cheerfulness was almost
menacing. My heart rate kicked up.

"We'll stay close," I told Jamie. "Ask to use their bathroom so you can go inside. Try to see everything and anything
you can."

"They look like giant gingerbread houses. I'm sooo
fuckin' scared," Jamie smirked, but his cheeks colored. He

was more nervous than he let on. He turned to me, and his smile quickly faded. "Hey guys, I don't even have a box. If I'm selling candy bars, I'd have a box." He wasn't exactly the same dumb kid I'd grown up with who leaped before he looked.

"Come on, Jamie," I pushed.

"Jacob." Lucas narrowed his eyes and shook his head. "Don't make him do this. Let's forget it."

"It's okay, Lucas." Jamie turned to me. He placed one hand on each of my shoulders. "You've got those cow eyes," he sighed.

Cow eyes? Whatever worked, I guess.

Then he asked, "We're cool, right, Jacob?"

I paused, grinning. "Hell yeah."

Jamie punched me, but not too hard, on the shoulder a couple of times, and I lightly hit him back. It was official. We were cool again.

We formed a huddle. Our smiles vanished, and our mood sobered.

Jamie told us, "If I get killed, tell Deanna I love her."

"Deanna? Weren't you making out with Kylie?" I asked.

Lucas frowned. "We're all being dramatic." Regaining the leadership role, he calmly added, "None of us are going to get killed. If you do get invited to go inside, don't stay longer than fifteen minutes." It was smart to time the visit. "Or we'll call the police."

Jamie scratched his head and thought about it. "Make it ten. And don't worry, I'll pass on the Kool-Aid."

I handed him the Hershey bars we stopped and bought at the gas station before we began our trek. He paused. Did he still have cold feet? "I can do this, if you want." This wasn't fair. I was the one invested. "We'll still be okay if you change your mind."

"No. I got it." Jamie pocketed the candy bars. "Should I pretend to join the cult?"

"Don't mention the cult!" Lucas yell-whispered.

Jaime pushed. "But what if they ask me to join? Do I go undercover?"

"They're not going to ask you. Cults don't just invite people," I nervously explained.

"Well, how does anyone ever join?" Jamie wondered.

"We don't even know it's a cult. A cult would have a compound, not a house." Lucas seemed to disregard the whole thing as ridiculous.

"The entire neighborhood might be the compound," I reasoned.

"It's getting late. Let's get this over with," Lucas said.

"I've done way more borderline deadly things," Jamie boasted.

We had taken cover in the safety of the trees as our friend walked toward the house. I gripped Lucas's upper arm. The door sprang open, and a tall woman eclipsed the entryway. It was her. The one they called Mother. There was no going back.

23
THE PLAN

JACOB

Stunned into mental blankness, we watched Jamie disappear inside the house. Lucas finally said, "She let him in. Just like that."

"Yeah. Weird." I let out a heavy breath. What was going on in there?

Lucas wanted things to be normal again. "Maybe she's just a nice lady."

I didn't disagree, allowing him to say whatever made him feel better in the moment. Seriously, I hoped it was true. "I'm going to have a closer look."

"I don't know. Maybe we should just hang out here."

I paused, offering, "I'll be careful," and veered around the driveway, trying to stay covered by a row of three huge pine trees. From there, the yard was open, with nowhere to hide. I ran to the back of the house to meet the challenge of an eight-foot wooden fence. My nerves served as a shot of adrenaline, and I jumped, catching the top of the fence. I strained to pull myself over, then landed, not so gracefully, on my butt. My lungs did a shuddery thing as I explored the perimeter of the yard. I hoped there wasn't a guard dog or one of Mother's disciples there to meet me. But luckily, the yard was empty. There was a large stone patio and nice outdoor furniture that seemed brand new. In the center of the yard, dark water rippled in a man-made pond. My vision tunneled in on it, and for a jarring moment, I swore it was blood. After blinking, it resolved to murky water.

I got up and urged my feet toward the house. The first-floor windows were layered with shutters. So, simply peeking inside for a glimpse of what life was really like was out of the question. The back door was metal and painted white. No glass sliding door or French door even, like most houses had. Unexpectedly, my cell phone buzzed. I fumbled to shut it off, uttering a slur of obscenities. Worried someone had heard, I stood completely still for a minute before grabbing the cool, brass doorknob. I tried to turn it, but it was locked. Frenzied energy buzzed around me while my mind called for *Ary*. I needed to find her.

Then, looking up, I winced at a red dot of light, high above the door, recording me, seeing me the whole frigging time. I panicked and ran for the fence. I jumped but not high enough to grab hold of the top of it. "Shit." I mumbled. I heard the backdoor hinges creak, and a man's voice called, "Hey, you!"

I leaped higher, barely catching the top of the fence, and struggled to pull myself over. This time, I managed to land on my feet and ran to take cover behind the trees.

Oddly enough, the natural order of things seemed to shrink away, and with each step, the yard seemed to grow and grow. Sweat dotted my brow. I kept going until I was finally able to conceal myself behind a wide pine tree. Then I zipped over to the next one before making a mad dash into the woods. I stopped inches away from Lucas and slumped over, winded. After the rush of relief passed, the disappointment set in.

"Well? Did you see anything?" Lucas bobbed from one foot to the other to deal with either the cold or his nerves.

"Just a camera." I shook my head in frustration. "And a man yelled after me. We gotta get Jamie."

"Told you this was a bad idea." Lucas shook his head at me.

"I already know," I said defensively.

A twig snapped, and even more surprisingly, a voice said, "Hello,"

I turned to see that lanky kid, Ren. A smugness surged through him. He again wore that disturbing little smile.

"Oh, hi, I've seen you at church," Lucas said.

"You know what they say: keep your friends close and your enemies closer." I was wondering what the hell that meant when Ren asked, "*Why* are you here?"

I was taken off guard, but Lucas stuck with the plan. "We're waiting for our friend. He's selling candy bars."

A small figure tiptoed out from behind the cover of an oak tree. It was the little boy, Elijah. The creepy kid who had been in my house. Instead of Michael Myers, he now sported a mask of the scary bunny from *The Purge*.

Ren glared at Lucas. "Hey, Lucas, did you tell your cousin, Jacob, you're gay?"

Lucas's face went blank for a second, and he shrugged. "I'm not." His brows crumpled.

I broke in. "How do you know our names?"

"I just know," Ren said.

What was with this guy?

A boy lurched out almost drunkenly from behind a tree. He looked like an overgrown twelve, or thirteen-year-old and was a few pounds away from being obese. The muscles in his stomach had turned to fat and spilled over his cargo pants. He had an upturned nose and small wideset eyes, which made him look a lot like a pig, and apparently, it was his nickname.

"This is Piggy," Ren introduced him.

Piggy stopped only inches from Lucas.

"What's taking our friend so long?" Lucas wondered, his voice sounding wobbly.

Ren moved in a little closer too. "Aw, Jamie *is* your friend…Unrequited love's a bitch, ain't it, Lucas?"

There was no possible way Lucas loved Jamie, even if he was gay, which he wasn't. Was he? They were trying to intimidate him. "Piss off," I said, defiantly keeping my chin up.

Another kid, tall and gangly with black spikey hair, around seventeen or eighteen, appeared from behind the same tree. He had face tats of scorpions, cobras, and the word *death* scrawled on his forehead in cheap, do-it-yourself blue ink. A cigarette hung from his lips, which he shot toward me, launching it like a tiny torpedo. He eyed me up and down, posturing, but still took the time to introduce himself. "Hi, girls. I'm Maverick."

I squinted at the guy. What was their problem? They were all brimming over with thinly concealed excitement.

"Hey. Listen, we don't want any trouble." Lucas sounded composed and adult-like. Yet I noticed an uncomfortable glint in his eyes.

All three of the older boys circled Lucas. From the looks on their faces, you would have thought Lucas was raw meat, and they were hungry pit bulls. Quickly, things made a turn for the worse. Ren shoved Lucas, causing him to topple backward onto the ground, then the pig boy started kicking him in his arms and sides. A protective feeling flared. My right hand jerked up, fist clenched, and I landed a good one on the fat kid's cheek. My knuckles throbbed. I had never flat-out punched anyone. I hurried to help Lucas to his feet as Ren burst into a fit of laughter. So did the chubby kid, as he held his cheek where I had clocked him.

Ren bit back a smile. "You should really go now. Home to your mom and mentally defective brother."

I was thrown by his comments and took a moment to speak. "You don't even know my brother. So, shut up. He's way cooler than you, cult-boy." It was like he knew the right buttons to push. Shaky with anger, I gritted my teeth and struggled to stay calm. "And maybe you didn't hear Lucas. We're waiting for our friend." I grabbed my phone from my coat pocket and texted Jamie, "Time to go."

The tall boy with the face tatts, Maverick advanced. I stared at his stretched earlobes the size of pop cans. "We want to kill you, but Mother won't let us. She has other plans for you two," he said.

That wasn't cryptic at all. "What plans?" I asked.

Ren mockingly stared at me. He was sure he had the upper hand. Since it was three and a half against two, I guess he did.

"Mother wants all the kids in the world to join hands in song."

"You guys should start a frigging boy band, make Mother happy," I dryly quipped, my pulse still elevated.

"Ignore them," Lucas whispered.

Out of the blue, Ren said to me, "It would be fun to see you cry like a little girl."

I didn't get this guy. Since Mother hadn't given them the okay to *kill us,* it seemed like they wouldn't go crazy. "It's not gonna happen," I flatly assured him.

Maverick leaned closer to me, and his eyes rolled up until his irises were no longer visible, and you could only see the whites of his eyes.

"Nice trick," I said, still playing it cool. Then, in utter confusion, I looked on as his eyes darkened and darkened, progressing to a solid black. "Holy shit."

Ren smiled approvingly. "I like you, Jacob. You got gonads." He paused before adding, "I have an idea. A fair fight."

"I don't want to fight you," I admitted.

"Not me. That would hardly be fair." Ren's gaze turned to Elijah. "He's only eight."

Lucas and I glanced at one another, and the other boys laughed.

My gaze returned to the idiots. "I don't like to fight, and I'm sure as hell not fighting a little kid."

In a juddering motion, Elijah pulled out a knife and frantically slashed the air. Lucas and I stepped away.

Ren lifted his hand. "Elijah, I said a fair fight. Ditch the knife."

Elijah growled in Ren's direction, slowly slipping the knife back into his pocket.

Nodding his head in approval, Ren said, "Go get him."

The next thing I knew, Elijah lunged, sending me to the ground. One frenzied fist after another pounded my cheekbones, turning my head to the left and then to the right until I managed to get the crazy little shit off me. I started to get up, but the kid was on top of me again. This time, he pummeled me repeatedly in the stomach, knocking the wind out of me, and finished with an uppercut to the mouth. The impact cracked my lip wide open.

The kid paused, and I took the opportunity, tightly gripping the bony shoulders of this little maniac. I tossed him off me with all the strength I could muster and rolled over, getting on top of him. My blood rained on his Halloween mask. As I raised one shaky fist in the air, everything was spinning. "Tell him to stop. I don't want to hurt him," I warned.

Ren and the other boys again snickered.

"Oh, you don't want to hurt him!" Pig-boy bellowed.

"Everyone's got a plan till they get punched in the mouth, eh, Jacob?" Ren said with a maniacal smile.

Lucas bent down and handed me some napkins and a cloth glove from his pocket, and I held them to my severed lip.

Ren announced. "We've had enough fun for now. Let's go."

I pushed myself up and staggered to my feet with a sigh, and Elijah stood too. Holy shit, I always wondered how I'd do in a fight. Now I knew—an eight-year-old had pulverized me. Something wasn't right. I couldn't be that much of a wimp. The boys' laughter grew vague and distant, and I tilted my head, relieved to see the gang walking back to their house.

"Are you okay?" Lucas asked. He had the dazed look of someone who got plowed down in a hit and run. It was precisely how I felt.

"I'm fine." Sure, I was sore and dizzy as hell, but I lied. "Why didn't you get the little psycho off me?" When I swallowed, it was blood and not saliva.

"Sorry," he offered, squinting, thinking, before blurting, "But he was just so small."

I flicked him an angry glance. "So...you want to fight that kid?"

Lucas quickly responded with a "Jesus! No." He shook his head. "I never seen anyone move that fast."

I placed the cool palm on my foggy head, still holding the glove to my lip with my other hand. I tripped over questions this incident prompted. I decided to ask, "Why did he say you're gay? I mean, you can tell me anything. It wouldn't change things." I wanted him to know this. "I hate bigots."

"Just shut up," Lucas snapped. He threw an intense and anxious look my way, almost like a warning. A warning for me not to dare tell his secret. Finally, Lucas explained, "My dad would disown me." I hadn't realized my uncle was homophobic. "That would make you happy, huh?" His eyes teared. At that moment, I knew it was true.

Had I been shitty to Lucas? Was it partly true? I said, "No. Come on, I'm not a complete dick." I just knew I loved Lucas and didn't care if he was straight or gay. But I was confused about what to say next.

My head cleared, and I returned to the here and now.

"Where the hell is Jamie?" A prickling sensation ran down my neck, the feeling something just wasn't right. I decided enough was enough. Mother knew we were here. At this point, it was already a dangerous game. I was going to the door to get Jamie and even ask about Ary.

24
DOOMED

JACOB

I stuffed the bloody glove and napkins in my coat pocket as Lucas pointed out, "Um, you've got blood all over you." His tone was tinted with disapproval.

I popped the collar of my jacket. "Don't care. I'm going to get Jamie."

My God, what were these people? And what were they doing to Jamie? The discomfort in my neck dripped down my shoulders and spine. Still, I kept my head up and walked until I had ascended three steps and planted my feet on the cheery welcome mat, animated with bluebirds. Giant lilac bushes obscured the front window, preventing me from getting a look inside. I rang the bell as Lucas lingered at the end of the drive. My heart thudded. I waited…and waited. When I started to doubt anyone would answer, the door swung open. I jumped back. It was only Jamie.

"What happened to you?" he asked me as the door closed

behind him.

"It's not important." We shuffled away from the house and joined Lucas at the curb.

"What took you so long?" Lucas wondered.

But before he could answer, I questioned him too. "What's it like inside? Did you see Ary?"

"No, I didn't see her. They seem like normal people, I guess. The lady's pretty."

"Mother?" I asked, confused.

"Yeah. She said everyone calls her that. There was a guy. I almost thought I'd seen him before." Jamie squinted and shook his head, then seemed to relax. "Oh, and guess what?" He proudly held out a twenty-dollar bill. "I sold all the candy bars. You're welcome."

"You do know this mission wasn't really about selling candy bars?" Could he really be this dumb? Irritation and panic tickled my skin.

"I know, but I sold them…Uh, what happened to you?" Jamie fidgeted with his hoodie's zipper.

"How much of the house did you see?" I pushed, needing more information.

"Just the entryway and part of the living room."

"Oh, God. You've got nothing. All this for nothing." I shook my head in frustration.

Jamie turned to Lucas. "Who gave him the Botox?"

"Some kid attacked him. One of Mother's foster kids." Lucas answered but remained edgy, saying, "Now let's get out of here."

"Yo bro, you need to learn to block," Jamie told me, putting his hands up in the air and shadow boxing around me in demonstration.

Jamie was Jamie. His dorky, unencumbered self. Soon he was singing his tuneless lungs out. His singing was as bad as his rapping. It should have lightened the mood. Here and there, I studied Lucas and Jamie, thinking about what Ren had said. That was all *pretty* weird. Was he somehow all-knowing? Psychic?

Through the trees, I saw the sunset with golds and eerie reds. Halfway, home, even Jamie got quiet. The wind sounded almost human. It was Ary calling my name. Over and over.

I asked Lucas, "Do you hear it? A girl's voice. She's calling me."

"It's just the wind," Lucas assured me.

An uncomfortable cold set in, and I just wanted to make it home before dark. So, I jammed my hands into my pockets and kept going. When we finally arrived at my house, the guys and I fist-bumped, and they went their own way.

Once inside, I kicked my sneakers off and collapsed into a weary heap on the sofa, but Mom discovered me and, of course, asked, "Jacob, what happened to you?"

I could feel a strained expression ripple across my face before I made up a lame story. "Jamie accidentally slammed the door on my face."

"I'm a nurse, for God's sake. You got into a fight." She crossed her arms, and her eyes narrowed. Her initial worry quickly turned to annoyance.

"Yeah. Sorry," I offered.

But she wanted to know more. "Did you fight with Jamie? I never trusted him."

"It wasn't Jamie. A random kid jumped me. I don't know his name."

"You're not hanging out at that trailer park anymore." She

was small but managed to tower above me. "Well, go put your coat in the laundry room and wash up for dinner."

When I stood, she melted a little and reached out, gently stroking my hair. "Oh sweetie, I think there are peas in the freezer for your lip."

"Okay."

A little later, Mom, Michael, and I split a frozen lasagna. I held the cold bag of peas to my mouth in between small bites. Michael only pushed the pasta around with his fork, so our mom got up to make him a salad.

My brother turned around in his chair to say, "Remember, no dressing."

My mom rummaged in the fridge, placing a head of lettuce and a tomato on the counter. After rinsing and chopping them, she created an unimpressive salad but promised, "I'll get some more veggies tomorrow."

"That's all you're eating. You've got to be kidding me." I remarked, irritated at my brother for wasting away.

"Those frozen dinners are toxic," he said and mumbled, "You look like shit."

I didn't have the attention span to argue more. Then, my mom casually said, "I meant to tell you, that girl stopped by."

My posture stiffened. "Uh." My voice caught in my throat as I fell into a state of shock. "When?"

"An hour ago, maybe two. You were out with Lucas and Jamie. She seemed unkept...frazzled."

"Oh, crap!" I sprang up. "I missed her."

"Just finish dinner and call her," Mom reasoned, eyeing me curiously.

"I'm not hungry." I kept nodding my head. "Okay. Okay.

You said she was unkept but was she alright?"

My mom looked at me like I was nuts. "Yeah, I think so. Why are you freaking out?"

Michael replied, "He loves her."

I shot him an annoyed glance and looked at my mom, reassuring her, "I'm not freaking out."

"She's your girlfriend?" Mom asked.

"No. I don't know." I rushed to the front door and flung it open, shouting Ary's name.

"When I said call her, I meant on the phone."

I turned around to find my mom behind me, glaring. "I thought she might still be hanging around," I tried to explain.

"What's going on, Jacob?" Her forehead creased in a mix of suspicion and concern.

My gaze dropped to the floor. I wanted to tell her everything, but it was complicated. I didn't know where to begin. "Nothing."

"Call her if you want." Her tone became sarcastic, overemphasizing the words, "On the phone." Mom's mouth puckered up as if she'd tasted something sour. "I think I want to meet her parents. She has parents, right?"

"Yeah, sure, Mom. Whatever."

My mom's eyes bored into mine. She crossed her arms. I forced my fat lip into something close to a smile, hoping to reassure her. But her suspicion was like a noose tightening around my neck.

At least Ary was alright, and Mother didn't have her. Yet I had to wonder, where would Ary have gone? I was clueless. I should've felt a sense of hope and relief, but an inexplicable sadness made me feel doomed.

25

THE SIX O'CLOCK NEWS

JACOB

October 30th, I ditched school, canvassing the woods for Ary instead. I meandered up the worn dirt path, listening to a single bird chirp before others joined the chorus. A spray of pale sunlight broke through the treetops, though the air was crisp and cold. I thought I heard something—possibly a whisper—prompting me to call Ary's name several times. But nothing.

I peered up a hill at scrub oaks and a slew of fallen branches but didn't see anyone and stayed on course, venturing to where the dead deer had been just yesterday. My eyes combed the ground, but there was no sign of the deer now. I even made it to the edge of the woods and peeked at that picture-perfect house. The place Ary had been held prisoner. The phrase, 'so near yet so far,' played in my head, making my heart rocket to my throat. Ary had stopped to see me last night, and somehow, we'd missed one another. I had to wonder if Mother could have found her again.

My eyes roamed the woods. From trees to stony paths and the remnants of a one-room shack with a moss-covered roof.

"Ary," I called, pushing the rickety door open, but didn't dare step inside.

There was a maze of places to hide. And I began to feel like I was going in circles, and who was to say Ary wouldn't show up at my house again. So, I decided to turn around to start my hike back. All the sounds of the forest fell away. It was eerily quiet. Like I was the only one in the world. After about forty-five minutes of walking, I cut back to the street and made it to the gas station. I stared at impaled hot dogs underneath a heat lamp. I was so hungry that they looked appetizing, so I bought one.

Out of the blue, a small ginger-haired girl thundered up to me, her two crooked braids bouncing. She was a sturdy little thing, no older than three or four. "Mother's not happy with you," she said.

A stream of obscenities spilled out from my lips as her mom charged up.

I slapped my hand over my mouth.

"Come on, sweetie." The mom gave me a dirty look as she gathered the small child in her arms and huffed away.

The little girl whined, "Mommy, I just wanted a hot dog," as they left the store.

Even the twenty-something cashier with cool rainbow hair rolled her eyes my way in disapproval. I exited, feeling ashamed and tense. I ate my lunch by the ice machine. I wished I'd bought a water bottle but didn't want to go back in.

After I cut through the woods toward my house, a familiar

ache from my track days invaded the muscles in my legs. The sunset and evening breeze swelled to blustery gusts. There was still no sign of Ary, and the day was spent.

Glad to be home, I found the door unlocked and slipped inside. Careful to keep my footsteps light, I checked Ary's secret hiding place, only to find it empty.

"Is that where she stayed?" Mom asked.

This wasn't good. I closed the half-door and stood, though it felt like the ground had been pulled from underneath my feet. I forced myself to turn around. My mom radiated heat like she was full of atomic energy.

I tried to play it off. "Um, I'm not sure what you're talking about?"

"Where were you?" She crossed her arms, waiting for an answer.

"I just went for a walk after school." I strained to remove all emotion from my face.

"Really, Jacob? Because the attendance office called. When did you start lying to me?"

I hadn't meant to. For a few agonizing seconds, I was blank on what to say. "Just ground me or something." I shook my head and stared at the floor.

"I'm not stupid, Jacob. I know this is all about that girl, the runaway. But don't you worry. I got someone to take my shift, so I'll be here to babysit you."

"Mom, you don't—"

"Just stop!" she roared and put her hand up. Then she scowled at me. "You know what? Go to your room. I can't stand the sight of you."

My mom had never said anything like that to me. Never. My heart crashed in my chest. "Fine!" I bolted up the steps.

She had lost all trust in me, and I still had no idea where Ary was. Collapsing on my bed, I stared at the ceiling until I calmed down enough to jam the earbuds in and blast some rock music. The rhythm beat and thumped. After a few songs, my mom appeared at my door. I tore out my earbuds and sprang up to a sitting position. The guilt made my posture straighten.

Mom had a sandwich and a glass of milk on a tray, telling me, "Don't come downstairs until you're ready to talk." She set it firmly on my dresser, and her eyes swept across my room. Her anger had faded, and now even her curls looked limp and sad.

Yeah, I wanted to talk to her, but where would I begin? What would I say?

"And you better go to school tomorrow, kid."

"I will, Mom," I promised.

"If you see her, *we are* calling the police," she said and left the room.

I ate a few bites of the turkey sandwich and drank the milk, feeling burned out.

Once in my bed for the night, the door opened. I lifted my head from the pillow. An unmistakable Michael-shaped silhouette lingered at my door. Hovering there, motionless.

"What is it, Michael?" He drifted off without even answering. Normally, I'd go see what was up with him. Instead, I reacted with an irritated, "Whatever," and thumped my pillow to fluff it.

I turned this way and that way, and before long, tumbled into a restless sleep. I dreamed of a burling gray smoke and screams but couldn't wake myself up. Morning came, and I still couldn't open my eyes at first. A sleep paralysis had set

in. I focused on my *fingers* with a concentrated effort before I
could even move them. From there, I patted my face and
pressed down on my eyelids, groaning. Only then was I able
to open my eyes.

I groggily explored my room and slowly got up and
dressed. Next, I stuffed everything into my backpack, slung
the strap over my shoulder. I didn't check in with Mom or
Michael on the way to the bathroom. My swollen lip had gone
down. Yet my reflection in the mirror resembled a bowl of
fruit. The area below my eye had a lump the color of a lemon.
A strawberry welt marked each cheek, turning a plum color at
the edges. *That little shit packed a punch,* I thought, flicking
off the light behind me and exiting the room.

I felt weird inside but didn't want to miss school and piss
Mom off even more. I hurried out the front door to make it on
time for the bus and noticed a cigarette butt on the porch. Oh,
great, I had driven my mom to smoke again.

Lucas had to go to school early for student council and
had got a ride. So, I sat by myself on the bus.

Once at school, a parade of footsteps and indistinct voices
swam around my head. I dizzily made my way to class.
Maybe I was coming down with the flu. I was out of it. Even
when lunchtime rolled around, I just went through the
motions.

When I approached my locker after fifth period, I overheard Deanna asking Hunter, "Why does Jacob have to be in
our friend group?" I didn't stick around for his reply. Overall,
it seemed like an uneventful day.

It was sixth period, Trig. Lucas and I again grabbed seats
next to one another. He asked, "Are you doing anything for
Halloween?"

"Nah, I want to look for Ary but can't since I'm on house arrest." I had complained a little to him about being grounded at lunch too.

"I could take a walk around and look for her," he offered.

"Wow. Thanks."

There was more on his mind. "You've been acting distant today. Almost like you're stoned. You have to give it a chance here."

"Sorry, I'm just preoccupied. My life can't get any weirder."

Just then, the teacher, Mr. Besson, came in. He was an average looking, middle-aged, balding guy with rimless specs. He cleared his throat as his eyes sharpened in on us. "I need Lucas McKay and Jacob Kelly to go to the office."

Lucas and I exchanged shrugs.

Then time sped up. Lucas's mom and dad had waited for us in the school's front office. My Aunt Veronica tried to keep a tremor out of her voice as she explained there had been, "A family emergency."

Lucas asked, "Is Grandma alright?"

My aunt told him, "Grandma's fine."

His parents wouldn't tell either of us what this so-called family emergency entailed. And the clink and clank of my aunt's heels followed us through the school like a shadow as we weaved between rows of lockers.

Of course, at the car, Lucas and I took the backseat. A rectangle of light shined in through the sunroof. My aunt only said, "You guys need to hang out at our house for a while. Uncle Pete and I will get all the details." It didn't take long to realize something serious had happened.

"Is my mom alright? Is it Michael?"

"We'll talk as soon as we get more information," my aunt snapped.

"Please just tell me they're okay." I didn't ask but pleaded.

"I'm sorry, Jacob. We're not sure yet," Uncle Pete said.

I kept asking, and Lucas did too. We didn't get any straight answers. I called the house phone and my mom's cell, and they went to voicemail. After ten minutes, my aunt and uncle parked the BMW in front of their place. I got out of the car, planning on finding out what was going on for myself.

Lucas reached over, resting his hand on my shoulder.

My aunt and uncle drove away, and I took off, running down the sidewalk, cutting across lawns, jumping fences to get home. Within minutes, I made it out of the subdivision and onto the main road. I barely noticed the cars racing by.

I ran faster than I ever had, full speed for as long as possible. My mind blurred. I ran with such momentum that even Lucas, who was breaking state records in track, couldn't keep up. Even though it was chilly outside, I quickly warmed up. After about a mile, I briefly slowed to a jog and held my cramping stomach, breathless. I panted and panted but didn't stop again until I saw my house. Dizziness set in. I bent over with my hands grasping the part of my legs just above my knees. The SOLD sign was still displayed on the front lawn. However, bright yellow crime scene tape now circled our house. A television crew hauled out lights and cables from a white van as my worst fears raced through my mind.

"No," I murmured in response.

Panicked screams rang out in my head, unable to find their

way out. Nausea curled in my throat. I wiggled my damp shirt, which clung to my chest. I approached the man holding a microphone to his hip, suddenly feeling like I was set in slow motion. From the corner of my eye, Lucas appeared, rushing up to me. He grabbed me by the arm to pull me back. Anger flared, and I broke away. The guy from the news turned around to acknowledge me.

At first, I opened my mouth, but no sound came, and I struggled to catch my breath. The man and I just stared at one another for a few seconds. The world was suspended in time for that horrible moment where nothing made sense.

"What happened here?" I finally asked.

"It was a gruesome scene. The schizophrenic son murdered his mother and a runaway girl he was hiding in the cellar."

The shock blasted through me like gunfire. "No! That's not possible."

"That can't be true," Lucas echoed my disbelief.

"You never really know what's going on in your neighbor's house," the guy said. "They were new here, right? Did you meet the family?"

I was frozen for several seconds. Then my knees buckled, and my body withered to the leaf shrouded lawn. I covered my face with both hands and wanted to shrink into the ground, lose all consciousness, and never get up again. Instead, tears poured, and a horrible pain throbbed in my chest.

Lucas let me bawl for a minute before helping me to my feet. "I'm sorry, Jacob," he breathed in my ear. His eyes were shiny, and his face streaked with tears and confusion.

The man stuttered, "I, uh, didn't know."

The breeze's icy edge took hold, and I trembled all over. The disbelief returned. Hope. "Wait, are you sure they're…dead?"

The man somberly nodded.

"No. My brother wouldn't do something like that." My words drifted in the air. No one heard them.

A woman's voice rang out, "We're rolling in ten."

One person's tragedy made the perfect opening for the six o'clock news.

26

OPEN AND SHUT

JACOB

Yellow crime scene tape fluttered in the breeze. My eyes explored the distance to the front door, and I had to go inside. It was a horrible mistake. So, I ran until I broke through the tape. I entered the house, and the door banged behind me. I made it to the foot of the stairs. "Mom?"

A man's voice called from behind me. "You can't be here. This is a crime scene."

I twisted around to see a plainclothes police officer in a tie with a badge on his hip.

"This is my house," I explained.

"Do you need to get some things?" The officer asked.

I couldn't believe it. "Is it true about my mom? And Ary?"

"Sorry." He frowned and added, "They're at the morgue."

I croaked out the word, "No," and choked back tears. It

felt unbearable. "My brother's innocent. He and my mom always get along. He's never violent. And I was the one hiding Ary, Sanctuary Daniels, but then she disappeared. She wasn't even here. I swear to God."

"You were hiding the runaway?" Another officer in uniform asked. It was the guy with the red hair that had been here during the search.

"Yeah. She stayed under the stairs."

The ginger haired cop coolly informed me, "Your brother had the knife and the victims' blood all over him. They're calling this an open and shut case."

More footsteps echoed. I looked over to see Damler, and I let the detective know. "It's him. He's involved with them." There was something about the detective I trusted, so I kept talking. "This lady, Mother, and her family. They're like a cult. They did—"

"The kid doesn't know what he's talking about," Damler interrupted.

The man ignored him and introduced himself. "I'm Detective Zane. You must be Jacob." He shook his head and squinted hard at me. "Did you hear anything last night?"

It hit me. "I think I did. I heard a scream, and there was smoke in my room. I thought I must have been dreaming."

"What time did you hear the scream?"

Had I slept through my mom's dying pleas? I winced in pain. "I'm not sure," my voice cracked. "I didn't wake up until morning. Things seemed...fine." My chest ached. "I need to see them." What else could I do?

"We are a little busy here." The corner of Damler's thick sausage lips twitched, and he sighed impatiently. His bald skull glistened with perspiration. He knew something.

"I'll take you," Detective Zane said. He had a broken looking nose on his lined face and messy black hair. Yet he was handsome, in a tough guy kind of way.

"Thank you," I muttered. It was all too much. A dizzying feeling made the room tilt, and I wasn't even sure how I was still standing. I zoned in on his shiny, pinstriped tie. He seemed to be my only hope. Hope for what? I wasn't sure because everything, everyone, was gone. Everyone but Michael—my brother was still alive. A fog lifted, and it hurt. I wanted to see my mom and Ary even though it petrified me. But I had to talk to Michael. "I need to talk to my brother. He might know what really happened. But he didn't do this." It was weird that my words came out strong when I felt so shaky and weak.

"If it will help you, kid. Let's go. We need someone to ID the bodies." The detective started toward the door.

Not wanting to do this alone, I pivoted toward Lucas. I didn't have to utter a word. My cousin said, "I'm coming too."

The next hour closed in around me. Zane escorted Lucas and me to the basement of the hospital. Stepping off the elevator, we arrived in an empty lobby with chairs along the wall of the L-shaped room, leading to a double door made of Plexiglas Words on the door read, *Brighton County Morgue*. Zane pushed a button and the doors parted. My chest tightened.

Once inside, we rounded a corner. It was a sterile and deserted place. We faced a wall full of beige file cabinets next to a silver sink, and a dry erase board, which read: BODY FRIDGE ROOM STATUS in big, bold letters. And the heading: "Bodies for Claim," on one line with the number two written in marker. The next one was: "Missing Body Parts," and the number one. I cringed. Next to the board was a large stainless-steel door. I knew it was where they kept the dead. Oh, God, that's where they were keeping my mom and Ary.

"Are you sure you're up to this?" Lucas asked, clenching his phone in his hand. "My mom could do this for you. I got a text from her. She's on the way."

"I have to," I said.

My cousin sadly nodded and stayed behind as I followed Zane through the stainless-steel door. There she was. It was a cold place, yet the sight of her on a table seared my heart with hot, crushing pain. It was hard to breathe.

I muttered, "No, Mom," walking closer to her.

She appeared almost artificial, with her skin a paler, waxy shade of white. An unnatural pinched expression on her face made it look like she'd swallowed a hundred sharp things. I wanted to run but stood completely still, catching sight of a band of thick stitches on her lower neck. Stitches that seemed to have sewn her head onto her shoulders. I shuddered. Ached. The officer positioned the blanket back up over her neck, and relief poured over me. Then, unexpectedly, my mom's dead eyes opened. I leaped back. A pure light blasted from empty sockets.

"What? What happened to her?" I turned to the officer, and a man in blue scrubs, who I guessed was the mortician. Looking confused, the two men squinted at me. "What happened to her eyes?" I demanded.

"What about her eyes?" Detective Zane asked.

When I looked back, her eyes were closed. Had I imagined it? Lost it? I stared back at her. "Mom?" I said with a question mark and inched back. Each breath I drew was strained like heavy weights were set on my lungs.

"I'm sorry," the officer said.

This wasn't right. Seeing my mom on that table made me hurt all over. Zane said he was sorry. I didn't want him to be sorry. I wanted him to arrest whoever really did this, or better yet, wake me up. It all felt like a nightmare.

I rubbed my hand down my face. Then, suddenly, Ary's voice floated in a sing-song whisper in my mind, *I'm still alive, Jacob. Help me.*

I blinked blearily but spoke firmly, "I need to see Ary now. Sanctuary Daniels," I clarified, my heart beating hard, filled with raw anguish.

"Sanctuary Daniels is missing," the coroner admitted, nervously rubbing his large hands together.

"What do you mean she's missing?" the detective asked, cursing under his breath, and added, "The dead stay where you put them."

"Her body has been... misplaced. We were just getting ready to phone it in."

"They've got her," I said. She was still alive. The voice I heard in my head was really her.

"Find her...I'll be in touch," Zane firmly told him.

I studied the mortician. He was an overgrown Hobbit standing over six feet tall with curly hair, doughy skin, and pointed ears, his ample form stuffed into rumpled scrubs. There was something oddly familiar about him. His name badge read: Gary Morgan.

"Gary?" I said, my head full of accusations. "You're

Gary." I pointed at him. "He's in on it. He's with them." I turned to Detective Zane.

The detective asked, "He is too, huh?"

They exchanged a look and some non-verbal communication.

Zane's expression crumpled in sympathy, and he gave me the, *I'm sorry you're crazy look.* "You'll get through this, kid."

I glared again at the mortician. At first, I figured he just had one of those faces you think you've seen, a passing thing. But no. I recognized him.

"How do I know you?" Then it struck me like lightning. My mouth tumbled open as I recalled where I'd seen Gary years ago. If I added a long beard and a few extra pounds, he'd look exactly the same. I mean, he hadn't aged a day. He was the one who'd attacked the girl in the park and stomped on my rib cage. I felt my muscles tense but tried my best to seem composed. Pieces were coming together, but it still made no sense. My lips parted, and my head turned to Zane. I stopped talking. It just seemed like my life was too messed up. The more I said, the less people believed.

Finally, after a hefty silence, I remembered, "I need to see my brother."

"Okay. Let's get out of here," Zane said.

27
THE BODY

ARY

Earlier that day

First, there was a tomb-like silence. Then a memory flashed.
A memory of Gramma. *A lady with sweet eyes and a worried
forehead, who was as loving as she was astute. She told me
things. Things I couldn't quite understand. "You're very
important. You can tip the balance of things for the good of
mankind." She tied my hair in a ponytail. "As long as you're
here, she can't destroy the world as she wishes. Now
wash up."*

*I climbed the step Gramma put for me to reach the sink's
tap in the bathroom and splashed my face with cool water. As
the water streamed down the drain, it seemed unnaturally
loud, and I shut it off. I saw Gramma behind me in the mirror
and heard her say, "Look, Sanctuary, your reflection comes
and goes."*

Even when I stared hard, careful not to blink, my image flashed in and out. I leaned forward and pressed my wet palms to the mirror, leaving marks on the glass. I turned to her and asked, "Why, Gramma, why?"

"You are in this world, but not of the world." she said.

Now I floated above my old self, which was cold and lifeless. I was something other than my skin, bones, or blood. High above me, a beautiful glowing light shimmered. I reached yet couldn't touch it. I struggled. The irresistible pull stopped me from going there.

My soul, and consciousness, inched closer and closer, and I was down the rabbit hole again. Colors came in and out, and I dropped back down, lured by some magnetic force. I never understood the inner workings of my anatomy even as my body slowly put itself back into working order. Stitches were popping open, and skin was growing back together as I reentered my body. My muscles and bones began to convulse on a hard metal table. Gasping for breath and disoriented, I shook and quaked, admitting a small, strangled cry.

Coming back was an agonizing and laborious process, although dying had been even worse. I existed again of supple flesh, returning to my encasement. My once dead eyes opened, and I shaded them with my hand. Narrowing my gaze at the glare of electric light, I choked on the antiseptic scent of formaldehyde. I had woken up in a room like this once. This was the morgue. Muffled voices slipped through the cracks in the doors. Ever so, gingerly, I put my feet on the tile and stumbled, naked and disoriented, until I grabbed a paper sheet, hurriedly wrapping it around my body. Shivering and cold, I looked over my shoulder. Left and then right. No one was in the room besides a newly departed man and woman. I saw them out of the corner of my eye but didn't desire to take a closer look.

My head jerked up as the door opened. At first, there was only a shadowy figure, a shifting mass that took on speed, and like a flash of light, Mother appeared. A statuesque and beautiful monster cleverly disguised as a nurse.

She tipped her chin toward me. "Sanctuary, darling, you've seen better days. Let me take you home."

I was still dizzy from an unfinished death. "Let me go," I begged with a brittle voice, knowing it was useless right after the plea left my lips.

"You know you're between the dead and living. There is no place for you but with me." Gary walked into the room right behind her. Mother kept talking. She always talked. "You, my only child. A descendant of a noble and superior clan." She paused, then asked, "Do you think I wanted to cut into you like that, causing wounds to bleed into wounds?"

"Yes." My answer came out quite unemotionally. There was no use in fighting. The numbness faded a little, but the nausea got worse.

Mother took another step forward. "The humans were ready for your autopsy and embalming. But you have another party to attend."

"Party?" That meant a procession of evil guests would arrive. A blood sacrifice at the door would bring them. I grimaced. I couldn't remember much of the past few days. With so many hours lost to me awakened fears, and I had to know. "Is Jacob alright?" My voice trembled. "Did you hurt him?"

"I didn't touch him." She came closer, her smile pious. Her most striking features were her large white smile and perfect skin. "Did you even tell this new boyfriend of yours that you're not human?"

I shook my head. "No," I said, carefully adding, "I didn't tell him anything."

"Oh, you are a pitiful liar." She laughed, gaining some great satisfaction from my sorrow. She leaned in. "But your death certificate is here. That's how sure I am you'll not run away again. We both know where you belong." She caressed my hair.

"You didn't do anything to Jacob, or his family?" I asked again, needing to be sure.

"His family?" Her mouth curved into an evil grin. "You never asked me about his family."

"No." My heart climbed to my throat.

Mother leaned into the glare of the overhead light, illuminating her now black eyes. She clutched hold of me by my arm and squeezed on the spot where a weak pulse beat. My hand shot up, and my anger rose as Mother flew back several feet, smacking into a concrete wall. I was strong enough to move Mother. My mouth dropped in shock. But then I remembered that was how I had gotten away before and given myself the chance to run to those woods and then to Jacob's house.

Mother rose, swiftly levitating back to me. She snarled as her hand closed over to my nose and mouth. I tensed and shuddered, retreating to learned helplessness.

"Sleep, sleep, you cheeky thing." Her words were warm puffs of air against my ear as Gary moved closer, and I fell into his arms. I was in and out of consciousness. Mother tore the paper gown away from me, and I could barely move, let alone fight. My body seemed soft, boneless. I was like a big rag doll she adorned in a sweet, flowing dress. She propped me up in a wheelchair. A roar tore at my throat, sounding primal but muffled because I could barely open my mouth.

Mother's pupils danced in hues of gold and bright greens. The whites of her eyes were restored. Only another's misery could light her eyes like that. She wheeled me with an urgent stride and only slowed to withdraw a key card from her pocket. She slid it through the panel beside the back door. My mind called for Jacob to help me as Mother snuck me out through the back of the hospital, a piece of string and cardboard with a hand-written number still on my big toe. My death tag.

28

MICHAEL

JACOB

I was still dazed as Detective Zane ushered me out of the morgue. "I'll take you to see your brother. If you're sure you feel up to it today?"

"Yeah, I need to." My voice came out pinched like my chest was too tight, and words had trouble getting out.

My aunt V showed up. She might have even hugged me. Then she and Lucas clustered to my side. Michael was at the psych unit at the hospital temporarily until these idiots could book him and charge him with the murders of our mom and Ary. And they hadn't even questioned me.

On the elevator going up, I said, "You know my brother didn't do this." Everyone remained silent, and I wondered again if anyone had heard me. I turned to Zane. "Aren't you even going to take my statement?"

"One thing at a time. We can do it another day."

I didn't believe him. "It's not an open and shut case. You have to hear me out."

"I will, Jacob," he promised.

I couldn't give up. Not yet, at least. "You have to check out this Gary, guy. The mortician. I swear, Ary mentioned him by name. He's with them. They keep kids chained up in the basement." I needed to speak for my brother, but I also needed to speak for those children. Zane looked at me differently. I had said too much, and he'd stopped listening. "You will at least check out the mortician, right?"

"I will," he hesitantly responded, and he and my aunt shared a concerned look.

"I know it sounds crazy, but everything I'm telling you is true." Heat prickled across my scalp, yet my body was still cold all over from being in that freezing and desolate morgue. I shivered from the temperature, or maybe I trembled from being in a world where something this ugly could happen.

Detective Zane didn't say anything as we followed him down the corridor to a hospital room. Sterile white walls dotted with paintings of serene landscapes and shiny floors made it dream-like. Then the detective warned us, "Your brother hurt himself. That's why he was brought here instead of the police station for questioning."

My stomach went hollow. "Hurt himself. How?"

He paused for a beat, then stated, "He scratched most of his eyelids off. He looks…bad."

"No." I shook my head in protest and bewilderment.

"That's not even possible," my aunt reasoned.

"I never heard of it either, but he did," the officer said matter-of-factly. He shrugged and bowed his head.

Two female nurses were whispering amongst themselves

as they left my brother's room. They immediately fell silent at the sight of me. I dropped my head and braced myself before entering. They had Michael restrained as if he were Hannibal Lector. Arms and legs strapped down in leather restraints to a hospital bed. What the hell? He was good…a sweet guy. Smart but childlike. Yeah, he was a pain in the butt, but weren't we all?

My aunt gasped, and Lucas clutched his stomach, waiting by the door. I slunk to Michael's bedside.

"Michael," "Michael." I said his name and slowly worked up the courage to lift my gaze to his face. Oh, God. His eyelids. His eyelids had really been torn away, and it hurt to see him like this. He stared straight ahead, detached. His blood-red eyes were bruised and strangely unblinking. Yellowish discharge amassed around his sockets, or maybe it was medicine. My gaze dropped to the floor, and my stomach flinched. Aside from seeing what resembled my mom on that slab, it was the most messed up thing I had ever witnessed. Vomit pooled in my stomach.

"I'm sorry. I'm so sorry," I said, shooting Lucas a pleading look.

When I turned back to Michael, he mouthed the words, "No. No."

I managed to pull it together enough to speak. "They're saying terrible things. They're saying you killed Mom and my friend, Ary…But it doesn't even look like Mom, not really, and Ary's gone. What happened? Talk. I need you to talk to me." My jaw clenched as every muscle and tendon in my body tightened so much, I thought they'd snap. "You can't do this. You can't just go away. I need you, Michael."

My aunt came close enough to put her arm around me.

"We should go, Jacob," she said, her voice thick and throaty with emotion.

"No." I jerked away, and she stepped back. I couldn't go. I had to breakthrough. Seeing my brother like this nauseated and saddened me, but I had to reach him. "I'm here, and I know you didn't do those bad things."

Moving slowly, he tilted his head toward me.

Hope flickered. "Michael, can you hear me?" The sorrow returned as I asked him, "Tell me, who hurt Mom?"

"Go away," he mumbled.

I gripped his metal bed rails. "Michael, I know you didn't do this. Talk to me, damn it."

"They're monsters. I heard them in my head. I still hear them," he said.

"I need to know if they talked about Ary? Anything you can tell me? What are they? How can I kill them?"

"Jacob!" my aunt exclaimed, her voice coated in admonishment.

I shot her an irritated look. "Can I please be alone with my brother?"

My aunt crossed her arms and didn't budge. "To talk about killing people. No."

I couldn't blame her. I sounded like a crazed psycho for sure. My anger rippled at the base of my neck, and I slapped my hand on the spot and concentrated on my brother. "Michael, tell me what you heard. Everything you know."

"They're only scared of one thing...the girl," Michael said.

"Ary? They're scared of Ary? Why?"

A terrible vacancy again overtook Michael's face.

"We're leaving now, Jacob," my aunt insisted.

We exited the room. A tremor passed through my body, and I rubbed my arms and said, "We have to go back to Mother's, confront her and those little bastards. Prove Michael's innocence. Find Ary."

"Jacob you're not making any sense," Lucas said, but his head dropped in contemplation. I turned my gaze to see that my aunt was squinting at me with a face full of concern.

"Can I have a minute with Lucas, please?"

She seemed taken back by this but eyed Lucas. He lifted his head and nodded. Then she said, "Meet me in the waiting room, boys. And Jacob, I'm not the enemy." Tears trickled, and her mascara ran in two slender rivers down her cheeks.

"I know, Aunt V." Our grief made us collapse into a long hug.

Then I listened to the echo of her heels as she trotted down the corridor.

"Don't you see Mother is running a cult? And the morgue is in on it too. That's why Ary is missing. I don't believe she's dead...But if you don't want to go with me, I'll understand. I'll do this myself." My voice was a choked whisper.

"I'll do anything."

The idea of finding Ary was all that kept me grounded in this world. She was the one person who could help me prove Michael's innocence.

As soon as we joined my aunt in the waiting room, she got up from her chair and announced, "We're going home now."

"Home?" The word confused me.

"Of course, you're staying with us."

29

A COLD DARK PLACE

ARY

Light glowed from the top of the stairs until the heavy door slammed shut. I'd resumed my place, chained by handcuffs to a metal pole. The cuffs dug a painful trench into my wrists and ankles. Gary had made them extra tight. My weakened muscles trembled, and helplessness flooded my body with terrible impotence.

The stagnant air was musty and hard to breathe. I was in the cold, dark place again. Never quite sure if it was a basement or an abyss. Returned to an unfathomable life. Escape had only brought ruin and pain to anyone who tried to help, and suicide was no option. Not that I ever attempted to kill myself. However, I'd been murdered several times and never stayed dead for long.

I groaned and lifted a hand to my head. It was as far as the chain allowed my arm to stretch. I strained at first to see, my vision adjusting to the dimness. The flickering light from

THE STARS FORGOT US   201

candles on tall pillars dimly lit the room. They burned in homage to her. To Mother.

My eyes shot over to a boy tied to another pole only a foot away, his mouth hanging open, his eyelashes pointing toward the floor, and loose hairs obscuring his face.

I focused on my new neighbor across the way. "Can you hear me?"

He lifted his head and turned in my direction. He was in the shadows, and I couldn't get a good look.

"I'm Ary."

"Ary?" he questioned. "It's you."

"How do you know me?"

"Sorry, I think I did this to you," he said. I didn't understand what he was talking about. "I'm Jamie. Jacob's friend."

My heart charged at the sound of Jacob's name. "Is he alright?"

"Yeah. I think so. He was looking for you."

"Were you with Jacob...wh-when they got you?" I worriedly asked.

"No. My dad was on a bender that night. I went to the woods alone to wait it out. I thought I heard someone behind me and took in this big tank of a guy. I sped up, but out of the blue, a little boy came out from between two trees...He said he was lost. The next thing I knew, I got taken from behind and went down hard, eating dirt...I'm not sure how I got here. Shit. I don't even know where I am."

A sudden paranoia washed over me at the realization that we were not alone.

"We aren't here to talk, Ary."

I tightened up at his voice. "Elijah, you betrayed me," but

my tone quickly weakened. He was so young. "You can't listen to them. You're a good little boy." I often tried to remind him of who he once was.

Elijah, in a Frankenstein mask, and Maverick both emerged from the gloom, now looming above us.

"Sorry. Not sorry." Elijah sounded like a small, nasally boy. A bratty kid brother.

"That's the kid," Jamie said. "He wore the same mask."

"You two, less word spew." Maverick put a finger to his lip. He had been into bad things even before Mother changed him: drugs, slasher films, even dabbling in the occult. Feeling ugly and forlorn mixed with a morbid curiosity made him a fan of anything dark. His family had all but disowned him. And that was prior to Mother claiming his soul. He produced a knife from his pocket. It had a serrated blade designed to cut through meat.

"No." I shook my head at him.

Maverick looked down approvingly at Elijah, who held a razor. "I'm so proud of this kid," he said. The straight edge closed into its handle until he flicked his wrist, and it swung open again.

"Stop, Elijah!"

Normally I'd be worried that they'd come to bleed me, but they hadn't. Not this time. Instead, they were here to get a taste of the new boy. An infraction that would only cause an eye roll from Mother. As if they were children, sneaking a treat from the cookie jar.

A shudder ran down my spine. Jamie's chains rattled as he struggled in vain to break free as the boys rapidly approached.

"Mother will kill you if you bleed him too much," I reminded them.

They ignored me, throwing themselves to the ground and descending on poor Jamie like two hungry wolves. A blue hoodie flew across the room, and the air around us became thickened and charged. I closed my eyes but heard Jamie's protests and shackles clatter.

I kept yelling for them to "Stop!"

The commotion died down. I finally looked up to see Elijah and Maverick wiping blood from their lips.

Maverick said, "He tastes like fast food."

"I think we drank a little too much," Elijah worried, staggering around dazed, like he always did after feeding. His knuckles were bluish-white as he gripped his knife, and his bottom lip trembled. Then his full focus returned to me. "Ary, I'll bring you a pillow and blanket."

"We promised one another we'd never be like them." I let out a small sound, holding back the hurt and disappointment.

"Come on, Ary. Why can't you just be bad like the rest of us?" Elijah took a quick step toward me, putting his mask back on.

"Forget her. We better get out of here. Mother might be pissed for real. We'll pin it on Piggy," Maverick added, and they snickered, sneaking up the stairs.

"Can you still hear me?" I called.

"I'm bleeding bad." Jamie's voice shuddered, and I could tell he was crying. "Like what the hell is wrong with them?"

"They're vampires," I said.

"No, they sliced my arms up with knives…and…" He had trouble even finishing his sentence.

"If their fangs come out, they will go into a state of blood-lust and risk drinking you dry. Mother likes them to make their meals last. That's what I was told." I said all this as if it was normal. Reasonable. When one lives with crazy long enough, it becomes the way things are.

"Shut up with that bullshit. They just think they're vampires. They're nuts." His breath came out in choppy waves. The chains rattled again. "Get me out of here."

"I wish I could."

Jamie brought his arms up as far as the chains could extend and halfway hugged himself. Perhaps to stop or slow the blood seeping from his wounds.

We didn't talk for a while.

Then he spoke again. His voice dropped and was barely loud enough for me to hear. "If I don't get out of here, tell Lucas I love him. I mean, tell Lucas and Jacob that I love them." Jamie sounded weak and sad.

If I hadn't run away and met Jacob, would his friend, Jamie, even be here? I regretted the part I had played in this. But reality eventually fell away like it always did when I was in this dungeon, and I remained somewhat numb. Detached. All the nerves and pathways in my brain dulled. I was nowhere and no one. I hummed my crazy song, "Mmm, mmm, u-huh, mmm."

I heard Jamie let out an irritated sigh. "Can you stop? Either sing or rap or something. Humming adds to the fuckin' creepiness of it all."

I mumbled, "Please don't curse," feeling worn and flat inside.

We sat in silence. I asked myself how many kids had come and gone? How much despair and loneliness could I withstand? Light flashed in and out, and the stairs creaked as Piggy appeared with a handful of chocolate bars and a knapsack flung over his shoulder.

"Go away!" I shouted. I knew well his ill intent.

Piggy ignored me, shuffling over to Jamie and handing him chocolate bars. The wrappers rustled to the floor. Jamie opened his mouth, taking big bites. "These are the candy bars that I sold you the other day."

"Uh-huh. Now, I get a taste." Licking his lips, Piggy pulled out a large butcher knife from the bag. It was way too big.

Jamie called out in a hoarse, breaking voice, "Stay away!"

I started to close my eyes but couldn't. "Stop! He's weak. Please. You can drink my blood instead. I'll heal myself and won't tell Mother." My blood was off limits. Only reserved for special guests.

The boy waddled over. In his limited human years, he had been a mediocre schoolyard bully who got picked on as much as he dished it out. A disappointment to his bruiser of a dad and brothers, Piggy just ate his sorrows. He wasn't so much different as a monster.

"Do you know how long I've wanted this? Thank you, Sanctuary." He smiled at me before dropping to the dirty floor, his utility sack thudding down beside him.

Then, he tried to lift my dress up as I yanked it back down and with steel in my voice, said, "My arm Piggy."

A rivulet of slobber seeped from the corner of his open mouth. He let out a series of disheartening sighs. "Okay."

"Don't cut deep."

He sank the knife into my outer forearm and lunged down, sucking, and slurping from the gash.

"Stop, stop. That's enough," I demanded.

I heard Jamie yell in protest.

But Piggy only moaned, lapping up blood like a starving dog. It burned, and I whimpered and flailed about enough to get him off me. That was when I caught a glimpse of his white fangs. I had to act quickly. I wrapped my chains around his neck in a chokehold. Only then did he tip over. The cuffs had cut into my wrist in the struggle, and they were bleeding more than the laceration on my arm. I concentrated on stop the flow of blood. A fresh batch of sweat sprung onto the back of my neck, along with the tingling feeling of my body healing itself.

Piggy was breathing hard as we untangled, and I unwound the chains from him. Blood trickled down his chin. He gaped at me as we both sat in a puddle of red, our clothes damp with it. I was still miserable, but the gash was now closed.

"But you taste like dessert, Ary. So sweet I could die of happiness," he said, holding his throat, still full of hunger and lust. "I couldn't keep my fangs in."

I warned, "Don't touch me again! Or I'll call Mother or Ren."

"No! Please don't tell." Piggie scampered away.

I must have been crying because there was water on my cheeks. No matter how much torture I endured, blood always panicked me. Pain always hurt.

"I'll try to get us out of here, Ary. I promise." Jamie's voice was full of emotion and warmth.

"Thank you," I muttered. My head dropped. *Jacob, I'm alive*, I repeated in my mind. Though my lips never parted, my thoughts echoed around the large hellish room in an audible mantra. It was curious, the things I could do.

But it was no use. Jacob was much better off without me.

I'd never forget him, although, in time, he'd be no more than a few memories I had tucked away.

Mother didn't come. Perhaps she had other plans that night. She sent a gray smoke in her place. An ashen taste filled my mouth as fumes rolled over us like swells of ocean waves. Mother never wanted us talking too much. I was bleary-eyed and foggy. The stupor had set in, and I drooled just a little from the corner of my open mouth. Minutes may have passed or hours. Even days. I had no way to know.

30

SAY GOODBYE

JACOB

The hospital parking lot had thinned out. I inhaled fresh, crisp air, cleansing the smell of death from my senses. Under a pool of light from a streetlamp, we slipped into the car. Lucas tidily buckled himself in, and I resented his calmness. Every fiber of my being was whipped into knots. I was ready to jump out of my skin with anxiety but managed to close the car door and breathe.

My aunt fumbled with her seat belt and stuck the key in the ignition. Then she glanced at me through the mirror. "It wouldn't hurt to see someone. I'll make an appointment for you. You've been through a lot. We all have."

"I don't need a shrink." Of course, my aunt thought I was nuts. Hell, I would think I was nuts too. I turned to the window and exhaled, fogging the glass. I ignored my aunt and the sinking feeling in my stomach.

"Should we stop and get some of your things?" She asked.

I couldn't. "No. I'll wear Lucas's stuff."

"Yeah, Mom, I don't mind," Lucas said.

My aunt usually drove fast, but now the car crawled. She did no more than thirty the whole way home. Turning her blinker on, she ever-so-carefully switched lanes like a student in driver's ed.

"Can you please drive faster," I snapped and shifted as close as possible to the car door. Yet maybe she crept along at a snail's pace because she was barely holding it together.

Once in Lucas's room, I called Jamie on my cell. I had to get him on board with going to Mother's house to confront her, but I just got his voice mail. "Jamie's still not answering."

I flopped onto the computer chair while Lucas paced, saying, "He's not responding to any of my texts either. It's weird. He's on his phone even when he's on the toilet." Lucas wore his thinking face, eyes narrowed, and lips slightly twisted. "Unless he's with a girl."

I sprang up. "We don't need him. We can go ourselves."

"No. We'll wait for Jamie."

"Forget Jamie. This is way too important."

"He'll call back any minute," Lucas promised.

But Jamie never called that night. Lucas let me take the bottom bunk, which was a futon, and he took the top, which was a full-sized bed. It had seemed amazing when we were kids. "Only you can still have a bunk bed and not be a joke," I said.

"Yeah, I need a real bed soon," Lucas agreed.

I pulled the blankets back and climbed in. The worn

springs squeaked as I drew a stilted breath. I didn't really care about the bed or anything for that matter.

Gusts of wind and rain hit the house, rattling the panes of the windows. My mind just kept darting between my mom, Michael, and Ary. My eyelids fluttered in confusion, and I couldn't keep them closed. The more I thought about things, the wider awake I became.

After days of blinding rainstorms, the cemetery was flooded. The burial wouldn't be held until conditions improved.

At the funeral I was unsure what to think but bitterly noticed there weren't that many people. There should have been more people. My mom always put Michael first and lost touch with practically everyone. Friends and relatives who did show cautiously gave their condolences as if I was on the ledge of a tall building, and they didn't want me to jump.

The minister from Aunt Veronica's church stepped up to the podium. The small crowd leaned forward as he spoke. My puffy eyes kept going to the door. I tried to listen, to focus, waiting and waiting for my dad to show. After about ten minutes, the eulogy ended, and the minister had everyone bow their heads in prayer when the door opened. Sure enough, my father waltzed in, causing a minor raucous as he fought to close an umbrella. He was always late. Now he'd missed most of my mom's funeral. He settled into the pew behind me. His hand touched my back.

I shifted around. My dad wasn't a business guy like

Lucas's father, but a truck driver who looked out of place in the suit he had on. His brown hair was gray at the temples.

"Jacob," he quietly said.

"Hey, dad," I sounded nonchalant but felt twitchy, and his being here didn't make it any better. Nothing could. I turned back around to face the coffin.

The minister said, "Please feel free to pay your respects." With that, he abandoned the pulpit.

There was no need to put off the inevitable. I shuffled down the aisle past mostly empty chairs. I drew painstakingly nearer with each shaky step. Grandma tearfully mouthed, "Love you, Jacob," and the girls, Kylie and Madison, offered sad waves. Deanna and Hunter were there too. Deanna's head was hung low, but Hunter was crying. He must have imagined it was his mom's funeral. Just the passing thought could rip a guy to shreds. But for me, it was reality.

My mom was gone, and they suspected my brother of committing her grisly murder. I was left alone to pick up the jagged pieces. *Was this our fate?* I wasn't the type to use such an over-the-top word. Fate was a word reserved for fairytales and fantasies, but now my life was over the top.

I collapsed onto a padded kneeler positioned right before the closed coffin. Then my brain called *Mom!* Desperation invaded my body, and my mind played back a part of the conversation we'd had on the ride to our new house.

"I want to be buried with Freckle's ashes. And please bury me with my cell phone in case, I wake up."

"Oh God, I forgot," I whispered. I grabbed my cell out and cracked open the coffin's lid just enough to slip it in. It was all I had to give her.

I was glued to this terrible moment for the longest time. I

loosened my tie, my chest heaving against the fine threads of my dress shirt. I felt like if I left, it was really goodbye. Then the tears poured out.

The hardest times seemed infinite. Until, finally, they were over, ending in the blink of an eye.

My dad exchanged words with Aunt Veronica and Uncle Pete in the lobby before coming over to me. He didn't know what to say any more than I knew what I wanted to hear.

"I'm sorry," he repeated, patting my upper arm.

I'm sure he was. He'd be stuck with me unless my Aunt V or Grandma took me in. Crap, I couldn't live alone at fifteen. Could I?

"Can we talk?" He asked.

"Sure. I'll start. Why'd you show up late? Why'd you bother to come at all?"

"I was with Michael. He looked bad. It's hard for me," he weakly said.

"Hard for you?" I bit my lip, holding in a storm of emotions. "It's not a great day for me either."

He closed his eyes for several seconds. "I dated your mom all through high school. She was my best friend. And we were happy for a long time." I didn't even want to share some kind of moment, but his eyes screwed into mine. "I'll always love her."

My dad's voice was so gentle I ached.

He pulled me close, and I hugged him back as tight as I could. When we parted, my forehead was wet with his tears. He wiped his eyes with the cuff of his shirt.

The words, "I love you, Dad," oozed out. But the resentment left an aftertaste in my mouth. "That's what makes what you did even more shitty."

"I know, but I love you too. Brenda's moved out. Why don't you come and live with me?"

"Let me think about it. I want to stay here for a while." If I'd learned anything, it was that life was short. But I had too much unfinished business to even think about working things out with my dad.

After the wake, I retreated to Lucas's room and collapsed onto the futon.

"I can't believe Jamie didn't show. This isn't right. Hunter and the girls haven't seen him either." Lucas's fingers curled at the nape of his neck, and he released an audible breath. "I'm going to go take a shower, alright?" Lucas asked, oddly seeking my permission.

"Fine," I replied.

Just then, his phone beeped, and he jerked his hand up as his eyes narrowed at his iPhone. "It says the call is from *you*."

"What?" I sat up. Only then I recalled slipping my cell into the coffin to fulfill my mom's request. "Um, I left my phone at the funeral home."

"Oh, they must have found it," Lucas replied and pushed his phone toward me.

I answered with a cautious, "Hello?"

A rustling cackled across the line. Someone was there, but they didn't say a word.

"Hello?"

A whimpering sound intertwined with the static.

Then I heard, "Jacob, where am I?" It was my mom's voice. Yet, it couldn't be. My jaw dropped, and I became totally disoriented. "What? Who is this?"

"It's dark here," she said. "I didn't want to go."

It sounded just like my mom. But how? "Mom? You're alive?" A chill ran through me, followed by a rush of hope and adrenaline. "Mom! Is it really you?"

Then the call dropped. "Hello. Hello." But no one was on the line.

Lucas's eyes traveled to me as I bolted up and pushed his phone to him. "It's my mom. She's alive. We have to go to the funeral home."

"Wait. Jacob, someone must have found your phone and is playing a cruel prank."

"I know my mom's voice." But how was it possible? I remembered with horror, "She's going to be buried tomorrow. There's no way in hell I'm not checking this out."

Lucas's face slumped in frustration. "Listen to yourself. What you're saying doesn't make sense."

He was still talking when I was halfway out the bedroom door. I tore down the stairs and flopped down onto the bench to tug my sneakers on. Lucas had just made it to the landing as I slipped the second shoe on. "Can we talk, Jacob?"

I burst out the front door and into the night, hearing the whisper of wind, and paused, shivering. The air blowing in filled my lungs and whipped my hair around. Dark clouds parted to reveal a full moon. It was a long way to the funeral home but screw it. I was going no matter what when I heard Lucas behind me. I had wanted him to follow, despite playing it cool. "You don't have to go with me."

"Of course, I'm going." He struggled to put on the jacket

he must have grabbed on the way out. Then he took a cap from his pocket, which he placed firmly on his head. With the cap on, he looked like he belonged in the 1920s. "Do you want me to go and grab your jacket? I can." He offered, remaining helpful and friendly even though the world had fallen apart.

For a fleeting second, I almost smiled, telling him, "You're such a geek." The November wind had an edge, and I started shaking harder.

"It's freezing. I'll just be a minute," he said, not waiting for my answer, and tore back toward the house.

I impatiently eyed the partly opened front door. The rain had finally stopped, but yellow leaves floated down the street like tiny boats. It was dark, serene, and quiet. It was hard to believe this was the same world where my mom and Ary had been savagely murdered.

Mom? I thought about her being on the other end of that call. Unable to stay still, I bounced back and forth on my feet. Charged with mounting anxiety, I couldn't wait any longer and halfway ran. My sneakers thumping the wet sidewalk. Rain puddles sprayed from beneath the soles of my shoes. Everything rushed by in surreal flashes. Lucas called for me as his pounding footsteps sounded, so I slowed down.

"You were supposed to wait." Lucas made a low humming sound of disquiet. His nostrils flared as he pushed my jacket into my chest. "You're welcome."

"Fine, I'll wear the stupid jacket." The bristling breeze made me glad he had brought it. I slipped it on and started walking.

"Why are you doing this, Jacob? You know it's just a cruel joke," Lucas said.

"I don't know anything anymore." My voice sounded higher pitched than usual. We stopped talking and just kept going. Drooping branches swayed on the other side of the road. We passed houses and the quiet downtown, maneuvering around the bigger puddles. My fingers trembled in the cold, but I was on a mission. Adrenaline coursed through me and sped my steps and mind with a laser focus. Finally, we saw it. The funeral home. It was an old Victorian house converted into a funeral parlor before I was even born.

"We came all this way, and it's just going to be locked," Lucas reasoned.

I plodded up to the front door and grabbed the door handle. It felt cold and sleek. The door squeaked open, swinging in on its hinges. First, we saw a table with a large bouquet of flowers and brochures. A single lamp was on by a landline phone in the corner of the entryway. It hardly gave enough light to challenge the darkness, but we moved farther in.

"This is nuts." Lucas clasped his hands together. "What if we wake the caretaker?"

"Screw the caretaker." I rubbed away the sweat from my forehead with my knuckles and spotted the soft overhead light illuminating *The Sarah Kelly Funeral* sign. I tore over, trying to pass through the double doors. At first, something pushed back.

Lucas tried too and said, "They're locked."

Mysteriously, the doors opened and then closed behind us after we stepped in.

We exchanged a questioning look. Lucas whispered, "You want to say goodbye again, I get that, but uh, let's try to make it out of here before anyone sees us."

I would have said, let's hurry this shit up, but Lucas was more polite than me. I told him again, even if he'd never believe me. "She really did call. I know my mom's voice."

Lucas seemed all but glued to that spot. I moved forward into the dim sanctuary to my mother's closed casket. It absorbed what little light there was in the room. An inner voice told me that something wasn't right. Along with that warning voice, fear swept in. My gaze shot back to Lucas as he exited through the double doors. But why had he abandoned ship? "Thanks a lot," I mumbled, stopping in my tracks. Then my focus returned to the nearby casket, and I started walking again.

Once there, I kneeled and squeezed my eyes shut. Bracing myself, I rose before lifting the lid of the coffin. Mom's body was there. Curls spread around her head in a halo. A slash of red lipstick was vivid against her pale skin, and somehow, the cell phone was clutched in her hand. Even more unexpectedly, her lips parted, and I could have sworn I heard her moan.

"Mom?" I called out like a question. But I grimaced at the clotted band of stitches around her neck and recalled the fact that we'd had her funeral earlier today. What the hell? It was impossible. She couldn't be alive. My heart battered my chest and skipped a beat as her eyes popped open. Dark eyes dilated with fear, wild with catching terror.

I took a clumsy step backward and turned to run. Hardly able to find my next breath, and unable to think clearly, I stumbled over to the double doors to find the image of my mom directly in front of me. It seemed incredible, but the horror was also real. Why the fear? I wanted her to be here so badly. To be alive, but how? "Is it really you?"

She nodded, and I knew it was her. Only in this moment,

she wasn't in her body but spirit-like, radiant, almost transparent.

"I love you, Mom. But what's happening?"

"I came to tell you, she did this." Her pretty, white skin glowed in the darkness, stained with tears. "The monster, Mother. She said if someone crosses her, she takes what they cherish most."

"And she took you and Michael," I uttered aloud and only thought *Ary.*

"You need to help him. He's scared. Alone. Please," she pleaded, her voice weak, and then she blinked out of existence.

Now I wanted her to come back. "Wait! Don't leave me, Mom."

Lucas burst back in through the doors. His face was contorted in a pucker of disgust until he calmed down a little, and his eyes narrowed. I thought he might open up about what he'd seen, but instead, he decided, "We have to get out of here."

"What happened? What did you see?"

"Let's go. *Now*," Lucas said before he torpedoed past me, and I hightailed it, trailing a step behind him.

We plunged into the lounge area, wanting to get the hell out. It was dark. Distant voices echoed. Indistinct whispers shot off around us. I had the feeling something was following us or was waiting just around the corner and would jump out at us at any time. Our flight and fury of steps went on forever when we spotted the outer doors, and Lucas turned back to make sure I was still there. An automatic light flashed on, flickering noisily for a moment until it quieted to a low buzz, bathing the lobby in a yellow glow. Lucas threw open the door. Something in my gut said to go back, but my survival instincts kept me going.

The doors slammed, and outside it had started to drizzle. A velvety night sky lay like a shroud over the town, concealing any stars and filtering the moon a misty gray. We were alone in the night. Lucas remained silent and continued to lead.

I grabbed ahold of his shoulder, and he stopped, and a taste of rain touched my tongue when I again asked. "Tell me what you saw?"

He turned his head my way and opened his mouth and sighed. Whatever he had seen freaked him out so bad he couldn't even talk about it. Suddenly, the world seemed to tilt just for a few seconds. I grabbed his shoulders to balance myself. He had slumped down, making his eyes level with mine. We lingered there for a minute. Stunned.

"What the hell just happened?" I asked.

"I'm not sure. It felt like a small tremor," Lucas reasoned.

I sensed that something unholy was coming.

Then I thought if I shared what had happened with Mom, it might help him open up. "I saw my mom. She talked to me. She asked me to help Michael. But how can I do that?"

Lucas just frowned in my direction and started walking again. Though my feet pounded wet asphalt as we crossed the street, I felt oddly detached from my body. Fear had taken root, sprouting, growing at a hectic pace. The air was thin and hard to breathe. Stepping onto a patch of soggy grass, bare trees lined in formation like skeletons. Were they even here before?

Soon a nearby train whistle shrieked as our feet closed in on a row of storefronts. We passed under the awnings for brief breaks from the rain, splashing through puddles on the swampy sidewalk, drenched to my shoelaces. Trash and leaves floated by our feet. A Twinkie wrapper and used tampon. I read *Main Street Café* and the *closed* sign in the window and then saw the darkened laundromat. We passed *Ted's Bike Repair,* which had a metal gate pulled down over the front door. A normal memory of having my bike fixed there years ago flashed in. Yet, nothing was normal anymore.

I kept up with Lucas's brisk pace, peeking at the sky through a cluster of swaying branches. I caught a flash of something, maybe lightning. Rain pelted down, and we ran through the downpour until we made it back to Lucas's house. Once in the foyer, we took deep breaths, trying to slow our racing hearts and not wake his sleeping parents. My cousin turned my way with that same desperate look.

"Come on, Lucas. What did you see?"

His lips screwed to the side, and his fingers worked their way through his short, wet hair. "I don't want to…I won't talk about it."

We took our coats and shoes off in a tense silence and left muddy puddles on the ceramic tile. I almost tripped, following Lucas up the dimly lit stairs. Thunder rumbled in the distance. I rounded a corner, passing a China cabinet, and made my way down the hall.

"Do you have to go?" Lucas asked in an oddly parental tone. I was lost until he spelled it out. "Do you have to piss?"

"Um, no."

Lucas turned into the bathroom, and I listened to a quick stream of urine and the toilet flush. Then he reappeared, silently blinking at me.

"Um, I could go," I realized and hurried to the toilet. I didn't put the seat back down or even bother to flush. Lucas waited just outside the door. Stony countenance. Arms crossed. Impatience rolling off him.

As soon as we stepped foot in his room, Lucas pushed his dresser to barricade the door. He didn't pause but quickly stripped out of his wet clothes, his arm muscles cording as he hung them on a hook on his door to dry. Moving about like a robot, he remained emotionless. Our eyes barely met as he put on a pair of shorts and T-shirt and climbed to the top bunk, ordering me to "Put some dry clothes on and go to sleep."

The façade of everyday life had been shattered, and my cousin wasn't able to deal with it any better than I could. A cold went through me. Yet, I had to know what he'd seen. "Just because you don't talk about something doesn't make it any less true. Tell me."

Lucas didn't answer. My dead mom visited me tonight, and the only person I had left in the world had checked out.

The following day, at the burial, the sky was the same blue as a birthing blanket. Oddly beautiful and innocent looking for such a dark day. The smell of damp earth and mist hung in the air. The casket was placed in the ground, and I felt sad as hell, of course, but off somehow too. Dazed. Detached. Then a hissing sound grew from behind me. It was the voice of a demonic woman, whispering, "Sssooon, Jacob," and finishing with a growl.

I whipped around to catch a glimpse of Mother by a

weeping willow tree. She loomed just rows away from my mom's grave in the cemetery. The mere proximity of her had lent a peculiar sensation even before I'd heard or spotted her.

I squinted at my aunt Veronica, feeling horrified but even more outraged. "What is she doing here?"

"Who?" My aunt asked. When I looked back, Mother wasn't there.

Anger beat inside of me. Gritting my teeth, I quickly weaved around tombstones, stepping on the walkway, which glistened with dirty puddles. By the time I made it to that tree, there was no sign of Mother. Again, I spotted an 'M' carved in the grain of the bark.

Lucas caught up with me. "Still no Jamie. He would have been here today. I finally got his dad on the phone, but he hasn't seen him or bothered to file a missing person's report." The light in his eyes dimmed, and his voice went flat. "I'm scared." His Adam's apple bobbed. "They're monsters, you know?"

"What did you see?" Lucas didn't answer for a long while. I repeated the question. "What the hell did you see?"

"I heard voices from the other chapel and went to check it out. I thought it was a prayer group or vigil, and that's why the front doors were open. People were wearing red cloaks and chanting. And Mother... Mother was watching a man eat a corpse," he said, a pitiful tremor in his voice.

My mind spun as I comprehended what he said. I wasn't ready for that. It was so wild for a second, I almost forgot I was at my mom's burial.

He rubbed his nose, his eyes watery. "Do you think I'm crazy?"

I said what I thought. "No. Steely, Pennsylvania is crazy. Maybe even the whole world."

"They have Jamie. I feel it in my gut," Lucas gloomily said.

"And Ary." Her pretty face whirled in. This horror had been so much of her life. She told me they were monsters. Now I believed her. "I think they're vampires."

"Vampires don't eat dead people. They might be zombies." A line flickered between his brows. "I can't believe we're having this conversation."

"We only know about movie, or book vampires," I reasoned.

"What if we call the police?" Lucas asked.

"I already told Detective Zane. He isn't a bad guy, but he didn't believe me either. And Damler and probably at least some of the others are in on it. We need to go there ourselves."

Something akin to sadness and defeat showed in his eyes. So, it surprised me when Lucas replied, "What are we waiting for?"

"We'll go later this afternoon." I remembered Ary asking, '*How do you kill demons...vampires?*' And I added, "But I need to get a few things first." Whatever they were, they weren't human, and we needed weapons.

My gaze skimmed over grave markers as I walked back to my mom's final resting place. And I could still feel her, but I could feel the horrible presence of Mother too. My adrenaline sped up, and I felt each beat of my pulse. What were we up against?

31

DEALS WITH DEVILS

ARY

Creaking steps disturbed the silence. I was still fighting my way out of the stupor as a hand slapped my cheek.

I faintly heard, "I turned the smoke off. Get up, Sanctuary."

I blinked my eyes and woke up partway but was still entwined in my dream. It was Jacob I saw. When the hand struck my face once more, I really woke to find Ren crouched down next to me, his face all but touching mine.

Ren was different from Gary. Different from his vampire brothers. Rebellious. Yes, he was soulless but not as loyal to Mother as the others. He had been chewed up and spit out by the world like all of them and landed here. He was a foster kid and runaway.

"What?" I groggily asked. He looked wild-eyed, unhinged. Not the cool vampire he had become. A leader to the other boys and an advisor to Mother with a sixth sense the others didn't have. "Are you alright?"

"Am I alright?" A smirk briefly curved his lips before it curdled. "I've little free will. I'm infected with Mother, numbed by her phantom smoke. Always waiting for the next fix. Infected with a terrible thirst, and it hurts." His lip curled in anguish, but it was the sincerity in his eyes that alarmed me.

He took out a blade, a blade that would slice into my flesh. He had tasted me against Mother's wishes. Yet, he would threaten to destroy the other boys if they ever tried. Curiously, he cut into the palm of his hand. "Drink it, Sanctuary. You'll be bound to me and stronger. Together, we can defeat that hag."

"Even if you're telling the truth, I'd be chained to you, and you're chained to darkness. So, I'd be Mother's too."

"If that was true, she'd let us change people. There's a rule against it, a reason she brings in the vampires." His arm dangled, and his hand dripped something darker than blood.

"Just let me and the new boy go. Please," I begged as a storm of emotions swirled in my chest.

He pinched his laceration together with the fingers of his free hand. "I tried. You should have burned this whole God forsaken place down. It is the only way to destroy them. But here you are again and as pitiful as always."

"I'll do it this time, Ren. I swear I will. Just let us go," my voice broke as I pleaded.

"Just drink my blood and you will be able to break those chains."

"It means I'll lose my soul." I wanted to save Jacob's

friend and the future victims from any more ruin and despair. That was a line I was unwilling to cross.

Ren spoke with rising inflection. "You're pure soul. Don't make me laugh. You can't die. Are you even human?" He paced in circles around me. His hips swayed from side to side, almost girlishly. Then the floorboards above our heads creaked, and he lowered his voice, though it was still full of resentment. "Even if you were human, what about the kids who were discarded like leftovers? What good did hoarding your precious soul do for them? Warm ones are no better than us. If they're not giving into their carnal temptations, they're looking the other way while others do."

"I was young. I didn't understand what was happening to them." I felt it. The scorching pain of guilt and anger. "Stop it!"

"You know now, bitch. Just drink the blood."

"No! And stop calling me the b word." I gritted my teeth.

Jamie broke in. "I'll do it. I'll drink it."

"Shut up!" Ren told him. "You're not of an immortal bloodline."

He had sharper instincts than me. I feared he would have noticed. Then he moved closer to Jamie and quivered. "You? You've got a little something. You might die instantly, but we'll give it a try. Don't drain me, trailer park. Just a few sips. Or you'll end yourself and weaken me."

"Don't do it, Jamie." I warned and turned to Ren, demanding, "Tell him the truth."

"Shut up. Okay. The truth is there's a teeny-tiny catch. You have to be dying before you drink." Ren dropped to the ground onto his knees. He brought his face so close to Jamie's that their breath became one. He brushed his lips over Jamie's mouth, and it looked like they might kiss, but instead, he playfully said, "This is going to hurt a lot."

I yelled, "No! Please!" as Ren's mouth bit down on Jamie's neck.

Jamie said, "Stop, stop." His cries grew weak. It seemed a small forever my twisted vampire brother drank.

I protested on the top of my lungs, "Stop! You're killing him!"

After Ren drew away, he yanked Jamie's head up by his hair. Jamie moaned and asked, "Will I be a superhero now?"

Ren was evil, but unlike the others, he didn't usually lie. He was too arrogant.

"Something will feel itchy beneath your skin and your heart will stop beating. Your blood will congeal, thicken, and sour like old milk. You will be a vampire."

"Oh, dude, am I going to sparkle? I hated the *Twilight* films," Jamie spoke softly, dazed.

"You're an idiot. You won't hunger for food and if you try to eat, you'll vomit. So, you can't enjoy your trailer park food. No weenies or McDonalds anymore. Blood will be your food. And that ain't even the kicker. You will be the undead and never have another erection again." He groped Jamie's private area, leaving a handprint of dark crimson. "Blood will be sex."

A shiver of agony passed through my flesh. "Stop!" I yelled. I couldn't stand to hear anymore.

"I changed my mind. I don't want to do this," Jamie weakly said, nearly passing out. He clamped his hand over his neck, which was still bleeding out.

Ren let out a humorless chuckle. "Well, if you don't drink now, idiot, you'll die."

Jamie's voice cracked. "I don't want to die."

Ren pushed his hand to Jamie's mouth, and he began to drink.

I couldn't bring myself to look away. I watched Ren struggle, finally getting his hand away from Jamie. After, Ren clambered to his feet, staggering over to me. "Fix me. Now!" He ordered and put his injured hand close to my face. "It burns. Bad."

"You'll heal yourself. I can't heal others," I said.

"Just try."

The last thing I wanted was more confrontation. So, humoring him, I shut my eyes. A white light glowed, and something stirred inside of me. In my life, I'd searched for signs of God in church, etched in the beauty of nature, yet I never came closer to experiencing the divine than when I healed Ren. But he was evil, a vampire.

He held his hand out to examine it. "You did it." He tossed his head back and snorted. "I knew it." Then, his mood sobered. He slowly sank to the ground and began gently caressing my cheek. "You should have given me a chance and not that loser human…You grew up, and I started to catch feelings." He studied me with elevated eyebrows. "You just needed one drink to be powerful. You're such a stupid girl. We could have ruled the world together." His expression painfully tightened.

Then he rose with his head bowed, placing his hand on his chest. Blue veins showed when he lifted his head, pulsating beneath his skin. "What did you do to me, you little witch?" His lip twitched. "It hurts so bad." Ren began to moan in excruciating pain, hunched over and hobbling about the basement floor.

"What is it? What's happening to you?" Had I hurt him when I believed I'd healed him?

He wasn't the only one suffering. Jamie's cries grew and reverberated off the cellar walls.

"You did something to me. I can barely stand," Ren said.

Our eyes were drawn to Jamie as he bolted to a sitting position, feverishly struggling with the chains before becoming silent. His gaze fell to the red stains on his shirt, which now appeared a glossy maroon. Finally, Jamie's jaw dropped, and he emitted low, wheezing sounds.

Before I could react to either boy's plight, a light flashed from the top of the stairs as the door crashed open. Footsteps. Then Mother and Gary appeared as I feared they would with all the commotion. I flinched. Mother wasn't happy. She had her dead face and horns out as her blackest eyes raked over me before crossing over to Jamie. She stooped down and lifted his arms, which were still bound together, and inspected them.

"Those naughty children. Who's already bleeding the new boy?"

Her anger first unsheathed in a low, guttural noise until it became beastlike, and she pounced on Jamie with a loud thud. The pair wrestled about the floor. After the quick tussle, Mother was on top. Then, on all fours, she sniffed Jamie high and low and growled in a fit of fury. Her neck twisted, and mouth opened gruesomely wide, showing her gleaming canines.

My hand was shaking as I covered my mouth, seeking to rein in my panic. It was always as if my mind played tricks on

me. Mother rose, clad in her human skin once again. Jamie
curled up in an embryonic position on the floor.

"What a shame. I wanted to have a coming-out party for
him. Now you've tainted his blood, we can't even eat him."
Her eyes landed on Ren. She smugly lifted her chin. "You
disobeyed me. You're not even a real vampire, but a mosquito
of the underworld. Do you have any idea the kind of pain I
can inflict on a boy who can't die? My darling, Sanctuary can
tell you a little about that."

She looked around—her attention suddenly diverted. "But
lucky for you, my pet, someone's here." She lifted her hand,
and Ren flew into the wall, sliding down to the floor, uncon-
scious and completely still.

From my peripheral, I noticed Gary slumped to the
ground. He had stuck his fingers in a puddle of blood near me
and began sucking on them like he was a toddler.

"Get up," Mother ordered, in a deep throaty voice, annoyance pulling her features.

Gary obeyed.

Then Mother took a deep breath before she spun to me.
"Your boyfriend's here," she said with wicked delight.

3²

PLUMMET

JACOB

(One hour earlier)

It was 4 o'clock. Lucas fed my aunt and uncle some excuse about us wanting to ride our bikes to escape all the darkness of late. He over-explained things, but his folks didn't seem to notice. It was early November. A chill grew in the air, and a shimmer of frost sequenced the ground. We each wore one of Lucas's bomber jackets, mine brown and his black. We quickly cycled away from the cul-de-sac and didn't look back. We pedaled hard as the road shot up over the brow of the hill, flying down with a dizzying sense like we were on a roller coaster.

We took a shortcut to a narrow potholed road with trees to either side. I skidded over a puddle before we met the grind of another incline, and my legs burned. On the other side of the hill, I was relieved to coast down. For a fleeting moment, we almost forgot where we were headed.

This time, we entered from the front of the subdivision. It was marked by a five-foot-tall sign that read *Heaven's Gate.* A fountain with water cascading down rocks sat underneath the sign. Now it was becoming real.

Minutes later, we rode onto Morning Glory, Mother's street, and my heart was a fistful of thunder. I knew anything could happen now that everything had. We slowed down on the sidewalk, passing the tree-lined street and cheerful cookie-cutter houses. We were getting closer and closer. Finally, a visual of Mother's house laid straight ahead of us, and I cut Lucas off, the brakes of our bikes screeching as we came to a stop.

Lucas knocked his kickstand out and came closer.

"So, what's the plan?" I asked, but we never really had one.

"I'm not sure." He shrugged.

We stood face to face. As lost as he was, Lucas remained an optimist by nature. I had to tell him. Warn him. "We might not live."

He cleared his throat. "I know."

Yet the thought of my mom's murder, Michael in that hospital bed, and Ary in some dismal dungeon—generated and fueled the desperation I needed to do this. "I have to go. Anyway, I have nothing to lose."

Lucas raised a slash of his dark eyebrow, sounding uncharacteristically deadpan. "Me either."

"Nothing but your mom and dad, and your freaking bright future," I reminded him. "Why should we both die? You could be the first independent president."

"George Washington was technically an independent president, but wow, you were actually listening." He released a big breath and smiled just a little.

"I guess I was."

His stance and mood shifted. "Whatever these things are, they have Jamie."

I contemplated his face, shiny with potential but marred with angst. He cared about Jamie more than I ever knew. I said, "Alright, we'll do this together, but you need to wait outside. Then you can get help if I don't come back out. Yeah, call Detective Zane. If it gets too crazy, Zane can see for himself and then he'd have to believe it." This seemed like the smarter thing to do. I pulled out the detective's card, and Lucas took it.

He studied the card and considered my idea. "That makes more sense." Lucas hesitated, scratching his head. "Not that anything makes sense anymore…I'll take cover in the woods for now."

I slid my backpack off and reached in, fumbling around inside. It was time for the big reveal as I drew out a revolver, a Glock 42/43 that gleamed in the setting sunlight. I heard my uncle talking about it.

"What the hell? That's my dad's gun."

"Yeah. I borrowed it." I had shot pop cans with a BB gun, played video games, but had no experience with the real thing. "It's supposed to be blessed, so I prayed over the bullets, but maybe you should do it. You're cleaner than me somehow."

Lucas shook his head and pushed it back to me. "That's not true. You're a good guy and you need it more than me. Anyway, you're the idiot who's going inside, Jacob."

"Good point." I flicked my eyebrows, reclaiming the gun, and stuck it in my jacket's inside pocket. "And I grabbed some other stuff. You need something too. Remember what you saw at the funeral home?" He didn't say a word but turned pale and nodded. "At least take this." I rummaged through the backpack and pulled out a knife enclosed in a leather sheath and then cloves of garlic, jamming them into his pockets. "Pretty lame. But I didn't know what else to bring."

Feeling exposed, our eyes darted all around. Yet the street was oddly quiet. No kids played outside, or cars drove by. I zipped up the bag and slid it over my shoulder. "Let's do this," I said.

He led, I followed. Twigs and frozen leaves crunched under our feet and wheels as we guided our bikes off to the nearby woods.

"Do you think Jamie's really there?" Lucas asked, second-guessing himself.

"I think so," I said, quickly deciding, "He is." Saving Jamie and Ary was a long shot, but we at least had to try. We owed them both that.

"Be careful," he whispered. We knew we might never see each other again. "I love you, Cuz."

I nodded. "Me, too." I thumped him lightly on the arm, and he did the same. "You're the best friend I ever had," I admitted, and we both smiled a little with effort. A sad goodbye smile.

I leaned my bike against the trunk of a large oak tree. I moved toward the house, glancing back at Lucas, and he waved a final time. Honestly, I never thought we'd have the guts for any of this. In my case, loss and pain made me either brave or stupid. The wind stirred my hair and the grass in a feathery rustle, and I shivered just a little. My gaze lifted to the back of the fence. Squinting my eyes and gnashing my teeth, I let the sorrow and anger take hold. Then I took a running leap, catching the top of the fence on the first try, hauling myself partway over. My legs dangled for a few seconds until I let go, making it to the other side but with a kind of hard fall.

Standing up, I stared at the back of the house. Taking a moment to compose myself, I inhaled a deep breath. Anything was better than letting my mom's lifeless body and Michael's wounded face come back into focus. Anything was better than being in this world without them. Yet, it was saving Ary that I concentrated on. At least there, I found an inkling of hope. It made this more than just a suicide mission.

The wind died away though it was noticeably cooler on this side of the fence. I drew the gun like a detective from TV but proceeded on wobbly legs. Yet, fear was a reprieve from the gnawing despair. I hadn't yet reached the shadow the house cast on the lawn when I remembered the cameras. I muttered a few curse words and socked the gun away in the pocket of my jacket.

I dropped to the ground, army-man style, and kept going, crawling on elbows and knees through the grass. Finally, after passing the lawn furniture on the stone patio, I made it to a first-floor window and tore down the shutters, placing them on the ground, where they rattled. The glass of the window-pane was cold under the palm of my hand. A rust-colored sofa and coffee table were in the family room. A nice ordinary house. Then I grabbed the windowsill with both hands. My breath hitched when the window opened all the way. It was

way too easy. A trap. But I told myself they wouldn't know I
had the gun.

Only now, when I peered in, it was pitch black inside the
house. There was no possible explanation for what could
prevent the daylight from pouring in through an open window.
How it remained completely dark inside was a mystery. My
nerves spiked. "What the hell?" I whispered. Part of me
wanted to run, but I pushed myself and climbed in halfway
through the window. My legs churned in midair when panic
got the best of me. I started to turn around and climb back out,
but some unknown force sucked me in. I was falling as if I
had plummeted there from the sky. Bright spots flew crazily
across my vision, and I couldn't see a thing. I threw my hands
out, trying to grab hold of something. Vaguely, I recognized
my own screams. I was sure I would die, but there was no
bright light, no angels, or my mom waiting on the other side. I
wasn't dead at all. My head ached, and consciousness hit me
like a hammer. I shoved the base of my palms into my eyes,
trying to crush the pain away.

Smoke billowed around me, and my mind spun in disbelief. Terror and confusion caused tears in my equilibrium.
Whatever the hell just happened was out of my realm of
understanding. I squinted, barely coming to my senses. Barely
able to see a thing. Then I held my breath and heard it. Laughter. I felt those giggles in my empty stomach as a boy's
menacing voice whispered, "Jacob."

Then blurry images came into clearer focus. Elijah stood
there, in a Frankenstein mask with the chubby kid with a
snout for a nose, Piggy next to him. The boys I'd encountered
in the woods.

"Welcome to our lovely porthole to hell. Mother will be

glad to see you," Elijah said in an oddly chipper voice.

"You've come just in time for dinner," Piggy added. The two boys drew something from their jean pockets, and I was looking at the glint of two sharp knives.

My head continued to throb, and a hot, dull pain radiated down my spine, but I ignored it the best I could. I drew the gun, pointing it back and forth between them. "Shut up and don't come closer or I'll shoot. These bullets are blessed."

Pig boy let out a rumbling chuckle.

"You'd shoot a little kid?" Elijah asked, his voice tinted with mockery.

Hectic energy pounded in me as I nervously scanned the room. It was again an ordinary family room with a plush and expensive-looking sectional and marble fireplace, but there was an odd smell of rot emanating from beautiful hardwood floors. Then a tall figure entered the room. It was Mother. My mouth dropped as her shadow engulfed me.

The boys shrieked and begged, "Mother, may I? Mother, may I?"

Mother gave them an icy stare, then turned to me. "Oh, Jacob." The witch glowered down at me. A dark expression stitched itself into the hollows of her bones. "Getting in is the easy part. It's leaving that proves troublesome."

I should have shot her on the spot, but I fumbled to cock the gun before firing, and with superhuman swiftness, she was on top of me as the gun misfired into the air. The next thing I knew, my throat muscles moved under her icy fingertips until her index finger stopped on my pulse. I tried to raise my arms but went numb. My limbs tingled with a sensation of pins and needles. Next, my body and brain turned to ashes, and I dropped the gun.

What had she done to me? A rush of fear took me, but I tried to be strong. For a moment, I didn't know where I was. Hell, I didn't even know who I was. My awareness was in little broken pieces in a pile and only slowly reassembled themselves.

"What did you do? What's happening?" I tripped over my words, attempting to think straight. Bit by bit, it all came back until I recalled one of the horrible truths, "You killed my mom." A terrible heat charged through me like an electric current, and I shook my arms, relieved that I could move again. I was angry but helpless too.

Her eyes turned midnight black, and her skin began to decay. Oh God, she really was a hideous monster, and a bit of her true self showed. After, she returned to her human mask. I stepped back, horrified, and repulsed as the question spilled out, "What the hell are you?"

"Humans need names for things. So, you called us vampires, zombies, witches. I am all these things and more. I am from an ancient and noble clan, superior beings…And you are insignificant." Her forked tongue darted out, and she licked her lips. "If my children didn't need your sweet blood to live, I'd kill you all."

Swallowing hard, I tried to keep her talking, hoping for a chance to reclaim the gun. "If you're so superior, why do you need to drink our blood? Because I don't need crap from you." My voice was both bitter and shaky. This dirty *thing* took my mom, framed my brother, and tortured Ary.

"If you don't want anything from me, then why are you here?" The monster asked.

I inched back. The two boys and Hobbit mortician flocked to her side like a protective wolf pack. At first, they appeared to be a portrait of an average family. A tall, attractive blonde lady posed next to her middle-aged husband and two sons. But then black veins began to pulsate and rise to the surface of their thin skin as they closed in. It was a scene straight from a horror movie.

Mother held up her index finger. They all stopped in their tracks. "Oh, you want something, or someone alright."

Ary. She was alive. And she was here. Close. I could feel it. "Yeah. I just need Ary and my friend, Jamie back. And I won't kill you. Not now, at least."

"He won't kill you," Pig boy laughed. Mother eyed him, and he withered under her gaze.

Then she said, "Jamie's father never cared about him. All the children I take are unwanted, abused. Elijah's dad held his face in boiling water. It was I who saved him. I saved them all." Mother gestured to Elijah, and he removed his mask. Bubbling pink flesh as fresh as raw meat and only a few clumps of hair remained on his glistening red scalp.

Shockwaves crawled the length of my body. I cringed and teared up at wounds that looked curiously fresh, like they'd just happened. "I'm sorry, Elijah," my voice broke.

Elijah bared his teeth in a searing snarl.

"You're doing this to him." My eyes danced nervously between Mother and Elijah, but his injuries were suddenly old again.

Mother said, "I've done nothing but given these kids a good home."

"A good home where you drink their blood until they die or worse, become monsters like you." My voice was laced with outrage, but fear clawed its way in. I had to be brave... get the gun back.

I paused and lunged for that revolver on the floor as Gary's fist landed on my cheek, rotating my head slightly and causing blood to fly out of my mouth. I fell backward to the hard floor and hit my head. Flicking my tongue out, I tasted blood on my lips. My ears rang, and vision blurred. I was still desperate, determined, and rolled over and crawled, reaching for the gun. My fingertips skimmed metal, but it was just out of reach, and I was kicked again in the gut. It knocked the wind out of me, and I was laid flat on my back once more.

"Asshole," I muttered. The room spun. A familiar type of boot sidled up to me. Instinctively, I tucked and covered my head and face with my forearms and weakly asked, "What the hell kind of name is *Gary* for a monster, anyway?" There was still a sliver of satisfaction in being a smartass until the boot kicked me again in the stomach and head. The vicious attack continued until I choked on liquid copper that ran down my throat, and everything went black.

I let out a convulsive exhale. Lights sparkled and blinked out. A wave of unease swept through me, and pain shot up the sides of my body. An electric shock that fell away with the dark. I was drifting, floating, tethered to nothing.

Then I heard it. Muffled and faraway. A soft purr of the engine in between Michael's snores. I sat on the passenger seat next to my mom, shielding my eyes from the sunlight pouring in from the windshield. I contemplated a long stretch of open road. Even then, something sharp brushed against my subconscious, and my head hurt.

"Can we please go home, Mom?"

"No. I'm afraid we can't go back," she told me.

Oh God, she was pretty. Why had I never noticed? Then I remembered, but only fragments. "I had the world's most fucked up nightmare," I leaned my head against the car seat, but a searing pain shot up my hip and ribs.

I expected my mom to tell me to watch my language, but Ary's voice rebuked me. "Don't curse, Jacob."

"Ary." The sound of her voice dragged me to the rim of consciousness. I partly opened my eyes. My body and brain ached, and I knew my mom and brother had just been a dream. My eyelids were heavy. I struggled to open them wider, and when I finally did, everything was fuzzy. Mismatched shades of white became no more defined the harder I focused.

"Rest, and I will tell you a story." It was again Ary's sweet words that lulled me.

I tried to sit up but reclined back on something soft. A bed. Mercifully low yet lumpy. Ary's lips briefly caressed mine, and I tasted a ghost of blood. My own, I think. The warmth produced at the mere idea of her briefly lessened the pain.

"I missed you. I looked for you." I spoke in a scratchy, barely alive voice, but she had to know this, even if I told her with my last breath.

Ary said, "I need to tell you, Mother wasn't always this way. She hunted in the forest to live. Stronger than any beast. They called her a Wendigo, and some worshipped her. She gave them great wealth and grew strong. After centuries there was hardly any woodland left. All had forsaken her. She became an urban legend, a campfire story. She took their human form and traveled far and hid in plain sight, but something terrible happened. She pretended to be human for so long humanity sunk in. An aloneness. It debilitated her."

"She's not a vampire? A Wendigo. How the hell do you kill one of those things?" I attempted to sharpen my gaze on Ary, but the light was too bright, and it hurt to move. To breathe. Oh crap. My ribs were broken for sure, and every part of my body hurt. I fought to stay awake, but my eyelids flickered shut again. I was just with it enough to feel scared. "Ary, we need to find Jamie. Get out of here."

Ary kept talking as if I hadn't said a word. "An old one, a cunning witch, promised Mother she would take the terrible weakness that grew in her away. Purge it into the form of a flesh and blood child. That was when Mother gave birth to a daughter, but the old hag betrayed her and left with the infant."

Fear shot through me, and my eyelids fluttered open. Through the haze of pain, stark glimpses quickly became a horrible reality, and I beheld the picturesque vision of the monster. Mother, in her human form. Striking features with tight poreless skin.

Oh my God, Ary had never really been here. "It's you." My mouth dropped. "Where's Ary? What have you done to her?"

"Oh Jacob, I'm right here," Mother said, perfectly mimicking Ary. Then losing all pretense, she heatedly asked, "What do you want with my daughter?"

The question burst out. "Ary's your daughter? She's not human?" My blood ran cold, and I shifted, causing intense pain to shoot through my body.

"I collected others. Male ones since Sanctuary was such a

disappointment. What you would call my vampire children, I suppose." She ran her long animal-like claws down my chest. "The mortal ones break so easily." Slicing through my leather jacket, shirt, and first few layers of skin, she stopped at my waist. She slashed her hand in the air, displaying monstrous claws. "I could scratch off your little man part."

My back arched, and my hands flew to cover my private area, wincing in real and anticipatory pain. She circled around me with the slow and careful movements of a predator.

Next, the horror show unfolded as a shadow fell over her irises, coloring her entire eye black and a fanged smile appeared on her face. No longer using a human voice at all, her words came out in an evil rasp. "Be assured Sanctuary is my daughter and is a part of me."

"What? No. I don't believe you." I felt weird all over.

In another what the hell moment, Mother sniffed me. "Oh, the pain and rage, you're not a pure sacrifice. Not at all. I can't serve you in this state."

"Serve me?" I drew back as her razor-sharp nails retracted. Her newly formed human fingers passed over my head, and I shuddered until seconds later, it was as if all my injuries had never been.

The creature was birdlike in a black feather dress and sprouted what appeared to be horns from her head. She turned, so her face was in the darkness and faded into it...and was gone?

"What? What? What?" I chanted. My mind spun. Now I had to get out of here, but was Mother watching me from just around the corner? Lurking? Waiting to attack? Then I turned to prayer. "Please help me, God."

Briny decay and the smell of rot cloyed in my nose as my

head spun from side to side, only to find myself seemingly alone in a gloomy basement. I halfway sat upright, lifting my arms up, and anxiously scooted around, surprised to be unbound. It no longer hurt to move, but I felt something pop beneath my weight when I sat up. My breath stuttered, revolted to be not on a mattress but a bed of dead mice. I jumped up. Their little corpses were being smashed below my sneakers with each panicked step. They popped under my feet like balloons filled with air and not creatures with bones. I tried my hardest not to freak the F out, but my heart drummed, and I trembled all over. I had trudged past the bed of tiny corpses and stopped moving altogether.

A chill shivered down my spine, thinking this was where Ary had been imprisoned for all those years. Yet the question nagged me, was Ary really not human? A part of that monster? No. Even if I hadn't fallen for her, she was good. Pure. How I longed to see her one more time.

I discovered I was surrounded by concrete walls that flashed in and out to limestone. There was no explanation except that I was between two worlds. The only rays of light filtered in from the corners of a solitary door. It couldn't be that easy, but what other options did I have? Jerking myself into motion, I crept closer and closer to that door. It illuminated a harsh, otherworldly glare.

Terrified and hesitant, I quietly called for my "Mom." It was what any scared-ass kid would do. But my ghost-mom never showed. Then I drew a deep breath as my senses tingled, warning me not to do it, but my grasp tightened around the handle, and I slowly turned the doorknob...

33

FEEDING

ARY

The time I spent with Jacob had lit a spark in me. But I was small. Weak. My bony ribs and arms were a testament to a life of famine. Once more, I hadn't eaten or drank for days. I twisted my wrists, this way, and that way, and my chains clanked. I tried and tried to break the chains but couldn't. Instead, the handcuffs, which had already cut into my flesh, dug deeper, causing blood to run down my skin. It stung. My neck trembled with the effort of holding my head up. Finally, I realized what I had to do. Before Ren even bartered with me, I knew I didn't need his blood to be a monster. Whenever possible, I tried to deny my birthright, my heritage, but I was born a monster.

"I'm sorry," I said. I held my arms up as far as possible in the chains, and my hunger created a gravitational pull, bringing mice to my open hands. They squirmed in my grip as I squeezed until their essence faded away to nothing, and I grew stronger and stronger. I feasted without ever opening my mouth, dropping handfuls of dead vermin to the floor. Carcasses now stripped of their tiny bones and organs. They were just a pile of skin and fur. Then I called for more, and they simply flew into my greedy hands. I had filled up on these poor creatures in this dreary cellar, even snuck a few at Jacob's house. This time, I ate till I felt I'd burst and grew stronger and stronger. Blood rushing in my veins. Heartbeat thudding in my head. I tore the chains off as if they were made of paper and not steel and stood, burning with energy. My feet briefly floated just above the ground before thudding back down.

I knew Gary was a common ghoul who feasted on corpses. The boys lapped up human blood while Mother indulged in drinking blood too. It was her fine wine. Yet, she was a different beast and consumed her prey by gulping down a creature's vital organs and skeletal structure. Leaving shells of all she devoured. I couldn't lie to myself anymore. I was a monster just like her. I trembled with the realization and wanted to die on the spot but was immortal, or so it seemed.

I heaved an audible sigh, clinging to the idea that I was still me, but it was hard. I shrank to a dark corner, scared and frightened. An animal with nowhere else to run at the end of a hunt. Jamie's moans beckoned. Like me, he was now between two worlds. The world of the living and the dead. I swiftly made my way to him. Laying hands on him. Concentrating. And then, within seconds, he stopped suffering but was he gone?

"No." I shook him and shook him, and his eyes fluttered open. He stared at me.

"What happened? Where am I?" he asked, sitting upright.

"In a not so good place," I admitted. "How do you feel?"

"Thirsty," he said, twisting and turning, throwing his weight against the chains.

Reluctantly, I stared at him. Skin too pale. Eyes too blue. Then his lips parted, and fangs jutted out. "What's happening to me?" Jamie rasped in an eerily layered voice. Several other lost souls spoke in unison with him. Then his eyes rolled back in his head, and I heard his agonizing cries.

If I had found my strength earlier, he could still be Jacob's same old friend. The human boy he had been. He was like the upstairs children now. Undead. Regret churned in my gut. But I had to try to help him. I dropped to the floor. I didn't know what words to say as I broke Jamie's chains. If the transition from human to vampire had worked, he'd have easily broken his own chains. I slowly placed my hands on the side of his face. A vampire was cool as clay to the touch, but he was burning up. His eyes gleamed pure white, and his face twitched. "Don't, please, don't," he begged, as his mouth twisted in fury and his fangs jutted out.

Warmth invaded my body. A tingling heat. I focused, and something beautiful moved inside me. But Jamie slipped through my arms, falling onto the floor, and his eyes closed. My vision had long ago adjusted to the gloom as I studied him. He was ghost-white with a streak of blood on his lip.

"No," I said.

I spotted a flicker of movement above me.

"Is he gone?" Ren asked, standing over me. "Why didn't it work?"

"I did something wrong. Didn't try hard enough," I said, my voice coated with pain and regret.

Confusion drained from Ren's face, replaced by a

different and more resolute expression. "No. It's not your fault. I killed him, and others," he said. "And I hurt you. I didn't mean to." He paced a few steps away.

"But… you did."

Ren told me, "You should be grateful. Humans would want to do such dirty things to you, little bitch." Even the night, he'd freed me from my chains. He tossed a dress and then a pair of black ankle boots at my feet. "Wear this."

It was one of those dresses from the late 1800s Mother kept around

"Better to look plain around humans," Ren advised.

I hurriedly slipped the shoes on. The boots made a substantial sound as I clumped around. "I like them, but they're a little too big."

"I'm not a fuckin shoe store here. Now quick get dressed." He leered at me.

"Just turn around." I tried to sound firm but ended up pleading. "Please. Please, Ren."

"Why should the warm ones have all the fun?" He took a flat silver blade from his belt.

"So… you're going to weaken me before you throw me out into the night?" Outrage and fear tinged my voice.

"Or I could put the chains back on." A thin smile formed at the corner of his mouth.

If Ren wanted absolution, now was not the time. I pushed ugly memories away and rocked Jamie in my arms, the way a real mother would hold a small child, praying and hoping he might come back to life. Concentrating on goodness, love, and God. Nothing. There was no response. He remained limp in my arms. So, I laid him gently on the ground.

Ren came closer with his familiar swagger. Only now, his

chest was heaving with ragged breaths as he offered his hand to me.

I was more than capable and didn't need or want his help. "No, thanks." Once on my feet, I shrank back, putting a space between us.

"I'm sorry," he said.

I'd never dreamed I'd hear those words from him. Secretly, I needed them. He should have been like a big brother. "That's a start. I'm not the one to forgive you, Ren. But a wise lady once told me heaven loves a good redemption story."

Oddly, he seemed moved and fell into deep contemplation.

I learned a lot today, too, that had my head spinning. Healing myself wasn't my only skill. I could heal others, even bring monsters back from the dead. Some at least. I glimpsed at a lifeless Jamie. Not able to look at him for long.

Ren's eyes were sad and worn. "It sucks to be human... But you're not, Sanctuary."

I stood and briefly lowered my head. Ashamed. A taste of the world left me longing to be normal. But what was I? "Am I really like her? Am I really like Mother?"

Ren stroked the nape of my neck before lifting my chin. His voice was hoarse as if fighting emotions. His crystal blue eyes were too wise and ancient to match that boyish face. "You've harnessed much of Mother's power, even though your body's human. I was too dark to realize it before, but you're an angel, Sanctuary."

"An angel?" I asked in awe.

A memory flashed. *My gramma knelt by her bed in prayer.*

Warmth filled my heart as the pulse of something occupied the room. I was so happy I floated. Literally.

Gramma looked over at me and smiled. She said, "Magic can be incredibly good. Holy. You will use it one day to defeat a terrible monster."

My feet landed on the ground. "Monster?" I fidgeted with my hands and stuttered, "Ba-but Gramma, I'm sc-scared of monsters."

"You won't be when the time comes."

The fine hair on my arms stood remembering.

A heavy feeling punctured the room, bringing me back to reality. And then, in an eye-watering flash, I again glanced at Jamie's crumpled body on the floor. My mind buzzed. Something told me I hadn't tried everything. I dropped to the floor next to Jamie. I gently removed a twig lodged in his dirty and matted hair. Try the mortal way, a voice said. Gramma's voice. I squeezed his nose shut with my fingers. Placed my lips on his as my breath crawled from my lungs to his. A bubble of air caught in his throat, and he gasped and even choked. My shoulders finally relaxed. He was alive.

As if simply waking from a slumber, his eyes popped open. A dull blue once more. Color revisited his face. "I want to go home." There was a mounting unease in his voice. "Can I go home now? What the hell? Can I just go home?"

His all too human voice made my limbs go watery with relief. "You'll be home soon," I promised but didn't really know.

Ren rushed to help me bring Jamie to his feet.

But Jamie recoiled at his touch. "Stay away from me, freak." He harshly said and took my hand instead and stood.

Ren had blood above his lip, like a macabre Kool-Aid

mustache. I gestured to it, and Ren brushed his lip with his hand.

Jamie's head jerked to me. "Wait, am I? A…vampire?"

"You were for a terrible minute, but I healed you. You're human again." I puffed out my chest. With the help of a higher power, I had saved him and restored his very soul.

"So, I've got no superpowers?" Jamie frowned and pressed his hand to his forehead. "Oh, great. Lamest vampire story ever," he said, finishing with a series of jagged breaths.

My posture briefly returned to its natural slumped position, and I offered him a confused, "Sorry. We have to find Jacob." He was close. I sensed it. And I felt something else blooming inside of me. Strength. Power. "We are all getting out of here," I said.

34

HAUNTED

ARY

It was quiet like the whole desolate place held its breath. Utterly still. We started our adrenaline-filled journey cautiously and slowly. I wanted to remain strong, but my chest tightened in apprehension of what horrible things we might see.

Jamie asked, "Do you mind if I hold your hand?" Pausing to clear his throat, he added, "So, I can look after you for Jacob and not because I'm scared shitless."

I let out a nervous but amused laugh. "Alright," I said, "for Jacob." He took my right hand in his. Ren was to my left. I wondered if I'd get to Jacob in time, pushing my way through a force field of doubts and fears.

Because I knew all too well, this wasn't a regular base-ment. For one thing, it went on for fathomless miles, more like an endless tunnel of catacombs with a pungent sewer smell. The whole place was stone. Stone floors and stone walls. Deep fissures tarnished its surface. Passageways opened like gaping and hungry mouths to chamber after chamber.

For another thing, it was haunted. Once, desperate and bony hands reached out from cracks in the ground. Naïve as I was, I had tried to take the hand and pull the poor soul back up, but it only sought to pull me down—down to the grave. I had barely survived.

This menacing and senseless place was especially ripe with paranormal activity before parties. Wicked gatherings served as an open invitation to a hoard of spirits and monsters alike. Jamie finally released my hand from his tight grip and took out his cell phone. "I can't believe it's still charged, even if I don't have a signal." He used it as a flashlight, shining it on the ground to reveal fist-sized roaches scuttling past our feet, finding their way up from the nether world. I winced.

"I've never seen roaches like that!" Jamie exclaimed.

"Those are the babies," Ren dryly remarked and took Jamie's hand, directing the cell phone to the corner of the room. "That's the mother." The light flickered up and down on a roach-like bug the size of a medium dog.

"Damn!" Jamie exclaimed, now clutching his cell to his chest.

We slowly proceeded, squashing giant bugs with each crunching step. There was no way to avoid them. Nauseated, I groaned, my bare feet doused in bug juice.

"By stepping on these things, won't we piss the mother off?" Jamie worried out loud.

Ren now pointed Jamie's hand to spotlight the mother

insect feasting on some of her young, explaining, "We're in a hell dimension. No one cares about anyone here."

"I do," I said. "Sorry, baby bugs."

"Oh, please," Ren complained.

"We are in hell, for real," Jamie whined. "If I get out of here, I promise to stop drinking, smoking and ah, get a job," he bartered with someone, maybe God. "Cause I ain't coming back."

"Humans get religious once they get the shit scared out of them," Ren remarked.

"You're one of them," I reminded him because I think he had forgotten.

"Oh, yay," he twirled his finger in mock excitement, his voice deadpan.

The minute I shook my head at him, disembodied voices echoed from the walls. "He's coming, he's coming," they whispered. I froze, and a pair of crimson eyes glowed from across the way. An early guest had arrived.

"Did you see that?" Jamie jumped, pointing at the pair of eyes right before they blinked out.

"Yes," I nodded gravely, scanning our gloomy surroundings, bracing myself for a random strike.

"If you ignore the hell out of them, they stay small," Ren said.

"Yes. I'll ignore them," I reminded myself. Really, I wanted to curl up and hide under Jacob's stairs. Make pancakes. Binge-watch something on that big TV. But I was here for a higher purpose and had to keep going. We had passed the traffic of bugs as a shadow demon peeked out from around the corner—blacker than the darkness. A tangle of nerves worked its way through me.

Startled, Jamie backpedaled on the dirty rock floor, taking me with him. "This place scares the shit outta me," he admitted, pausing as his eyes darted all around.

I nodded, my voice cracking out the words, "I call it home sweet home. It's sarcasm. Jacob uses it sometimes," I timidly explained.

"I'm sarcastic too," Ren mumbled.

"*Damn,* and I thought I had it bad," Jamie responded.

I didn't reply to either of them. I just stayed quiet. Kept moving.

These kinds of apparitions had terrified me in my early childhood. Shadow people just existed to jump out at an unsuspecting someone. They lived only for the scare. And the red-eyed ones loved to watch and stare. I reminded myself that they couldn't touch me. They only became fully charged with fear. But neither of these manifestations was what had the ground shaking and quaking. That was what concerned me. "Mother used to say the dark one would come one day, when the door was close to being opened," I worried out loud.

Jamie asked. "What dark one?"

Ren answered, "The dark one is worse than Mother. Stronger. Keep in mind, I've seen her pull arms off a boy like they were the wings on a fly."

Jamie didn't even have a rebuttal or follow-up question.

"What about that door Mother obsesses over?" Ren wondered and added, "She says unlocking the door would give her control over earth."

"How can a door do that?" Jamie asked.

Ren speculated, "Maybe there is an army of devils ready to serve her."

"I don't think so." My mind spun, playing back the bits and pieces Mother had said about that door and what I'd heard from Gramma. Suddenly, a little light bulb went off in my brain. I finally understood what that door was.

We again passed through what was the basement in the real world. A small block window let in shards of lackluster light. A washer and dryer from the laundry room were noisily at work. Streaks of old blood in pastel stained the washer's vibrating door. A wooden shelf holding Tide and Downy. Real-world stuff. Then, we spotted Piggy up against the wall as Elijah pointed a gun at him.

"What are you doing?" I asked, alarmed.

"I wanted Elijah to shoot me for fun," Piggy replied.

"Mother wants me to bring her the gun," Ren lied and grabbed the gun from Elijah.

We walked past the boys. After we were at a safe distance, Ren spoke again. "Those boys are as dumb as rocks. They didn't even realize I'm human again," he said, and then his tone became more serious. "When the time comes, do you think you could change them?"

"I know I can," I said.

The farther we went, the darker it became. It was hard to see a thing. The ground gradually descended. My skin crawled just a little, and a drafty cold filled the air. A terrible silence settled in as more black candles on lavish gold pillars stood in a row, interrupting the darkness with a faint amber glow. Shapes formed just beyond the aura of candlelight.

A procession of figures in ruby red cloaks stoically passed like ancient druids. Each clutched a torch, which eerily illumi- nated their faces. They possessed dead eyes and had a waxi-

THE STARS FORGOT US

ness to their skin that made me think of disease. A gasp bubbled up in my throat, and I slapped my hand over my mouth to capture it.

"Who the hell are they?" Jamie asked.

"I was never quite sure." My stomach always went hollow at the sight of them.

"They were Mother's followers. Some were here long ago... pilgrims. But even in death, Mother refuses to relinquish her hold on them. They wander aimlessly, unable to cross over."

"I get it. This is just a nightmare," Jamie told himself.

"In a way, I feel bad for them," I admitted.

I broke away, blinking rapidly to compose myself. We kept going, and soon eerie mounds of bonfires glowed, throwing flickering obscurities on the walls as skeletons began to litter the ground. Pieces and piles of bones, along with glittering bars of gold and jewels, also cluttered our path. Jamie bent down, taking a handful of treasure.

"No!" I yelled.

"Idiot," Ren mumbled.

Jamie dropped it, and the three of us fell into a huddle, our heads ducked low.

"Fine. I'll get nothin' out of all this—this pain and torture." Jamie shoved his shaky, bloody hands in his jean pockets when his eyes again shot down to a gold bar. "I could take one. Just one."

"Sure, but you might join the nice red robed people," Ren warned.

Jamie clearly experienced an inner struggle, but in the end, decided, "No thanks. I'm pretty used to being poor."

We all stepped cautiously, respectfully around the bones, taking nothing from the mounds of riches.

A skull with a wig on top of its head and bright red jewels jammed in the eye sockets leered at us, appearing even more sinister in the glow of the firelight. Mother had brought me here one time, but this was a new attraction. It was the senseless work of Maverick, no doubt from the graveyard of cigarette butts under our feet.

From there, the three of us shivered as we ventured through a tunnel where the limestone glistened with ice. Immediately after, we entered another chamber, and the air grew warmer with each step. We just walked in silence, swathed in shadows. Twigs and branches peeked out from cracks in the moss-covered walls, and we gazed at a large tree that dominated the space. Its trunk was six feet wide, with spiky leaves and white flowers. Tiny iridescent birds glowed and buzzed, orbiting the tree.

"A Joshua Tree. What? This wasn't here," Ren muttered. "And birds? Well, that explains Mother's feather dress."

Before I could respond, the hummingbirds abandoned the tree, and in a dizzying swarm, they looped around, encircling me. They swept through my hair and tickled my face with the downy touch of a thousand feathers.

Soon they flitted about my body. All the blood and filth began to disappear from my dress as if it had been washed and bleached. These tiny creatures even tailored, creating a whole new design. The now flowing material sparkled, and beautiful lace adorned my sleeves. Then, as quickly as they came, the birds cliqued together, flying back up to flutter around the tree.

Amazed, I looked down at a crystal embroidered gown, which suddenly touched the ground. I placed my hand shyly on the sweetheart neckline. It was new, yet oddly familiar to me. I turned to the boys in a state of utter disbelief.

"I don't know what just happened," Jamie admitted, adding, "But it's no wonder Jacob has got it so bad. You're beautiful."

I felt my face warm and smiled his way.

"Alright. If you're done playing Cinderella, we've got things to do," Ren said.

He was right. We needed to stay focused. The boys didn't speak another word, and neither did I. We all kept going. The dress felt cumbersome and dragged on the ground as I battled and kicked a web of petticoats at my feet. I almost tripped twice, working hard to meet the boy's pace.

Then a warning bell rang in my head. A knot formed in the pit of my stomach.

"Stop." Ren propelled around, grabbing my lace-clad forearm as we halted in our tracks.

Jamie skidded to a stop less than a foot away but turned to face us.

Ren then said what I already knew. "We're close."

I pulled in a breath. The air was rank and oppressive. An odor like heady wool with a subtle hint of rot. The scent of Mother and of an immense evil that I had shrunk away from my entire life. An evil I now had to face. A live wire of fear and anger charged through me. The throb of my pulse lit my fingertips.

"I'll jump in when I need to. But it's on you. You must be strong, Sanctuary. Unleash all your power on her," Ren said as

Jamie intently listened. Then their gaze shifted. Now both of their eyes burned into me.

Ren's voice quieted to a passionate whisper. *"All of it."*

"I will. I'll use all of my power," I said, yet my voice was small and shaky.

"Oh, hell, do we have a backup plan?" Jamie asked.

35

A PURE SACRIFICE

JACOB

A brilliant light shone through the edges of the door, and I rattled the doorknob back and forth, but the damn thing wouldn't budge. I heard muffled cries. Close by. Voices of kids younger than me. They were scared. My eyes darted all around, but no one else was here. I wasn't sure if they were the ghost of children, or living, breathing kids being kept prisoner on the other side of the wall.

"I'm getting out of here, and will send for help," I promised. I hoped.

"Thank you," a small voice replied.

Again, I tried the door, and the room fell silent. A gnawing in my stomach compelled me to turn around. It was Mother.

"Don't talk to the children. They're in time out." She came closer, holding something behind her back with both hands. My best guess was a weapon. "You can't open that

R.J. GARCIA

door. I've summoned powerful demons who couldn't. I learned only a pure sacrifice will open it. So, I sacrificed virgin after tiresome virgin. Innocent animals, innocent children. Even my own daughter. No sacrifice proved pure enough."

Maybe this was all a nightmare. I wasn't sure. But the ground softened below my feet, and I looked at a dozen or more hands reaching up, breaking out from below like macabre blossoms. I gasped, teetering back and forth on trembling legs. My knees were all but buckling. Then, in the blink of an eye, they all disappeared. When the world felt solid again, I took a step and asked, "What the hell just happened?"

"You must pay better attention." A wicked gleam lit her eyes. "We were talking about all my sacrifices. In fact, I even sacrificed a police officer." She hoisted up the decapitated head of Detective Zane, holding it by his mane of dark hair.

"You killed him." I covered my eyes with my hand and recoiled back. Vomit creeping up to my throat. I clamped my mouth shut.

"He came here with your little cousin."

I pressed my lips together. Heat rising in my chest. "Lucas? He's here? No. You didn't…" I wanted—needed to know Lucas was alright to catch my next breath.

She dropped the head. It fell at my feet with a small thud, and blood splashed across my chest and speckled my hair. I turned away, wincing. Still feeling like I might be sick.

Then Mother commanded, "Bring the boy."

Gary came forward, holding Lucas by the arm. My cousin's eyes were wide with terror, and his hands clenched into fists at his side until he dug them into his pockets and pulled out a fist full of garlic. He dropped it at the monster's feet.

Mother only snickered and launched into a monologue, explaining, "This porthole I call home is one of many Hell-mouths. But opening this door means I'll have power over all the world. I will rule this dismal planet. Bring it to complete ruin. Armageddon at last." Her monster face flickered in and out, and then she briefly held up a finger. "I'm going to sacrifice one of you, two boys. So, Jacob, since you fascinate my dear Sanctuary, I shall let you decide. Who will die? You, or the perfect...perfectly boring Lucas? Choose!"

Lucas stood motionless and slightly slumped over, holding his tear-streaked face in his hands.

"I choose neither of us," I said in a firm voice, swallowing my fear.

Mother flicked her chin to Gary, and he shoved Lucas toward her. She ripped the tape from his mouth. "Well, Lucas, you win by default. Who should I kill, you or jealous Jacob?"

Lucas seemed to agonize over it, then answered, "Neither of us."

"So weak. Then I'll kill you both," she snapped.

Mother's eyes went to Gary, and he rushed to me. I landed a left and right to the sides of his ugly face in succession, but it barely phased him. He overpowered me in the struggle, grabbing me in a chokehold. My survival instincts kicked into overdrive, and with my arms free, I extended my hand, locked my wrists and elbows, and plunged my fingers into the hollow of Gary's neck to break free.

Mother had forced Lucas to a kneeling position. "Come closer, Jacob. Watch while I tear your cousin's precious head off."

"Don't!" I yelled at the top of my lungs. My love for Lucas and a sheer panic from the thought of losing him flooded me. "Let him go. Take me!"

"No. I'll be the sacrifice," Lucas said with finality.

The door shot open, and I could hardly see a thing. Lucas and I, even Mother and Gary, shielded their eyes from a blinding light.

My mouth dropped in astonishment.

"A human willing to die for another human. How sweet. How simple." Mother's face shined in the fierce glow of the light as she turned Lucas to face her. His eyes narrowed, and he whimpered right before she slashed his throat with her claws and tossed him like a rag doll to the cellar floor.

I dropped to his side. But it was too late. "No!" I yelled. He was glassy-eyed, staring up at me, lying in a pool of his own blood. "I'm so sorry, Lucas. I'm so sorry."

Mother's voice rose over my sobs. "This is it. Yes. Yes. This is finally it." Her skeleton face under patches of rotting skin and horns sprayed with Lucas's blood drew near. Her monster claws extended into five miniature knives.

A whole new level of rage burst to the surface. "I'll kill you," I threatened, lurching forward and catching her hands, attempting to stab the demon with her own claws. Feathers from her dress flew in the air, but she was too strong and seized control of my arms.

"You know I'm not even trying yet," she said.

Gary viewed the scene with humorless laughter.

I thrashed, kicked, and swore, determined to die fighting, but the gray smoke swirled in. "Stop!" I protested. She wouldn't even let me go out screaming and kicking. I choked down the murky air. It burned my throat and lungs.

Woozy. The room spun. Then the numbness started in my legs and climbed to my arms and hands. And with it, a sense of dread spread over my skin. This was the end. I reached down deep to find my senses but could barely wiggle my fingers.

Mother squeezed my arms. In agony, I felt and heard my bones break. A groan of pain rose in my throat and spilled out of my mouth. The smoke that paralyzed me did nothing to dull the pain. I was still reeling from it when Mother's features pulled down in confusion, and she partly turned to peer across the way. The air around me changed, the smoke cleared. My back straightened.

I could hardly believe it when I heard Ary's voice. "Leave my boyfriend alone and go back to hell, you bitch."

Mother's death grip loosened. The remnants of smoke faded. I fought my way out of the stupor.

"Sanctuary. I've never heard you swear. Naughty little thing. Do I have to cut you to pieces again?" Mother dryly asked.

"Stop talking," Ary ordered Mother before shifting her gaze to me. "Oh, Jacob, you've come to save me," she warmly gushed.

"Uh, yeah," I breathlessly groaned and was finally able to turn around.

There Ary stood, small in stature but stronger and more beautiful than ever. A smile fluttered across her lips. Ary alone didn't need to shield her eyes from that light. Instead, she absorbed it. Her velvety skin was shimmery and aglow. Her ball gown and hair gently swayed in a sudden breeze.

Mother shoved me away, and I fell to the hard ground.

Ary waved her hand, and a fierce wind blew in, slamming the door shut.

Gritting her teeth, Mother said, "How...dare...you undermine me. Open that door this instant!"

"No," Ary bravely replied.

I looked on, stunned, while Mother ripped off one of her knife-like nails, catapulting it across the way, straight to Ary's heart, but it bounced off the dress.

"You're wearing armor. Clever," Mother raged, hurling a second nail to Ary's exposed neck.

This one stuck. Ary groaned as her face registered the pain, and she briefly hunched over, holding her throat. Blood trickled through her fingers and onto her dress.

I called to Ary and staggered forward, wanting to help. Yet I could barely move my arms and was unable to stop my hands from trembling with fear.

Then Mother's human façade distorted and grayed to a shade of rot, and she began to talk. "Housewives' light candles in homage, with too few blood sacrifices. I should rule this world by now—but that hag tricked me. She trapped me in this body, and you...You're holding a bit of my power."

Ary removed the impaled fingernail, and it clunked down to the floor. Then she smacked her glowing hand over the wound. "No, I'm holding a lot of your power. And just for the record, she was a prophet and a Wiccan."

Mother jabbed her paws out, twisting and turning them toward Ary, whose limbs jerked mechanically and feet faltered, causing her to tumble backward. Ary's head and back, taking the impact.

No, I grimaced.

Mother stared with flat perplexity and growled, speaking a slur of words, no longer in a human tongue, and tearing off a second talon-type fingernail, which she hurled toward Ary's neck with a marksman's precision.

But Ary brought her arms up defensively, and it impaled her right hand. Her eyes flicked over to mine, and she mouthed the words, "I'm okay." Her face twisted with pain as she pulled the talon out and sat up.

"My lamb." Mother's low chuckle moved through the large, dank space. Soon Gary appeared from the corner and handed the monster a gleaming sword. "We'll see how okay you are when I slash you to ribbons."

My stomach turned over with fear.

"Use all your power, Sanctuary!" The boy, Ren shouted, emerging from the shadows. And I noticed Jamie standing just behind him. Jamie lifted his chin, and his eyes met mine. He was alive. I almost smiled. Almost cried.

Then, with more of my strength returning, I rushed to help Ary. Stand in front of her as a human shield, if nothing else. But Mother charged toward Ren, wielding her weapon. When I reached Ary, I realized she hadn't needed my help. She was up now, though her feet were no longer on the ground. Instead, she was effortlessly afloat. It was better than supernatural. It was magical. Tears gathered behind my eyes, and I had the impression nothing could hold her back now. I smiled up at her.

It happened in heartbeats. Mother had reached Ren and drew the sword back. Just then, Ary's arms shot up. And the sword was ripped away from the monster's clutches and hurled into the gloom. Next, Mother herself was launched up high in the air until she thumped against the ceiling, causing a cloud of bats to take flight. Seconds later, Mother violently crashed back down to the floor.

The amazing spectacle continued, and I felt heavily connected to each moment. Ary's body and face glowed luminously as her eyes burned with intent. Somehow, coordinated with the wave of her arms, the monster's body flew across the chamber, crashing against the limestone wall. There was a scuttling sound close to me. From the corner of my eye, I saw Gary heave, ready to pounce on Ary, but I extended my leg, causing him to trip and land face first. When he rolled over, I gave him a dozen hard kicks in the stomach and ribs. Despite being in intense pain, I must admit, it felt pretty damn good.

Ren pointed the gun at a bloody and bashed Mother, who clamored to her feet once more, calling, "Judas!" as she hobbled closer to him.

Gunshot after gunshot rang out as Ren unloaded the gun into Mother's chest, causing her to do a strange dance. Black monster blood splattered about the chamber. Finally, Mother let out a shrill, animal-like cry, withering in pain. How I wanted to press my hands over my ears, but my broken arms hung limp and useless. The cry reached an earsplitting crescendo, louder than the gunfire. My head rang—the din of madness magnified by the cave-like setting. The smells of gunpowder and blood hung in the air.

But then, in an instant, Gary got up and sprinted toward Ren. I could only move in slow motion, but Ary appeared healed of her injuries and unphased by the chaos. A fierce concentration remained sketched across her face as she waved her hand, raising Gary from the ground. Her feet levitated off the floor before she snapped Gary's neck and hurled him into the wall with the simple flick of her wrist.

The noise in my head died down to a low rumble as my eyes sharpened in on Gary, finally at rest on the floor next to Mother. The evil duo lay in a grotesque and motionless heap. Dark liquid flowed around them that resembled an oil spill.

My eyes shot to Ary across the room as she told Ren something. Then she turned to me, still in midair, and her voice echoed, "I'm sorry, Jacob."

It was then my eyes found Jamie weeping and rocking a lifeless Lucas in his arms. Every muscle stiffened. No. Lucas was really gone. I had been so sure I'd join him that I hadn't comprehended what his death meant.

Ary's feet alighted on the ground, and we met in the middle of that dungeon. Both dazed.

"You're hurt," she said and put one hand on each of my shoulders. Morphine had eased the pain at the hospital after Gary's first assault. What she gave me was like a shot of instant Morphine. I lifted my arms that had felt like broken wings. There was no pain at all. I started to ask how she'd done it, but Ary hugged me, and I held her tight. I needed this. Needed her.

"I have to go, Jacob," she said.

"I can't lose you too."

"You showed me the good things about being human."

"I want to show you more. Stay," I begged, and a tremor ran through my voice.

Our lips met, but it was different from our other kiss. It was slow, sweet, and full of comfort.

"For one glorious moment, everything else disappeared," Ary whispered in my ear as she broke out of the embrace.

"Yeah," I said. My voice was thick with emotion.

Her eyes raked over my face. I hadn't made peace with

losing my mom, hadn't begun to wrap my head around Lucas's murder, and now Ary was leaving. Even though she had healed me from the physical pain, I hurt all over.

"It'll all be better soon," she promised, but that wasn't possible. She strode closer toward the door.

I followed. Aching. "What's that door?" I asked. "Where are you going?"

"It's the porthole to time. Like a time-machine...It will be the day you moved here." Her sorrowful eyes flickered to Lucas's lifeless body. "I'm going to make things right. I couldn't do what I needed to before because it wasn't the boys' fault. But now I know how to help them. I can set them free, make them human."

I didn't have to understand. I just longed to be with her. "Can I go with you?"

She took a deep and shaky breath. "No."

I grabbed ahold of her hand, pulling her closer. "Are you coming back?" My voice cracked.

"I'm afraid not. Mother is waking up," Ary warned, and I glanced over my shoulder at Gary and Mother's remains just a yard away. The two mangled bodies convulsed. "I don't want to leave you, not even to go to the light, but I have to, Jacob."

"Will I remember?"

"I think it will be as if none of it ever happened," Ary said with a small, bittersweet smile.

Mother was moaning, growling aloud, and almost simultaneously, a vibration originated from somewhere below. A pulse grew stronger and made the ground rumble. Ary and I fell into one another's arms as a network of cracks spread on the stone beneath our feet.

We steadied ourselves and parted. "Mother has all but

healed herself, and she has summoned something bad. Powerful. I have to go." Ary instructed me to "Close your eyes."
She no longer hesitated but walked to the door. A full-fledged
halo fanned around her, encompassing her in pale gold light.
My head spun.

She merely touched the doorknob, and it opened for her. It
was so bright I couldn't see a thing but called, "Ary!" one
final and desperate time as the whole place shook violently
and the ground crumbled. I was free-falling for the longest
time, but I wasn't scared...

Sunlight poured in through the windshield. The engine
purred. Michael snored. And I was in the passenger seat next
to my mom.

36

WHAT YOU DON'T KNOW

JACOB

I noticed the closet door slightly ajar. It was closed before, but maybe my mom had put something away. I opened it and flicked on the light. Nothing was there except for my clothes and two cardboard boxes I had put there earlier that read Jacob's crap. Then I collapsed, sitting on the floor for a long time. Getting up felt akin to climbing Mount Everest. I couldn't say why. I guessed the move had worn me out.

The next morning, I still felt sluggish. I poured milk over my Frosted Flakes and found the newspaper on the table. I never read the paper, but I couldn't resist for some reason.

My eyes became glued to a headline about a fire. "*House burns down, and a young girl, identified as Sanctuary Daniels dies rescuing children and teen boys from the inferno!*"

Ary from the third grade…She was a weird kid, maybe too good for the world. I had a little crush on her back then.

No. A big crush. I wasn't sure exactly why, but I just stared into space for a while. Then, I read the rest of the article, my heart racing like I'd downed an energy drink. I strained to process what happened, or stranger yet, remember something. But what?

"Did you read about the fire? It was close to our house. Terrible. The foster parents died. And some of those kids were kidnapped... But that girl was a hero," Mom said.

"Yeah, she was." I looked down at my cereal, dazed and touched.

"Well, eat up. We have to register you for school."

I couldn't shake this odd feeling. Then my mind took on a maddening beat as I struggled through cobwebs of nightmare-filled memories. Flashes of terrible images triggering a sickening lurch in my stomach. Mom laid out on a table at the morgue. A statuesque lady transforming into a corpse-like beast. Random and horrible images that didn't tell a story. I fought through the threads of then and now. Until my mind turned a page, and I remembered the entire terrifying and heartbreaking story. I remembered Ary. Beautiful, innocent, magical, Ary. And an evil lurking all around, I could no longer be oblivious to. It was like a punch to the gut, knocking the wind out of me.

Struggling to keep it together, my eyes poured over my mom, now very much alive. Her hair was tied up in a twisty just got out of bed kind of knot, and she was still in her night-shirt. "You're pretty, Mom. I love you."

"Are you okay?" she asked.

Jittery and raw, I pleaded, "I need a mental health day. I swear, I'll register for school tomorrow."

"Oh, that's why I'm pretty." Her lips compressed into a thin line, and her eyes pointedly studied me. The chair creaked as she reached over to put her hand on my head. "Alright, you're a little warm," she decided. "I feel out of it too. I slept like the dead."

I grimaced at her choice of words.

"I guess it's the move."

"Yeah, the move. Thanks, Mom," I said and darted off.

Immediately, I checked Ary's space, inching my way inside. It was empty, but a faint vibration led me up the stairs. The strumming of a guitar grew louder and more distinct with each step. "Theory of A Deadman – Hallelujah."

Sure enough, when I peeked into Michael's room, he was playing his guitar like he hadn't in ages. He may have woken up early, but more likely, he'd been up all night. Finally, he shifted, facing me.

This was one of those times I had socked away. A memory of my brother effortlessly playing chords that made their own sweet song. Only it was happening in real-time. I opened my mouth to respond, but there was a lump in my throat. Michael halfway smiled, though his face was sweaty and reddened. Before long, our mom appeared and put her arm around me, all teary-eyed.

Michael finished the song and set the guitar down next to him.

Mom warmly said, "It was great, Michael."

I needed to know. "How do you feel?" Had he tapped into these evil things all along? Or had they haunted my brother, and now he'd be free? Psychiatrists had changed his diagnosis, and no meds had ever really worked. I was way ahead of myself with wishful thinking. "I mean, is the new medicine working?"

He shrugged. "I think so...It's just. I want to be alone." He seemed more than a little flushed and overwhelmed. Mom and I told him we understood. Then in the hall, Mom smiled in a can-you-believe-it kind of way.

"I know." I was hardly able to get the words out. She went downstairs, and I retreated to my room.

I shut the door, wondering how to process the enormity of it all when it never really happened. Then I squinted, thinking about Ary. An idea surfaced. I picked up a black Sharpie from my dresser and headed to the closet.

I thought for a second and wrote, "I remember. I miss you. And I won't forget." I dropped the marker and read the message I'd jotted down in big clunky letters. My stomach churned with anticipation, believing she might actually read it.

Dropping down, I sat on the floor. My fingers tapped rapid beats on my leg, and I stared at the wall for an hour like a guy waiting for a text. Then I paced the length of my room before flopping down on my bed and rubbing my palms across my comforter. Thinking. It was a wild dream, or I lost touch with reality. Maybe—but no. I knew. I just knew.

Going back to the closet once more, I talked to Ary, hoping she could hear me. "If you're in heaven, I get that it would be a long-distance relationship and I'll go on with my life." I had an empty feeling knowing that even in remembering, I would never completely understand. I only knew evil lived just below the surface. It had seeped into our world, welcomed, and invited too many times.

Melancholy and worn, I needed to know good existed

too… something beyond the grave. "In order to even budge from this spot," my voice cracked, "Ary, I just need to know you're alright?"

The lights in my room flicked on and off. Then, a drawing of the perfect Valentine's heart formed. I traced my fingertips over it. Happy. Broken. Amazed.

ACKNOWLEDGMENTS

Thank you to Midnight Tide Publishing for welcoming me into their amazing group of writers, and thanks to my talented beta readers: Nick, Gerardo, Hannah, and Dave.

I want to mention my beautiful family. My husband, Ernesto, and two kids, Sabrina and Matthew, for inspiring me. Sending love to my brothers, Ronnie and Kevin, and my best friend, Bonita, for always supporting me. Also, like to give a shout-out to my mom, who introduced me to scary stories. I think of you every day, Mom.

ABOUT R.J. GARCIA

 R.J. Garcia was born in a small Midwestern town you'd pass on the way to where else. She is a wife and proud mom of two smart kids and a chorkie named Zoey. She earned her MSW and worked with foster children and long-term care. Writing has been her other great love. She has been writing short stories for as long as she can remember. To her amazement, those short stories became novels!

Check out more of her books!
rj-garcia-writer.com

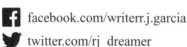 facebook.com/writerr.j.garcia
twitter.com/rj_dreamer
instagram.com/writer_rjgarcia

MORE FROM R.J.

Standalone

Nocturnal Meetings of the Misplaced

The Call of Death

MORE BOOKS YOU'LL LOVE

If you enjoyed this story, please consider leaving a review!

Then check out more books from Midnight Tide Publishing!

Merciless Stars by Candace Robinson

Two sisters. Two loves. And a secret that can destroy them both.

For years, Silver has used her magic to draw the same human soul,
Keelen, from the afterlife and place him into a wax raven she
created. Each visit, her impossible relationship with Keelen
deepened, leading Silver to want more than friendship. Yet it isn't
until after Silver and her queen sister, Afton, are forced to defend
themselves from an enemy king's guards, that Silver discovers a
way to give Keelen human life and become Afton's weapon.

Afton had never given her heart to another … until she met Ragan.
Just when it seems she's found true love, she must temporarily push
her feelings aside and accept a betrothal contract from the enemy
king to keep her territory safe. But when Afton uncovers a danger
that threatens all she has built, the sisters must put a stop to it before
everything they love, including their sisterly bond, shatters.

Available Now

Come True by Brindi Quinn

A jaded girl. A persistent genie. A contest of souls.

Recent college graduate Dolly Jones has spent the last year stubbornly trying to atone for a mistake that cost her everything. She doesn't go out, she doesn't make new friends and she sure as hell doesn't treat herself to things she hasn't earned, but when her most recent thrift store purchase proves home to a hot, magical genie determined to draw out her darkest desires in exchange for a taste of her soul, Dolly's restraint, and patience, will be put to the test.

Newbie genie Velis Reilhander will do anything to beat his older half-brothers in a soul-collecting contest that will determine the next heir to their family estate, even if it means coaxing desire out of the least palatable human he's ever contracted. As a djinn from a 'polluted' bloodline, Velis knows what it's like to work twice as hard as everyone else, and he won't let anyone—not even Dolly f*cking Jones—stand in the way of his birthright. He just needs to figure out her heart's greatest desire before his asshole brothers can get to her first.

Available Now

Frost Mate by Elle Beaumont & Candace Robinson

He's the captain, and she's the trainee. Will a mission get in the way of their fated bond?

Captain Korreth spends his days training Morozko's Army, wanting nothing more than to quash the Changelings as they wreak havoc on Frosteria. But when a new trainee enters the barracks, he feels an inexplicable pull.

New recruit Zira has one thing on her mind, and it's taking out the Changelings that slaughtered her family. She's full of vengeance, but she can't deny how difficult it is to focus in the presence of the captain.

With tensions rising in Frosteria and the mortal world, Korreth and Zira must work together, however, it will take the strongest of wills to ignore the call of a mate bond. That is, if they even wish to.

Available Now

Made in the USA
Monee, IL
03 April 2022

94039443R00164